BLOODY CLAWS

What Reviewers Say About
Winter Pennington's Work

"Winter Pennington's creative mind is a dark and gloriously erotic place. ...The twists and turns of the plotlines are written with the ease of an accomplished author, while the balance of horror and humor is achieved with seemingly effortless skill. Blood, sex, fury, betrayal, animal instinct, true love...they are as intrinsically entwined as the lovers within the pages. It may just be time to go over to the dark side..."—Candia of *Inkubus Sukkubus*

"[*Witch Wolf*] is a nice mix of urban fantasy with police procedural/ murder mystery. If Pam is your favorite vampire on *True Blood*, you're going to love Lenorre."—*Rainbow Reviews*

"It's a testimony to the strength of Pennington's writing skills that readers never lose track of the plot even as new characters are introduced and others are more fully developed. What follows is an engrossing read involving vampires, werewolves, and some very hot, kinky sex and excitement!"—*Just About Write*

"Kassandra Lyall is a likeable, sympathetic and frequently funny heroine, and Pennington sets her up well amongst a brace of other quirky, intriguing characters. *Raven Mask* an entertaining novel— highly recommended to anyone looking for a sexy, funny, escapist bit of fluff to bury themselves in for an afternoon."—*The Lesbrary*

"*Darkness Embraced* is a sinfully sexy read. Pick up *Darkness Embraced* and be enthralled."—*Bibliographic Book Blog*

"Pennington's novel is a fascinating look at the werewolf and vampire cultures. *Witch Wolf* is a rollicking story told with a wry sense of humor. It's an engaging read that leaves the reader asking for more."—*Just About Write*

Visit us at www.boldstrokesbooks.com

By the Author

Bloody Claws

Darkness Embraced: A Rosso Lussuria Vampire Novel

Witch Wolf

Raven Mask

BLOODY CLAWS

by

Winter Pennington

2012

ISBN 10: 1-60282-588-2
ISBN 13: 978-1-60282-588-8

This Trade Paperback Original Is Published By
Bold Strokes Books, Inc.
P.O. Box 249
Valley Falls, NY 12185

First Edition: January 2012

CREDITS
EDITORS: VICTORIA OLDHAM AND CINDY CRESAP
PRODUCTION DESIGN: SUSAN RAMUNDO
COVER DESIGN BY SHERI (GRAPHICARTIST2020@HOTMAIL.COM)

Acknowledgments

A big thank you goes to my amazing parents and my wonderful wife for offering their patience and opinions and for beta reading when asked. Many thanks to Candia and Tony McKormack of Inkubus Sukkubus for their brilliant music, British slang, and for being some of the niftiest people I've had the pleasure of getting to know. Huge thanks also go to Sasha and Michi, for sending support in the form of chocolate, tea, coffee, and other goodies (which were very much enjoyed!). And of course, thanks to my wickedly awesome editor, Victoria, for her invaluable guidance.

CHAPTER ONE

I spun in my seat, pressing the large black button on the wireless intercom. The intercoms were new and for the past several days, I'd entertained myself immensely by driving June insane with them. I didn't need to see her flying out of her seat every time the little box buzzed to know she still hadn't gotten used to them.

"What?" she grumbled.

"June?" I asked, waiting to see what kind of response she would come up with this time. The last time, she'd accused me of trying to give her a heart attack and threatened to throw the intercom systems in the trash. I was the boss, but June was my I-don't-give-a-shit-what-you-think-of-my-attitude secretary. She was one tough broad. I respected her for that.

"What is it, Miss Lyall?" Her words were polite. Her tone was not. I smiled to the empty room.

"Seeing if you're still here."

There was a long pause. "And where the heck would I go?"

"I don't know," I said, aimlessly strangling the pencil on my desk with a rubber band. "There's a strip club three blocks away. Maybe there?"

I waited. It wouldn't take long for her to lose her patience. I know it was petty of me, childish even, but a woman had to have some fun. June proved to be a good source of entertainment on a slow day at the office.

"To see what?" she asked, exasperated. I bit my bottom lip, trying to hold in the burst of laughter that threatened to erupt. "If I wanted to see naked hillbillies, I'd go home and tell my husband to strip."

I pressed the button and said, laughing, "Good one."

Ten minutes later the intercom screeched like a little boxed banshee and I jumped, stifling a growl.

"Ms. Lyall," June said in a voice that was way too nice to be authentic. "Your five o'clock appointment, Hunter Kinsley, is here."

I slipped my stocking clad feet into the heels I'd kicked off under the desk. "Send her in," I said, trying to pull my attire back together. I took the black blazer off the back of the chair and slipped it on over the white blouse I was wearing. If it weren't for the wide legged black trousers and the heels, the suit might've made me look more like a Secret Service agent than a Preternatural Investigator. I was fairly certain Secret Service agents were smart enough to wear flats, though.

I was wearing my gun, a Kimber Eclipse Lenorre had given me as a gift, tucked into the shoulder rig. The shoulder rig had been a late birthday present from Rupert. He'd said Lenorre wouldn't be able to rip it off me. I wasn't sure I believed it was indestructible, but Lenorre and I hadn't exactly tested the theory. Call me cautious, but I was reluctant to sacrifice another holster.

I checked the mirror in my office, making sure the blazer hid the bulk of the weapon. I tucked the white streak in my long black hair behind my ear.

Most clients tend to get uncomfortable around guns, but I was a cop before I was infected with the lycanthropy virus, and some habits die hard. I still work with the cops, but now I make my own schedule. I don't have to worry about the full moon interfering with my job and so far, I've done pretty good at keeping my secret from my ex-colleagues.

There was the barest of knocks on the frosted glass door.

"Come in."

The door opened. "Ms. Lyall?" A girl stood in the doorway, casting an uncertain glance into the room.

I went to the door and held it open. "Yes." I offered my hand. "I'm Kassandra. Are you Hunter?"

"Yeah."

She took my hand and gave it a firm shake. I motioned for her to take a seat and she did so, running a hand through her brown punk rock hair. The hair was cut short in the back, with the layers lengthening out as they arched toward her forehead. She'd styled the hair forward so that the longest layer veiled her brows but still left her vision free. Well, for the most part.

Hunter Kinsley was an androgynous beauty. The hairstyle suited the square line of her jaw. Smoky eye shadow brought out the brown and green of her irises. Her lips had a natural sullen pout to them.

She took off the jacket she wore. The buckles clinked as she draped it across the back of the chair. The pants she wore clung to her body with two bondage straps crossing over the back of her legs. She'd tucked the pants into a pair of ankle high combat boots. The outfit was modern punk rock chic, which made me guess she was in her early twenties.

I smiled, taking a seat. "What can I do for you today, Hunter?"

Hunter stopped scanning the room to look at me. "I heard rumor that you're family."

I blinked, leaning back in my seat, careful that my jacket didn't gape and that I didn't flash gun.

"Family?" I asked. I understood what "family," meant, but was she talking witchy, furry, or lezzy?

Hunter gazed at the painting of the wolf on the wall behind my desk, obviously a bit uncomfortable. The red wolf painting had been a gift from friend and beta werewolf of the Blackthorne pack, Rosalin Walker. I'd been surprised to find out that she was an artist. With the amount of artistic talent she had, she could've sold the sucker for a few hundred. I'd told her as much, but she'd insisted that I take the painting. The red wolf was also Rosalin's werewolf form. The gesture was sweet, and I wasn't sure of Rosalin's intentions with it, but every time I saw it, it reminded me that I'd accidentally claimed her. I really wished she'd sold the damn thing.

"You play for the same team?"

"What team are we talking about?" I asked.

"The all girls team," she said.

"Are you asking me if I'm a lesbian?"

"Uh…yes?" She didn't sound very certain.

"Then just ask."

"Are you a lesbian?"

"Yes," I said. "Is that what you came here for? To determine my sexual orientation?"

Hunter's cheeks flushed a bright shade of red.

"No, I'm sorry. I'm gay too and…and…I think my girlfriend is cheating on me."

"You think?" I asked.

Hunter picked out a corner of the ceiling to stare at while she spoke. "She's been acting really weird lately, telling me she has to work late, canceling lunch dates. We live together. Normally, she's home around midnight, but lately she hasn't been getting home until around two thirty in the morning. When I ask her why she has to stay late, she blames it on the new manager at work."

"Where does she work?"

"At a food joint," she told me.

"Okay." I folded my arms across the desk. "You think your girlfriend is cheating on you. If you want to hire me to find out whether she is or is not, I need specifics. Is that what you came here for?" It was important to me that I repeat the client's words, not only to get the specific details I needed for the investigation, but to make sure what they intended to pay me for was perfectly clear.

"Yes, that's why I'm here. Kamryn and I have been together for almost five years. This wouldn't be the first time she hasn't kept it in her pants." She held my gaze, looking uncomfortable and uncertain.

"Do you know for a fact she's cheated on you before? Does she have a history of being unfaithful?"

"Yeah."

I fixed her with a blank look. "So you know what I might find on this investigation. Are you willing to deal with the outcome?"

"Look," she said, sitting upright, "I'm not going to go psycho on her or anything. If she's cheating on me, I have a right to know. I told her last time if I caught her cheating again I'd kick her ass out of the apartment. I have a right to know. I intend to kick her ass out if she's fucking me over."

For the first time, there was no uncertainty in her. There was anger in her tone, righteous anger. I agreed with her. She had a right to know if her girlfriend of almost five years was cheating on her. Hell, I'd want to know so I could kick her ass out too.

I didn't often work on mundane, "I think my spouse is cheating," cases, and a part of me wondered if she'd paid any attention to the sign on the door that read, "Preternatural Investigations."

I sighed. "All right. I'll do it."

The whole spouse "might be" cheating thing could turn ugly really fast, but then, so did most of the cases I took involving the preternatural. At least this one had a sense of normal about it. Whatever normal is these days.

Hunter spent the next fifteen minutes telling me what she knew and suspected. She thought her girlfriend was cheating on her with someone from work, which is where I came in. It was kind of like a true or false question I got to answer. Kamryn Sherman worked at Al's Diner, a burger joint in downtown Oklahoma City. Hunter gave me the address.

I opened the top drawer on my desk and tossed in the notebook that I'd written Kamryn's name and work address in. I opened the second drawer and pulled out one of the contracts. The only time I'd actually let the contract slide was with Rosalin, because she was another werewolf, and she had wanted to keep everything on the down low. In all seriousness, it wasn't a smart move on my behalf. Fortunately, I still received payment.

When Lenorre and her vampires couldn't find Rosalin's brother, Lenorre sent Rosalin to me. One night, my friend and licensed Paranormal Hunter Rupert and I were investigating a series of murders committed by a werewolf, and we spotted Rosalin near the crime scene and followed her back to The Two Points, Lenorre's club in the city.

It was there that Lenorre offered her aid and we began working together and, well, dating.

I was usually very strict on the whole contract thing. I took the case with Rosalin because she was a member of the local werewolf pack and wanted someone outside the pack to help her. The contract protects both the client and me. It states very clearly that even if I don't find any valuable information, I get paid for my efforts. If a client doesn't think I'm doing a good job, they can still try to take me to court based upon what they perceive as a lack of effort. It's important when working a case to be able to bring physical evidence to the table. If I couldn't prove that I'd done my research and my job, I could be in deep shit. Sometimes, the threat of deep shit is a good motivator.

"I need you to read and sign this contract," I said. "It states very clearly that regardless of the outcome, I still get paid. If you don't feel I've done my part, you're welcome to challenge that. It goes over the privacy policy..."

Hunter took the contract, leaning over the desk and mumbling as she read it. I always gave a person the rundown of what the contract stated, but I still expected them to read it very carefully to make sure they understood what they were signing.

Hunter held her hand out and I gave her the pen.

"Thanks," she mumbled, scribbling her signature on the line at the bottom of the page.

I took the contract and signed my own signature on the other side of hers. I opened the bottom left drawer and took out the manila folder that had all her information in it. The information was basic: name, telephone, address, etc. June made my job easier by having a potential client fill out the document before coming in for an interview. An interview goes both ways, not only were we interviewing potential clients, but the client was interviewing us.

"Do you have any questions?"

She gave me a questioning look. "I just let you do your job, right?"

"Yes, and if I find anything, I'll contact you." I pushed a black and white business card with my cell number on it across the desk. "If you have any questions you're welcome to call me."

Hunter stood and took the card then slipped it into her pocket. I walked around my desk, offering my hand again. "Have a good evening, Hunter."

"If you call a client by their first name, does that mean they get to call you by yours?"

"If that's what you prefer," I said, smiling, hand still hovering in the air.

In the heels, she was only an inch or so shorter than I was. Hunter took my hand. A sudden burst of energy, almost like an electric shock, jolted between our clasped palms. Goosebumps crawled up and down my flesh.

Hunter jerked her hand from mine, a little too late.

I felt the wolf rouse inside me, raising her snout in curiosity, ears perking in interest.

"That was weird," Hunter said, rubbing her hand on her pants.

"Yes," I said, taking a step closer to her. My nostrils flared slightly. "It was."

Hunter Kinsley's scent hit me. She smelled of grass and rain and something not human. Humans have a different scent, sometimes sweet, sometimes salty, and sometimes downright putrid. The scents vary, but they're distinctively human. Mingling with the scent of rainwater, Hunter Kinsley smelled like fur.

Hunter took a step back, trying to put some distance between us. I followed her movements. She shot a worried glance toward the door.

"Hunter," I said gently. She took another step back. "Hunter," I tried again. The blood had drained from her face in a rush of fear. She glanced at the door again, and that one gesture of fear sent a tremble of excitement through the wolf, through me.

"Hunter," I said, "don't."

Hunter moved, lithe and agile. I moved with the quickness of the wolf, blocking her way, somehow managing not to trip in the high heels.

I barred the door, watching her, anticipating her next move. Hunter sank back. Her lips curled in a hiss that revealed elongated canine teeth on both upper and lower jaw. Black markings rose to her face, decorating her brow and cheeks like some Egyptian tattoo. Her skin took on a golden shimmer.

A rumbling growl beat like angry wings against my ribs. Hunter's pupils were too large to be human, too large and oblong to be wolf. I took another step forward, driving her further into my office. I was fairly certain if June saw her, I couldn't explain the marks on her face.

"Hunter," I said, "I think there's something you forgot to mention."

She backed into the client chair, sending it wobbling and crashing to the floor as she tried to get past it.

I stopped, trying to cage my instincts. If I kept moving toward her, she was only going to keep backing up until she had no other place to go, and neither animal nor human likes being backed into a corner. I tried to breathe past the scent of fear and adrenaline.

Hunter stopped, chest rising and falling quickly and jerkily.

"What are you?" she asked, voice trembling around the edges.

I pulled the jacket of my suit down, focusing on pulling the energy of the beast back into the core of my body, focusing on my shields, the metaphysical walls that kept the beast at bay.

"I should be asking you that."

She closed her eyes, as if she too were trying to calm herself. Breathing techniques help a lot when it comes to shifting. I had absolutely no doubt that Hunter Kinsley was a shape-shifter. I just didn't know what flavor.

It dawned on me. I'd seen those oblong pupils only once in my life, when I was in elementary school and had gone on a field trip with my science class to the zoo.

"You're a clouded leopard." I stared at her.

There was still that hint of panic in her when she nodded. "Yeah...you?"

"You don't know what I am?"

She inclined, sniffing the air between us. "You're not a cat," she said, snarling slightly.

"No, I'm not."

Her nostrils flared. "Canine?"

When I nodded she took a timid step forward, watching me warily.

"I won't attack you. You can calm down."

"Why did you block the door?"

"I don't need you running out of my office like that, and since you weren't up front with me, I doubt you want the rest of my office to know."

A blush tinted the skin of her face around the black markings. "I didn't know you weren't human or I would've been up front with you."

I moved, picking up the chair and setting it upright. Hunter scrambled to the other side of the room.

"Why are you afraid of me?" I asked.

"You smell dangerous."

"How do I smell dangerous?"

"Instincts? I don't know," she said. "When you moved to block the door you triggered all my instinctual responses. Those responses told me to run."

"I'm not going to hurt you." I offered my wrist. "Here," I said, "smell."

She knew I was canine, but she had yet to determine what type of lycanthropy I carried. She came to me and held my wrist lightly in both her hands. She glanced at me before sniffing just above the skin. Her mouth opened as her top lip curled slightly. She drew my scent in, like a cat would when having the flehmen response to a smell. On a human face, even with the dusting of gold and the black markings, it looked strange.

"Wolf?" she closed her mouth.

"It's really hard not to be insulted when felines do that."

"Do what?" she asked, leaning back against my desk.

"Flehmening," I said. "The feline stink face like you've just smelled something incredibly nasty."

She smiled awkwardly. "It wasn't bad," she said. "But the perfume was a little overwhelming." She scrunched up her nose.

"If I don't mask my scent with perfume—"

"Others will figure out what you are?" She finished my sentence with a question.

"Exactly."

"How long have you been infected?"

"A few years."

"I was six," she said. "My babysitter."

"Your babysitter attacked you?"

"No, she didn't mean to," she said. "It was an accident. I didn't understand until later that the strand I carry…we're easily spooked."

"I hadn't noticed."

She blushed again. "I brought a stray dog into the house and she freaked. Somewhere in the midst of her freak-out, I got scratched."

"Do your parents know?"

"No," she said. "I kept it to myself. What about you?"

"I was a cop working on a case."

"Was it traumatic?"

"No, I feel much better now that she's dead."

Hunter swallowed loud enough that I heard it.

"She deserved it, Hunter. She was out of control."

The tension between her shoulders eased a little. "Okay."

"What about your girlfriend?" I asked. "Am I going to face any supernatural surprises with her?"

"No, she's human."

"A human and a were-animal?" I raised my brows. "Does she know? Is that even safe?"

There's really no such thing as "safe sex" between a human and a were-animal. The tiniest scratch during the throes of passion could potentially infect a human lover. And unfortunately, there's no morning after pill to cure the lycanthropy virus.

"She knows. We've always been very careful with each other. She's careful not to spook me or do things that bring out my inner kitty, and I'm careful not to scratch or bite her."

I nodded, picked her jacket up off the floor, and handed it to her. "I'll see what I can find, Hunter." A thought occurred to me. "Can you not smell if she's been cheating?"

She paused in putting her jacket on, letting it hang from the tips of her fingers. As a were-animal, she should've been able to smell another woman on her girlfriend.

Slowly, she shook her head. "I smell sweat, burgers, grease, perfume, but I've never smelled another woman on her, in that way. And if she's hugged someone, you know...I don't want to jump to assumptions just because someone's smell rubbed off on her. We've gotten into some nasty fights in the past over that kind of thing. I need proof this time," she said, sounding reasonable. "Kamryn has always come home from work and hopped in the shower as soon as she walked in the door. She's just...she's distant. I don't know if it's from working so many hours or what."

"That's understandable, Hunter."

"I'm sorry I went all scaredy-cat on you." She finished putting on her jacket.

"Well, I did go bitchy on you first." I smiled. "Don't worry about it."

Hunter stopped in the doorway and turned back. "Thank you," she said.

"No problem."

I heard her draw in a deep breath.

"We should hang out some time."

I tilted my head. "You really think that's a good idea, considering?" I didn't get the sense she was hitting on me or flirting with me, but she was a werecat, and if she spooked as easily as I'd witnessed earlier, I was thinking a werewolf was the last person she wanted to befriend.

"As friends," she said.

"I don't know, Hunter. One, you're a client. Two, we're kind of opposite ends of the totem pole when it comes to our particular abilities."

The black markings and golden shimmer had faded from her face, but her pupils dilated, threatening to swallow her irises. That one look seemed to be saying, "I desperately need a friend."

Fucking felines and their Goddess-damned pussycat eyes.

I sighed. "We'll see, okay?"

She smiled brightly, pupils magically shrinking as if she could control it.

I had a feeling she could.

"Do you do that to your girlfriend?" I asked as she turned to leave.

"Do what?"

"The pussycat eyes."

"Yeah." She smiled widely, showing teeth that were no longer elongated. "You should see me when she opens a pack of lunchmeat."

I laughed.

Hunter left my office smiling despite the reason she'd come into it.

I returned to the seat behind my desk, wondering why I chose a line of work that ensured I inevitably ended up in someone else's mess.

CHAPTER TWO

It was ten minutes until six when I decided to call it a day. I shrugged into the black pea coat and fished my keys out of the side pocket. The phone rang and I frowned.

"Whoever this is, it had better be good."

"Don't I always have something good to tell you?"

It was Detective Arthur Kingfisher. Arthur and I had worked together since before I was infected with lycanthropy. He'd recently been promoted to detective.

"Do you want me to be honest or to hold my tongue?"

"I didn't know a lesbian could hold her tongue."

"For you, I'll make an exception."

Arthur joked pretty much nonstop, about anything and everything. When he wasn't joking, I was worried, because it meant shit had hit the roof. Arthur had only gone serious on me a few times in the past several years that I'd known him. It hadn't been a pretty sight. I always thought he was light-hearted, but I'd found out that beyond the joking attitude he had more depth than he let on. He was also an excellent cop and had been since the day I'd met him, but like most cops, the preternatural wasn't his area of expertise.

"Are you busy?" he asked.

I frowned even harder. Arthur only asked me if I was busy when the police wanted to call me in on something.

"Damn it, Arthur. If you tell me there's a body, I'm going to be pissed."

"You always say that and actually, no. We don't have a body."

I sighed in relief.

"We can't find the bodies alive or…" he added.

"If you can't find them, why are you calling me?"

"Neighbor called us," he mumbled. "She hadn't heard from the couple next door since yesterday evening. Said it's unusual. I'll explain more when you get here. I sent two uniforms out to talk to her. She had a key to the house but didn't want to go in. Well, uniforms used it."

"So you have a missing person's case?" I asked. Contrary to popular belief, the police won't always wait seventy-two hours to declare a person officially missing. It really depended on circumstance and evidence. If the absence was not common or the police found any indication of violence at the scene, they'll jump in and secure it for the crime scene investigators and possibly forensics as quickly as possible.

My stomach turned. "There's violence at the scene, isn't there?" I asked.

"There appears to be."

"You suck."

"No, but I know a guy who does."

"Are you referring to your boyfriend?" I quipped.

He laughed loud enough that I had to draw the telephone away from my ear.

"Man," he said, "I love your comebacks. So you on your way?"

"Does this have anything to do with the preternatural?" I asked. "If it doesn't, Arthur, I don't have to do anything. You know the rules."

"Kass," he said, "I'm holding the crime scene photos."

"I need a better reason than that."

"You want a better reason?" He said, and sounded a little angry. Arthur never got angry with me. What the hell?

"Here's a better reason. There are symbols painted on the walls in blood. You want to know something? They look a lot like that star necklace you used to wear. The couple's bed is covered in what appears to be blood. Something happened there, Kass. I can feel it in my gut."

He was referring to my pentacle necklace. A lot of witches wear jewelry symbolic of their spirituality. Thanks to the lycanthropy and not connecting the dots...I had a permanent white scar on my chest where I'd tried to wear my necklace after being infected. Yeah, silver and lycanthropy is a big no-no.

Arthur said. "We've got the house blocked off. I want your opinion on this. Come down to the department, Kass."

I heard his hand cover the phone as he mumbled something to someone else in the room. I had supernatural hearing, but covering the phone muffled the words enough that I couldn't make them out.

A man's bass voice suddenly boomed in my ear. "Lyall, get your ass down here immediately. That's a fucking order."

The phone clicked silent. I knew the man's voice. How could I not? Captain Holbrook was my old boss and Arthur had just sicced him on me.

That rat bastard.

I turned the lights off and locked my office door on the way out. June was still at her desk.

"June," I said, and she looked up from the stack of paperwork she was sorting.

"What?"

I ignored the attitude. "Next time, would you please walk the client to my office? They have a tendency to get lost."

"How hard can it be to find your office when there's only two up there?" she asked. "Besides, your friends don't seem to have trouble finding it."

I ignored the chastising tone in her voice. June had once met Rosalin, and the time she'd met her, Rosalin had walked up to my office without June's okay. June obviously was holding a grudge about that.

"There's a difference between a friend and a client. If it's someone you don't recognize and you know they're a potential client because they have an appointment, walk them up."

"Fine." She returned to sorting through paperwork.

"Have a good evening. Lock up when you leave."

"Don't I always?"

CHAPTER THREE

I parked in front of the sign that read City of Oklahoma Police Department and got out, locking the car doors with the keypad out of habit. I opened one side of the double glass doors and walked into the bright fluorescent lit room. I scanned the rows of desks looking for Arthur's face.

"Miss?" A young cop stepped forward. "May I help you?"

"Where's Kingfisher?" I asked.

"Kingfisher," he mumbled. He seemed to be talking more to himself than me, scanning the rows of desks too. I didn't say anything. His face was boyish and clean and I wondered if he even had to shave. I felt a pang of pity for him. He was new. I could smell it.

"Preternatural Investigator Kassandra Lyall?" a woman's voice called out from behind new-boy. He was slim but had enough muscle and was tall enough that I had to look around him to spot her.

"I'll take you back to see *Detective* Arthur Kingfisher," she said, turning to the younger cop and making it obvious she was reminding him who Kingfisher was. Sadly, I didn't really blame her.

Berkeley Ackerman and I had met before, but she hadn't been on the force when I'd worked as a cop. She'd been one of the cops around when Arthur had taken my statement and helped clean up a pile of dead werewolf a few months ago.

The last time I'd seen her, she'd accused me of torturing Lukas Morris, Sheila Morris's sociopathic brother. Of course, I'd assured her that if I had been torturing him, or intending to torture him, I wouldn't have used a gun. Since when did torture involve guns? Last I checked, you used a gun for a quick kill, not when you're going to be hunkering down and devoting an hour and a half to inflicting intense pain.

I watched her long fiery braid dance down her back as she led the way to Arthur's location. Like me, Ackerman was slender, but she was taller, longer of leg and arm, and definitely bustier. I caught up with her as we headed down the hallway, passing the interrogation room with its fading paint job. I sensed very strongly that Ackerman didn't like me. She didn't have to say it; her body language screamed it.

"I heard you were a good cop," she said, slowing her walk. It wasn't really a question.

"I like to think so," I said, slipping my hands inside the pockets of my coat.

"But you don't hesitate to take a life, do you?"

"I don't hesitate to protect innocent lives, Ackerman. I am a Paranormal Huntress. Taking out the bad guys is part of what I do."

"Taking out bad guys that are three times your size and supernaturally stronger?" She shook her head. "You don't look like much. I find it hard to believe you took down that werewolf a few months ago."

If she thought I was going to have a pissing contest with her, she was sorely mistaken.

"You were there when Arthur took my statement. I had help."

"From who?"

"How am I supposed to know?"

"Two random werewolves just decided to help you out?"

Actually, they weren't random. What I hadn't told the police was that Lenorre, Rosalin, and Carver had saved my ass. In fact, I'd completely left Lenorre out of it. The only thing the cops knew was that two wolves had showed up and helped save my life. Did I mention Lukas had kidnapped me? Did I mention I'm dating the Countess vampire of Oklahoma City? One would think kidnapping the girlfriend of a very powerful vampire is a bad idea, right? Or is that just me?

"Are you preternaturally prejudiced or something, Ackerman?"

"No…"

"What's with the twenty questions? You should know as well as I that size and physical strength don't always matter. I'm a trained professional, just like you, and when someone helps save my ass, I'm not going to bitch about it."

"More like a trained preternatural assassin," she whispered.

I stared at her, not knowing how to respond without making the situation much, much worse.

"Officer Ackerman," Arthur said and Berkeley Ackerman turned toward the sound of his voice. Arthur stood in the doorway to what I was guessing was his new office.

"Detective Kingfisher," she said, "I was just escorting Ms. Lyall to see you."

"Sounded more to me like you were chewing her ear off." He motioned with his head toward the main room. "Go back to your desk. I'll take it from here."

"Yes, sir," she said politely enough. She spared me a narrow-eyed look on her way back.

"Kass," Arthur said, holding the door open.

I walked past Arthur and into the room beyond. The room was painted off-white, and was fairly empty and plain. The wastebasket, however, was overflowing with stuff.

Yep, definitely Arthur's office.

"I don't think she likes me," I said.

Arthur chuckled softly, tugging uncomfortably at his tie.

"I'd be surprised if Ackerman likes anyone."

"Ah, she's one of those?"

"A bitch?" he asked. "Yeah."

The corner of my mouth twitched. "I didn't say it."

"Nope, I did." He sat behind his desk and pushed a manila envelope across the desk, "Sit down. Take a look. It ain't pretty."

A warning wasn't enough to prepare anyone for what I was looking at. The first photograph was a wide view showing the front door. The next showed the living room. The third was from deeper in the living room, facing a hallway that led to four bedrooms.

"The point of entry is the front door?"

"No signs of breaking and entering," he said.

The next photograph was closer to the hallway, facing a dark stain in the pale gray carpet that led from the hallway.

"A body was dragged?"

"We think so."

"Did you see these?" I asked, going back to the previous photograph. "The statues on top of the entertainment center?" The first statue was of Gaia, a woman figure holding the earth in her arms. "This is Gaia," I said, "Gaia was the earth Goddess to the Ancient Greeks."

Arthur slipped his hand inside his jacket then drew a pen from his shirt pocket. He pointed at the picture with the capped end. "Who's the devil?"

"That is not the devil. That is Pan. He was the God of hunting, music, and pleasure to the Ancient Greeks. They also viewed him as a sort of shepherd."

"Looks more like he'd scare the sheep away," Arthur mumbled.

"That's not the point," I said.

"What do the statues mean?" He straightened, tapping his pen against the palm of his other hand.

"Well, to me, the statues suggest that the couple were pagan."

"They were witches?"

"Not necessarily, no."

"Explain. What's the difference between a pagan and a witch?"

I thought about it. "Pagan covers a broad spectrum of nature-based and polytheistic spiritualities. But not all pagans practice witchcraft."

"What about the pentacle?" he asked. I hadn't yet seen the pentacle in the photographs.

"I don't know," I said honestly.

"Okay, so you think our possible victims were pagan?"

"It's very likely, yes. I just don't know what flavor."

Arthur tugged uncomfortably at his light blue tie. He pushed the messy tresses of his brown hair out of his face. "Keep going," he said.

I pushed the two photographs away and scanned one of the close-ups. Crime scene photographs go in order of a full range snapshot, mid-range, and close-up. I stopped at the close-up of what I guessed was the doorway to the master bedroom. A trail of blood, like a body had been dragged, went from the door to the right and toward the camera.

"A body was dragged from the master bedroom?" I asked, going to the next photograph. A red stained symbol stood out above the couple's bed. The celestial decorated blankets on the bed appeared to be soaked in the fluid.

"That's not a pentacle," I said.

The symbol looked disturbing, no longer bright and shiny red, no longer fresh, but dried, seeping down like the wall itself had bled. It didn't appear to be that big, perhaps a little larger than my hand. In the middle of the symbol, eight elongated triangles were positioned to form what appeared to be an eight-pointed star. Each triangle harbored a small symbol. I recognized the two symbols at the top of the drawing. The first was a sickle with a line drawn through the handle.

"Do you know what it is and what it means?" Arthur asked.

"Not off the top of my head," I said, gesturing for Arthur to stand. When he stood beside my chair and leaned over, I pointed at the first symbol. "This is the symbol for the dwarf planet Ceres. In astrology, Ceres corresponds to the mother."

"The second symbol is just a circle," Arthur said.

"Yes, but what do you get when you have a circle?" I asked, thinking aloud. "The circle can represent a lot of things, the sun, the moon, wholeness, completion. This entire drawing looks like a homemade seal of some sort."

"A seal?"

"Sometimes when a witch or Wiccan is doing magical work, they'll design a seal or sigil to represent the magical working. Usually, they'd carry the seal with them, on a piece of paper or talisman to aid the energy flow, intent, and focus. They could burn it, either by engraving the symbol on a candle or by burning the paper they've inscribed it on."

I sighed. No doubt, the media was going to go ape-shit with this. Leave it to one idiot to give everyone else in a community a bad name.

"I don't know why someone would leave this kind of symbol behind."

"You think whoever drew the symbol on the wall is pagan?" he asked.

"I can't answer that," I said, "as there's no telling just by looking. I can tell you that many of these symbols I'm not familiar with. They look alchemical, which isn't limited to a person who identifies as pagan. Has someone tested the stain on the wall to confirm it's blood?"

"We sent samples to the lab."

"Tell me about the couple that lived there."

"Miranda and Landon Blevins. Married for two years. Miranda was twenty-five. Landon twenty-six. The neighbor, an elderly woman named Emma Mullins, said they were 'sweet kids.' No known enemies. Miranda often helped her with her garden. She didn't say much about Landon. But she did say that Miranda told her a few weeks ago she was infertile. She and Landon were looking to adopt." He flipped the notebook closed. "That's all I've got."

I stared back down at the picture of the bedroom. "I don't see any signs of struggle. I don't see a weapon. The room is clean; nothing is knocked over or looks out of place. There's no body. Damn it, Arthur," I said. "I think right now, forensics is your best bet."

"Why do you think you're sitting in my office?" he said. "They're out there as we speak. We'll go when we're not going to be in their way."

It didn't surprise me he wanted to go in after forensics. It was easier than tiptoeing around trying not to contaminate anything. "And if they take stuff away to take back to the lab? It's better if I see the scene whole, Arthur. Judging by the dried blood on the wall, it's already some hours cold."

"I know, Kass. I'm doing what I can. Do you think it's a cult related crime?"

"I don't know. It could be someone trying to make it look like a cult related crime. It could be a discrimination crime. There are too many possibilities and not enough evidence."

"When I get the green light, we'll go in."

"You know, even seeing the scene, I can't guarantee any results."

"None of us can," he said. "We just try our damndest to find clues."

"Damndest?" I asked, smiling. "Oh, you were so born in Oklahoma."

Arthur flashed his cheesy grin. "I know. I sound like my Gramps."

"You sound like everyone's grandfather when you say that. It's not even a word."

Arthur sat up straight like something had startled him. "I nearly forgot," he said, opening the top drawer of his desk. He pulled out a chain with a square of plastic attached to it. "We had an ID made for you so I don't have to hold your hand and walk you onto a crime scene."

I took the neck ID. The top of it had my name and title written on it. The photograph in the middle of the ID was old, from before I'd been infected with lycanthropy, before the white streak had shown up.

It wasn't a bad picture, but I looked serious and not happy about having it taken. I could see why most people had never pegged me as a cop. I looked feminine and fragile with a darker edge that might make some mistake me for Goth. The dark blue uniform looked good against my pale skin, made my eyes greener, but it didn't make me look like a cop. Arthur had once said I had a dominant look, despite my stature. Gazing at the picture on the ID tag, I didn't see it. I looked bored more than anything. Which if memory served me correctly, I had been. I'm not a big fan of being photographed.

"This picture is so fucking old."

"Yeah," he said, "but it's all we've got on file. It still looks like you, so it'll get you into the crime scenes without a police escort."

"Hopefully, because every time I flash my license and badge they don't believe me."

"They'll believe you now. Look at the bottom."

I noticed the signatures. "Damn. You got Holbrook to sign it?"

"Yep." He beamed. "I bugged the shit out of him until he did."

"Thank you, Arthur."

"No problem. You deserve to be able to walk onto a scene all by yourself."

"I agree. Do you have a time guesstimate for when we'll check out the crime scene?"

"Later."

"Arthur, I really should be going in while the scene is still in one piece."

"Sorry, Kass, but this time we're kind of bringing you in as a last resort."

"I hadn't noticed."

"I'll call you," he said.

I got up, ready to leave. In part, I was glad I didn't have to go and immediately see the scene. The pictures were bad enough. It didn't sit well with me that he could call me at any hour of the night expecting my ass to roll out of bed, but it's not like he hadn't done it before.

"Have a good night, Kass."

"You too, Kingfisher."

With that, I opened the door and headed for the exit, ignoring the hush of silence that fell over the main room. Ackerman was by the door. Her crystalline gaze met mine as she held it open. The look she gave me wasn't friendly.

I ignored her as I walked past, hoping it would irritate her. I unlocked the car and slid behind the wheel.

Ackerman stood in the doorway, glaring at me. I had to force myself to resist the urge to flip her off.

Crime scene, murder, and a jackass police officer—three things that are not a good combination for a positive and cheerful mood.

Chapter Four

I had my foot on the brake and was stopping at a red light when my cell phone rang from the console. When in the car, I keep a headset plugged into the phone so that I don't turn into one of those people who is too busy yakking away to pay attention to the road. The sun was setting on the western horizon of Oklahoma City. The last few streamers of light reflected brightly off the skyscrapers, like it was the light's last chance to fight against the darkness. Still, it was too early for Lenorre to be awake.

I flipped the phone open and stuck the earpiece in my ear.

"Arthur, I just left. What the hell?"

"There's been a murder," he said.

I jumped as a silver Impala behind me laid on their horn and noticed the light had turned green and someone was impatient to get somewhere.

"You found a body?"

I could hear a woman's muffled voice in the background, but what she said, even my werewolf hearing couldn't translate. Arthur was covering his phone again.

"At the first scene? No. At this one? Yes. Where are you?"

"In my car," I told him. "On my way home. Why? Where are you?" I knew why. I knew the moment I saw his number on my caller ID that something was up, and I had a feeling I was about to get dragged into that something. Oh, joy.

"Penn and Eighty-Ninth," he said, spouting off an address.

"Arthur," I said. "I'm driving. I can't very well write it down!"
He chuckled. "Then look for the flashing lights. You can't miss us. We've got the entire street blocked off for the time being."

"Why are you blocking the street?"

There was a pause. "You don't want to know."

"Shit, Arthur. Do you ever have anything good to tell me?"

"You can bring your girlfriend or that one chick," he said.

"Oh, that's wonderful news, Arthur. Thank you so much for inviting my girlfriend onto a murder scene." I hit my turn signal and made a left. "Why and what chick?"

"That one vamp," he said. "Tall, dark, and drop-dead gorgeous." He seemed to find his last words amusing, chuckling in my ear.

"Eris?" I asked.

"Is that the one you don't get along with? The one that broke old man Cunningham's door down?"

"Yeah, that's Eris." I sighed again. "It'll be a while. It's still too early for Lenorre or any of the other vampires to be awake. Give me about forty minutes, and I'll be there."

"Forty minutes?" he said. "The sun is setting now. We could use her spidey senses. Not that yours aren't good enough or anything."

"I need to change and I am not bringing a hungry vampire onto a bloody crime scene."

He laughed. "That'd be a sight."

"No, that would be an entirely new crime scene."

"Hey," he said, "at least we wouldn't be busting our balls trying to find a suspect."

"I'll be there as soon as I can," I said, and hung up on him. I probably should've told him that forty minutes would be the minimum amount of time it would take me. I guided the car onto the highway and headed for Lenorre's, hoping I had something to change into that didn't involve heels.

The cops wanted to call me in last. Well, chances were I'd arrive last.

CHAPTER FIVE

R osalin opened the door. "Wow, you look pissy."
She moved out of the way as I entered and hung my coat
on a coat rack by the door.

"I'm not exactly happy."

"What's up?"

"I have a crime scene to go to."

"The police have called you in on something?"

Rosalin pushed the tangled auburn locks of hair out of her face.
It appeared as though she hadn't brushed her hair.

"Yeah. Did you just wake up?"

"No," she said. "I make it a habit to run around in my nighties."

I shook my head. Rosalin often slept in tank tops and a pair of
boxer shorts. The red tank top she was wearing clung to her figure.
It looked too tight to be comfortable to sleep in.

I followed her, and the smell of coffee, into the kitchen.

I leaned against the island as she poured herself a cup. "Do you
want one?"

"Nah, not right now."

She gave me a look full of phony surprise. "God, mark this
date. Kassandra Lyall, turning down coffee."

I ignored her and checked the digital clock above the stove. It
was almost seven thirty, which meant Lenorre should've already
woken for the night.

"You think she's up yet?" I asked.

She took a sip of her coffee. "Probably."

"Fed?"

Rosalin shrugged. "Go find out."

"I don't think that's a good—"

"She's awake." I turned to find Zaphara standing in the doorway. "And fed."

Two tiny bite marks were beginning to heal at the side of her neck.

"Thanks for the update."

Her dark brows rose. "You don't sound very appreciative."

"Hard to, coming from you."

Her generous mouth spread into a wide grin. "Which makes it all the more fun."

"Zaphara," Rosalin said, but her voice didn't have the command in it that Lenorre often used when someone was stepping out of line.

"Kassandra isn't in a good mood. I wouldn't push her," she said, but she wasn't meeting Zaphara's gaze. By doing so, she was admitting Zaphara was dominant.

"Oh?" Zaphara asked, making a show of touching the tiny drops of blood on her neck and wincing.

A low growl rumbled in my chest.

She laughed. "Seems you are correct, wolf. You don't feel like playing?"

"With you," I said, "very fucking rarely."

Zaphara had her moments when she was easy to get along with, but only to an extent. She'd treated me with a little more respect in the last several weeks and had taken it upon herself to teach me how to harness the raven magic in my blood. For that, I was grateful, but the teasing and testing got on my nerves. But that's exactly why she did it.

I left Zaphara and Rosalin to keep each other company, heading through the basement and the inner hallway. The door at the end of the hall opened, spilling light and color into my black and white night vision.

"Good morning." I slipped in as Lenorre shut the door behind me.

Lenorre wrapped an arm around my waist and brushed her lips across my cheek. "Good evening." She embraced me briefly before releasing me.

I leaned against the back of the couch, crossing my legs out in front of my body.

"How long have you been waiting?" she asked.

"Not long," I said. "Pretty much as soon as I arrived Zaphara started parading around."

Lenorre shook her head, black, waist-length curls slithering serpent-like over the wine colored blouse she wore.

"You are later than usual."

I crossed my arms, not defensively, but so I wouldn't get distracted by going to her, touching her. "I had an appointment that was scheduled later than usual," I told her. "Arthur called."

"A murder?"

"That's the only reason he calls, isn't it?"

"To my knowledge, yes."

"He called me in to look at some photographs."

"Photographs?"

"Mmhmm."

Lenorre's expression was thoughtful, trying to figure it out.

"Why photographs?" she finally asked.

"According to him," I said, "he's trying to give me a break."

"That does not sound like your detective friend."

"No, it doesn't," I said. "Usually, no matter who else is on the scene, investigators, medical examiner, forensics, Arthur lets me play with them. Honestly, I think he's trying to keep me away from the press."

"Why do you think so?"

"There's something distinctively pagan about it."

Lenorre caught it very quickly. "Ah." She moved, slightly, no longer so statuesque. "And if it leaks to the media that the police have a practicing witch working on their investigation…"

"Right," I said. "If it goes to court, the defense might use it as an excuse to play some awful cards. The whole department would probably get hit. So I think Arthur is trying his hardest to keep things under wraps."

"What else?" Lenorre asked.

I tilted my head. "What do you mean? What else?"

"Kassandra." She smiled and my knees felt weak. "There is more. I can see it in the set of your shoulders. You're holding something back."

This time, my brows went up.

Lenorre moved so quickly she was a blur of wine-colored silk. She gripped my shoulders, pressing me a little roughly into the back of the couch. She squeezed and I stiffened under her hands.

"I do not think it's just the photographs or Arthur's decisions that have created such tension."

"You don't think it's being around you?" I asked.

Her hands slid down my shoulders, across my back, resting at the base of my spine.

"No," she said simply, but something about the way she said it was too intimate.

I looked away.

She placed one long, tapered finger under my jaw and turned my face back to hers.

"Kassandra."

"Well, technically, I don't think they've officially declared the first scene as a homicide, since they're still gathering evidence. However, there has been a murder and Arthur wants me to take a look at it."

She took a step back. "I take it you want to change your clothes?"

I nodded. "Yeah, and you've been invited, by the way."

It wasn't obvious, but her surprise showed a little. "I have?"

"Yes," I said. "Do you want to come with me? Seems they want someone who's more sensitive to help sniff things out." I shrugged. "And because they know what you are you'll be able to point things out to the police that I can't."

She smiled, this time revealing the tips of her small fangs. "For you? Yes. For your detective friend? Not so much."

I reached out, trying to catch her wrist.

Lenorre moved too damn fast, turning her upper body away from me, just out of reach. The expression on her face was impish.

I pouted. "No fair."

She stepped into me, using her lower body to press mine against the couch. The breath caught in my throat.

"Darling," she said, "All's fair—"

I put a hand against her chest. "If you finish that sentence, I will not have sex with you tonight."

She laughed at me. "Oh you think so, do you?" Her mouth sought my neck as she placed a tiny kiss upon my pulse.

My heart gave a loud, resounding thump throughout my entire body.

"Fuck," I murmured. "I can try."

Her hand found my hip, thumb tracing distractingly over my slacks.

"I do believe," she mumbled, "we have played this game before."

Her tongue teased across my pulse a second before her teeth clenched lightly, catching and releasing the skin without breaking it. I gripped the back of the couch until the wood creaked in protest.

"I'm confused. Which of us are you teasing?"

She cupped the back of my skull. "Both," she said, tangling her hand in my hair and pulling my face up to hers.

Her lips were like silk against my own, cool and smooth. She tasted of cinnamon toothpaste, but beneath the cinnamon, I could taste the faint undertone of blood. Zaphara's blood. My stomach turned. It wasn't the taste of blood that made my stomach turn; it was the fact that it was Zaphara's and that it was everywhere in her mouth that did me in.

"What is it?" Lenorre asked, searching my face.

"Next time," I said in a near growl, "use mouthwash."

It was like watching someone slam the blinds down over a window. Lenorre's guard tumbled that fast.

"I'm sorry," I said. "That was harsh. Zaphara was teasing me again. I know she's your blood donor." I shook my head, wrapping my arms around myself. "But for some reason, I really want to punch her in the face right now."

It may have been childish, but it was honest.

The corner of her mouth twitched.

"Don't you dare laugh at me," I said.

"How can I not when there is an obvious solution?"

"What do you mean?"

"If you are so jealous of Zaphara being my blood source, why do you not offer yourself in her stead?"

A little flicker of discomfort went through me too quickly to hide. The muscles in my shoulders tensed.

I didn't know what to say.

Lenorre stepped back. "Does the idea of feeding me frighten you so, Kassandra?"

"You've bitten me before."

"I have drunk your blood during sex," Lenorre said. "You would not let me bite you, truly, or enchant you."

"Is that what they're calling it?" I made little quotes in the air. "Enchant?"

"Would you prefer it if I said you would not let me fuck your mind as much as I fuck the rest of your body?"

It felt like someone had pulled my legs out from under me. I clung to the back of the couch and bowed my head, hiding behind my hair.

Lenorre gave a short laugh this time. "Your mouth forms words that say one thing, but your body and your pulse say another, Kassandra."

I raised my face. "I think you're misinterpreting my physical reaction."

"How so?"

"I'm not excited, by any means, at the idea of you mind-fucking me, Lenorre."

"Fair enough," she said. "However, you are excited by the thought of being bitten. I believe we have already garnered such knowledge."

I held her gaze. "Yes."

"Will you let me bite you?" she asked bluntly.

"I don't know."

Lenorre let out a long, frustrated sigh. "I do not understand what is truly so bad. What makes you so uncertain when it comes to sharing blood with me? What is in the way, Kassandra? You have shared during sex. You have bled me during sex. What is the issue?"

"I don't want to be food."

"You are my lover," she said, somewhat incredulously. "Zaphara is food. You are my lover. You are the one I want most to share blood with. Do you know how mutually pleasurable such a thing could be?"

"I've upset you."

Lenorre's dark eyelashes fluttered closed. "A little."

"Why?"

"You are withholding a piece of yourself from me to avoid getting too close. Are you that afraid I will hurt you? Do you distrust me so, even now?"

I thought about denying her words, but I knew it was pointless. She was a vampire, and despite my job description, I'd never been much good at lying to the people I cared about. The best liars are the ones who are capable of convincing themselves of their lies. In this, I was too aware of myself to dissemble.

"Damn it, Lenorre."

"Damn it? You are not going to disagree or argue with me?"

"That would be a lie and pointless, wouldn't it? I'm not trying to hurt you."

"I know you are not trying to hurt me," she said. "But can you see how it would?"

I stood there, watching her as she fell into that vampiric stillness. She had this uncanny ability to see past my walls, to force me to turn around and look at myself behind them. It was exciting and frightening. Exciting because she understood me. Frightening because the more she understood me, the more in love with her I fell.

I sighed, breathing the word, "Yes."

She took a step back. "We have a scene to look at for the police," she said. "When you are ready, Kassandra."

It was obvious she wasn't referring to the fact that I needed to get dressed so we could go, but was referring to me opening up, letting down my guard, and giving that piece of myself to her.

That's one thing the stories don't tell you, that sometimes, love, real love, is a scary bitch. Love will ask you to face the things within yourself you'd rather just ignore. And the catch is, in order to make a relationship work, you can't. You have to face your inner demons and fears head on, or they get bigger, nastier.

Lenorre was asking me to face them. If I didn't, I risked hurting her.

Sadly, I'd always been better at dealing with the monsters outside myself than the ones within me.

At least the ones outside me I could shoot.

CHAPTER SIX

I found a pair of black boots I'd left at Lenorre's. The boots looked good with the dress slacks. Lenorre was wearing a white knee-length jacket that cinched at her waist. The onyx waist-length curls of her hair looked delicious against the white coat. I was wearing the same black pea coat I'd worn to the office. Between the two of us, the only splash of color other than black and white was Lenorre's wine-colored blouse.

Arthur was right. The entire street was blocked off, and the red and blue police lights were a flashing beacon. I put the car in park, unbuckled my seat belt, and reached over Lenorre to open the glove compartment. I retrieved the spiffy new badge Arthur had given me, draped the lanyard over my neck, and pulled my hair out from under it.

"We're going to get stopped by at least three police officers after getting past the tape."

Lenorre gave me a look. "Do you want me to make it so we will not?"

I shook my head. "Nah, after so many years, that would be weird."

She smiled slightly. "I shall follow your lead."

"Good idea." I got out and slammed the car door shut.

I ducked under the Do Not Cross tape, wondering if Lenorre could seriously use her vampire wiles and walk in and out of the crime scene completely undetected. The thought was just a little unnerving.

Arthur met us in the front yard and led the way through the house.

"In here," he said, and we stepped into what appeared to be the victim's master bedroom. The scene before me didn't match the signature of violence that hung in the air. Unlike the scenes in the photographs that Arthur had shown me, I didn't see or smell any blood, but just because I couldn't see or smell anything didn't mean anything. I could feel the tension in the air like the calm after a thunderstorm.

"Martha is on her way," Arthur said.

Martha Apostolos was the Chief Medical Examiner, and once she arrived on scene she'd be in charge of examining the body and collecting any evidence from it. I wasn't here to collect evidence to send back to a lab or to transport the body for further examination. That's not my area of expertise. I was here because I was supposed to help the cops figure out if this crime had anything to do with the preternatural and if so, how?

Lenorre stood next to me. I took the pair of latex gloves that Arthur offered. I'd put my hair back before we'd left Lenorre's. If Forensics was going to be all over the place, I didn't want them accidentally picking up any DNA I shed.

I went to the side of the bed.

The victim was laid back against the pillows. She was clothed, wearing a light pink nightgown that ended just below her knees. Her dark brown hair spilled out against the white pillowcase. Her eyes were still open, wide and terrified in that last moment, glazed with death. Something a lot of people don't realize is that it's easier looking at a body when the victim's eyes aren't open. There's always something more peaceful about it, a part of the childish mind that can imagine they're only sleeping. But when they're not shut, that last second of life seems frozen, like a film stuck on the last frame.

One thing I had noticed when we entered the bedroom was the small altar setup on a wooden dresser that was placed under the only window. The smell of some thick and cloying incense lingered, mingling with the soft and floral scent of soap on the body. She'd showered recently, though her hair was no longer wet.

I examined the white sheets carefully.

"Arthur," I said, as something caught my eye. He stepped up and I gestured toward the woman's leg.

"Is that a burn mark?" he asked.

The same mark I'd seen on the wall in the crime scene photographs was imprinted on the victim's leg, red and raw against her pale skin. I leaned closer to the body and realized it was a mistake. The smell of something musky and sour hit the back of my tongue.

I called Lenorre's name and felt her move to the opposite side of me.

"What can you smell?" I asked her.

I watched as she drew in a deep breath, sorting through the scents in the room more obviously than I would've done in front of the nice policemen.

"Incense," she said, "soap, fear, arousal…"

"Arousal?" Arthur asked. "You can smell arousal and fear?"

"Yes, Detective."

"So if you smell arousal, does that mean you smell sex?"

"'Tis probable," she said carefully.

"Our victim was raped?" He was looking at me now.

I touched the victim's wrist with my gloved fingers and the body was fresh enough to move easily. I turned the wrist and lowered it gently back to the bed. I got Arthur to move out of my way.

"She was strangled," I said, noting the faint bruising that was beginning to blossom like a necklace around the victim's neck. "I can't tell you just by a glance if the victim was sexually assaulted. I don't see any bruising at the wrists, which you'd commonly find."

"Not always," a voice said from the doorway.

Martha Apostolos entered the room wearing a flowing long-sleeved blue dress and heels. Her dark mane of hair was pulled away from her face, revealing her soft, Greek features. She gave a smile that reached her red-brown eyes when she said, "Kassandra, it's been a long time."

Arthur and I both stepped away from the body, getting out of her way. I returned the friendly smile. "I take it your night has been interrupted too?" I asked.

"It has," she said. "I was out with a friend." She fixed Arthur with an accusatory stare, as if it was all his fault.

Arthur handed her a pair of gloves and said, "Sorry to interrupt."

"Oh, no, you're not." She laughed. "As I was saying when I walked in, you won't always find signs of restraint and force left behind. I would say that it doesn't appear your victim struggled, but I'll know more once I've had the opportunity to examine the body more thoroughly."

"All right," Arthur said. "Thanks, Martha. We'll get out of your hair."

Martha offered a sharp nod, but she was already eyeing the body and intently setting to work. We left her to it.

Lenorre knelt beside the bed in the guestroom, which was decorated in a lot of blue and a lot of gray. I could smell the unmistakable scent of cat urine and kitty litter in this room. If I looked closely enough, I could see black cat hairs on the bed.

"We suspect our victim in the other room is Leana Davey," Arthur said. "She lives here alone."

Lenorre said, "Not exactly, Detective," as a black cat slipped out from under the bed. The cat looked at me, ears twitching, pupils dilating. Lenorre stroked a hand down the back of its head. The cat looked startled for a second before rubbing against her leg. Apparently, cats like vampires. Who would've thought? I would've petted the cat, but I didn't for two reasons. One, it wasn't my cat. Two, the look it had given me told me I'd be sticking my hand in a kitty blender.

"Familiar?" Arthur asked.

I shrugged. "Could be? Who knows. Tell me what else you know," I said. "Does this scene match the other in that there are no signs of forced entry?"

Lenorre continued to pet the cat, which was greedily gobbling up her affection.

Arthur looked at me as he leaned against the wall closest to the door. "Same," he said. "Do you think it's human or preternatural?"

"Honestly," I said, "I don't know. At this point, the only connection I can make between this crime and the last one is the victims' spiritual preferences and that damned symbol."

"It could easily be either," Lenorre offered.

"Do you have any idea what the symbol means?" I asked her.

She shook her head. "If I had, Kassandra, I would have spoken so. I am sorry. I do not."

Berkeley Ackerman chose that moment to walk into the room. She held a phone out to Arthur. "Holbrook wants to talk to you," she said.

"Shit," Arthur said, taking the phone and walking out of the room with it.

I heard him say, "Kingfisher, here," and a few, "Uh-huhs," as he made his way down the short hallway and out into the living room.

I felt Ackerman staring at me.

"So, it's true," she said, crossing her arms over her dark blue uniform.

I knelt, peeking under the bed. There might not be any clues there, but it didn't hurt to look. I stood carefully, trying not to scare the cat that was keeping a precarious distance and huddling against Lenorre.

"What's true?"

She nodded toward Lenorre. "That's your girlfriend?"

"My personal life isn't your business, Ackerman."

"I don't know why Holbrook keeps you on retainer," she said snidely. "It's not like you do much of anything aside from shooting people."

One breath. Two breaths.

"Ackerman," I said, trying not to sound as bitchy as I felt. "If that's what you want to think, then fine, think it. If it helps you sleep better at night, knock yourself out. I really don't give a shit what you think of me."

"What I think of you?" Her brows raised a fraction. "It's fact, Ms. Lyall. You're nothing but a fancy licensed killer."

I took three quick strides that put me in her face. Ackerman flinched as if she were afraid I'd hit her.

"If you thought what I did to Lukas Morris was terrible, you should have seen what he did to his victims. Why are you so oblivious to the fact that he committed murder? He was a serial killer, you idiot. He took innocent lives. Maybe you have sympathy for him. But I don't. I don't have a fucking ounce of sympathy for the twisted bastard."

She stood up, tall and straight, as if she were trying to tower over me. As if to say, "I'm taller, which makes me tougher." However, she wasn't as tall as Lenorre, and when she tried to use her height to intimidate me, I saw Lenorre stand out of my peripheral vision. I didn't hear her take a step toward me, but I knew she had when Ackerman's gaze flicked nervously past my shoulder. If there was one thing she knew about the vampire standing behind me, it was what and who she was. And it was obvious in that moment that Ackerman wasn't exactly comfortable around her.

I wondered if that's why she'd been staying so close to the door.

"Officer," Lenorre said, infusing that one word with the undercurrent of a smooth threat and warning.

Ackerman kept her gaze averted, refusing to look at Lenorre.

Was she afraid of all vampires or was it just Lenorre?

"I've seen the file," Ackerman said. "I saw what she did to that man."

"That man wasn't a man, Ackerman. That man was a serial killer and a lycanthrope."

Lenorre's energy crept up my spine like cold needles and I tried to ignore it.

Ackerman turned her head very slowly to look at Lenorre and something happened. The air felt heavier, humid, slightly tinted with the scent of mesquite. Lenorre's energy tingled along my spine and was met by a soft wave of heat.

The heat was coming off Berkeley Ackerman.

"You are not my Countess." I watched as specks of dark chocolate and amber rose to the surface of Ackerman's irises.

I automatically slammed my shields shut tight, very tight, like a steel glove encasing my body, and took a wide step away from her.

I did not touch Ackerman. That had been my mistake with Hunter. When one lycanthrope touches another, they're going to recognize each other as what they really are. I wasn't sure what Ackerman was, but I knew the flavor of shape-shifter when I smelled it. So far, Ackerman hadn't recognized me. I didn't know how she didn't recognize me, but I wanted to keep it that way.

"No," Lenorre said, "but I know what you are."

"That is why you found Lukas's fate so terrible," I said, bringing Ackerman's attention back to me. "You're not human."

"What I am isn't any of your business," Ackerman said, low and defensive.

I laughed and Ackerman jumped.

"I don't care if you're a shape-shifter, Ackerman. I care if you're a good one or not."

Ackerman's chest was rising and falling a bit too quickly behind her blue uniform.

I took another step back, giving her room. "But just because you're one of them doesn't mean you have to defend all of them. How the hell are you supposed to be a good cop if you're going to protect murderers just because they have the same condition as you?"

Her energy pushed against me like a wave of warm honey.

"You're not about to go furry, are you?" I was concerned. Ackerman must've been experiencing some very strong emotions. Anger, most likely, but there was fear there too, so it was hard to tell. Either way, in order to keep her control of whatever beastie she was, she needed to tone down the emotions a few notches.

Ackerman's mouth opened as if she was going to reply, but she didn't. I heard her panting softly.

Shit.

She was going to fucking shift.

I felt Lenorre withdraw her energy, her power like a gentle, cool night breeze.

"Ackerman," I tried again, her eyes were almost drowning in dark chocolate and amber now. "Fucking hell, Ackerman, in through your nose and out through your mouth. Get your shit under control."

She crossed her arms over her chest, the toned muscles of her forearms jumping slightly. If I thought I could have helped her by touching her, I might've, but touching her would've only made matters worse, would've magnified the energy between us. So I didn't. I kept my hands to myself and focused on shielding like a son of a bitch.

Her nostrils flared, but she did what I told her, she exhaled through her mouth.

"Look at me." I made my voice low, but firm.

Ackerman looked at me.

"Don't you dare," I said. "Not here, not in front of the cops."

The blue in her eyes receded, like watching sand swallowing water and not the other way around.

Ackerman pushed off the wall and without a word headed down the hallway.

"Where are you going?" I heard Arthur say before Ackerman replied, "Fresh air."

Arthur stepped in the doorway. "What'd you say to her, Kass?"

"Nothing," I said.

"Yeah, right," he said. "The day you say nothing is the day I'm joining a convent and becoming a nun."

I looked at him for several moments. "That's just so you."

"We're going to the other scene. You and Vampira can follow me."

"I have a name, Detective."

"So do I," Arthur said, "and it's not Detective."

"Would you prefer I drop the courtesy of using your title?"

"You can call me Arthur."

"And you can most assuredly call me something other than Vampira."

Arthur looked thoughtful. In fact, he looked so thoughtful I feared he was going to hurt himself.

"You wouldn't take to Fangs, would you?"

"Would you take to Stench?" she asked, sounding very serious. "Two can play that game, Detective."

"You called me Detective again," he said, obviously toying with Lenorre. I sighed, resisting the urge to bury my face in my hands.

"Did I?" she asked, swinging from serious to disinterest.

I finally interrupted. "Can we continue this episode of Fangs and Stench at the next crime scene?"

They both looked at me and I returned their looks with an impatient one of my own.

"Arthur," I said finally, "stop baiting her."

"Okay, Kassie," he said, grinning like a twelve-year-old boy.

"I could hit you in the face for calling me that."

"Wow. That hit a nerve."

"You think?" It was one of the few nicknames that would piss me off in a heartbeat. I let Arthur see that.

"I'm sorry," he said. "I'll stop baiting you, Lenorre."

"I would appreciate that, Arthur."

"Great, now that you've both proven you know each other's names, let's go," I said.

We were already out of the room when Arthur asked, "Wait, do I really stink?"

Lenorre and I both ignored him.

On the way down the hall, she touched my arm lightly. "You did well in there."

"Thanks for tolerating Arthur's sense of humor," I said, ignoring the praise or whatever it was.

"Ah," she said, "his sense of humor is fairly harmless."

"You say that now," I said. "Wait until after you've been subjected to it for over an hour."

Chapter Seven

We ended up on the southwest side of Oklahoma City in some housing addition between MacArthur and Meridian. It was an unfamiliar area to me. Granted, I've lived in Oklahoma all my life, doesn't mean I've seen every nook and cranny of it.

I put the car in park and unfastened my seat belt. We'd driven in silence so far. I broke that silence now, parked behind Arthur's Crown Victoria.

"What is Ackerman?" I asked Lenorre.

"You could not tell?"

"I can tell she's a shape-shifter, just not what kind, and I was too reluctant to touch her to find out."

"I was not close enough to her to sense precisely what she was. At a glance of her beast, I would say that she is a fox."

I was nodding my agreement when a loud metallic clink startled me at my window.

"Fucking ass," I said, swinging my door open and trying to hit Arthur with it. He moved out of the way with a chuckle.

"Made you jump." He grinned.

"Kingfisher," I said, "You're lucky I don't kick your ass."

"Oooh," he said, "That's a good threat. You're like what? Sixty pounds?"

"Closer to a hundred than that," I said.

His brows went up as he pushed his hair out of his face. "Huh," he said, "So you don't actually hit a hundred and ten, do you?"

I wondered if I did now that I was a lycanthrope, but let the thought go. It'd been forever since I stepped on a scale, as I'm a firm believer that no woman should own one, but I was still humanly the same size. "I don't know," I said. "Didn't used to."

He shook his head. "Damn, I knew you were small, but damn. I could pick you up and throw you."

I narrowed my eyes. "Don't even try it, Kingfisher."

He put his hands up in the air. "I won't."

Lenorre had gotten out of the car and walked around the front of it when we were talking.

"She is quite light," she said.

Arthur gave me an intense and serious look. "How do the bad guys not flick you like a booger?"

"Because," I said, "First, I don't let them get close enough. Second, I have a gun that is bigger than the rest of me."

I'm also a werewolf. That helps. Yep. Okay, so size really doesn't matter. I'd seen a woman smaller than me take down a guy at least three times Arthur's size. It was all about the training and knowing how to turn your opponent's size and weight against them, but the super-beastie part seriously came in fucking handy.

Arthur looked behind him as Ackerman got out of the passenger side of his Crown Victoria.

"Detective Kingfisher," she said, "We'll meet you inside."

Arthur's expression went from amused to questioning in a split second.

I shrugged and said to him, "I think she just wants to have another girl talk."

"Right, I'll be glad I missed that," he said. To Ackerman, he said, "Fine, but hurry your asses up."

"You don't want to go in there alone, do you?" I asked.

"Hell no," he said, "I don't want to go in there again." He shook his head, but he turned and followed the winding concrete pathway that led up to the door.

I turned to Ackerman. "What do you want?"

"I don't want the cops to know," she said.

"Fine," I said.

"I'm serious," she said.

"I said fine. I won't tell the cops, Ackerman."

"I could lose my badge."

"I know."

She gave me an unfriendly and distrusting look. "Just like that? You won't tell them? You hunt down and kill shape-shifters, yet you're willing to keep my secret, why?"

"Because it's your secret, Ackerman, and you obviously don't understand the job description of a Paranormal Huntress."

"You're a killer," she said, taking a step toward me. This time the wave of heat from her body was intentional and it caught me off guard. I was suddenly drowning in scents, musk, fur, and mesquite. I could smell her perfume, but it was so light, so subtle, it didn't mask the scent of her, not really.

Ackerman's gaze had bled caramel-gold. A resounding warmth, but something hotter, rose up like bile in the pit of my stomach.

Crap.

I squished it as fast as I could, like kicking dirt over a fire, trying to put the flame out. I didn't wrap my shields around me; I focused on holding them down like someone trying to close a stubborn window.

She took another step toward me and I gave my ground, stepping back.

"You," Ackerman murmured. Her lips parted sensually, and her tongue flicked out across them, wetting them.

Ackerman might not have seemed like much, but I realized in that moment that I had sorely, very sorely, underestimated her abilities. Had she not recognized me in the guest room only because of Lenorre's distraction?

I sensed Lenorre still standing by the car but didn't risk glancing at her.

The shocked expression Ackerman wore made my pulse leap into my throat.

I felt the wolf inside me like something steady and solid, unafraid of the woman in front of me. She had no qualms over revealing herself or being what she was.

I did.

Ackerman reached out like she was going to touch me. This time I backed up again before I realized she wasn't actually trying to touch me. She didn't have to.

Her hand hovered in the air between us and I could feel her warm energy playing against my skin like she really was touching it. For a moment, the wolf looked up, ready to run and meet that energy face-to-face, to take it head on because it was invading her space. I envisioned a curtain between Ackerman and me, a thick velvet curtain that confused not only my wolf, but Ackerman's energy trying to search through mine.

"You're different," she said, but the look on her face didn't match the tone in her voice. Her brows furrowed in fierce concentration. I realized, because she'd only had a quick taste of my energy, a flicker of response, that she hadn't gotten a taste of my wolf. In order for her to fully recognize me, she'd probably have to touch me, but touch could ruin both our controls, and I wasn't sure Ackerman was willing to take that risk, especially if she wasn't certain I was a shape-shifter.

"What are you?" she whispered, hand sliding down, closer to my heart chakra. My pulse sped. For some reason, I didn't want her playing her energy there. I stepped back, several steps, still focusing on a thick curtain between us.

"I'm different," I said, "We'll leave it at that." But my voice was breathy, distracted by that warm play of energy.

She moved her hand as if she were going to touch me again, and I made a mistake. I stupidly, out of instinct, caught her wrist to stop her.

The reaction was instantaneous. Heat. So much heat. As if my hand was going to burn her. As if we were both flames, and when the flames touched they burned hotter.

Ackerman leaned her upper body toward me, and this time I was too slow.

The curtain rippled as if the wolf was going to dive through it.

I heard Ackerman take in a harsh breath, trying to catch my scent.

Fuck.

Ackerman said, "That's how you took down a werewolf that was more than twice your size."

The look she gave me was a little too sly, mirroring her animal counterpart.

"The rumors aren't true," she said, shaking her head. "I knew they weren't when I confronted you earlier today, but…"

I was drawing deep, careful breaths, trying to stifle and soothe the curious wolf within. "What rumors?"

Her fox-like gaze shifted to Lenorre. "That she had turned you."

"What?"

Ackerman seemed to relax now that I was the one tense and struggling. "A few of the cops think that you've been turned."

She smiled when she said that last bit.

I frowned.

"If the cops have seen me in broad daylight why would they think that?"

She shrugged very slowly. "They think you're a Lightwalker."

"A Lightwalker?"

"That is purely fictitious," Lenorre said smoothly. She came to me, placing a hand on my shoulder. Her energy, for some reason, calmed the wolf, and she stopped impatiently and curiously skimming the curtain I'd envisioned. A part of me knew what she wanted. She didn't want to get out and raise hell. Ackerman had disturbed her and she wanted to investigate the source of the disturbance. I didn't know how the wolf would react to a fox, and I was unwilling to find out.

"A Lightwalker?" I asked again. "I'm guessing that's supposed to be some kind of vampire?"

"There are humans who believe we can walk willingly into sunlight."

"Without being toasted?"

"Something like that, but it is purely fictitious."

"Is it?" Ackerman asked Lenorre.

"Yes."

"I almost believed them." Ackerman turned to me. "God knows, you're pale enough and you move differently than the rest."

I'd have to watch myself from now on. I didn't know I moved that differently.

I heard a door open, before Arthur's voice carried, "Kass?"

I turned and held up a hand.

Ackerman said. "You keep my secret. I'll keep yours."

"Done," I said and went to turn to the house.

Ackerman caught my arm. Lenorre took a step closer, but Ackerman kept her gaze on me. "I want to talk more about this," she said. "You may not be a vampire," she whispered, "but you're not like I am, either."

I sensed the wolf prick her ears, mirroring my agitation.

"Ackerman," I said, "Don't touch me."

She pulled her hand away.

"We will talk."

"Maybe," I said.

Chapter Eight

One thing is for sure, even if you've seen crime photos, the scene itself still manages to catch one off guard. The pictures are never as horrible as having the real thing right in front of your face. There are some things you can't prepare for. You can only look and hope you don't run screaming.

Lenorre stood close to my side as Arthur led us through the house and around the huddling group of blue uniforms and the forensic team in their black jackets with bright white letters reading "Forensics" on the back. It wasn't a large house by any means, and having so many people, whether they were working or not, made it seem even smaller.

The one thing that was very different about this crime scene was that it smelled blatantly of blood, tangy and metallic. The smell of it hit me in the face like a ton of bricks, threatening to rouse the wolf. I drew my shields tightly around me, using those careful walls I'd spent years working on building to keep her contained.

Arthur led the way cautiously around the streak of blood in the hallway. He didn't bother pointing it out because it was unnecessary. Even if I hadn't seen the pictures, there was no missing the dark stain on the light carpet. We walked past a bathroom, a bedroom, another bedroom, and into the room at the end of the hall.

I looked up at the bloody symbol above the bed and a tremble went through me, making my hand twitch. For several minutes, all of us just stood there.

Arthur finally spoke. "Your turn," he said. "I've already seen this mess."

I sighed and moved closer to the bed. The dark blue and gold celestial blankets were black and brown with blood. There wasn't a lot of furniture in the room—two small nightstands, probably his and hers, a dresser with a large vanity mirror, a potted ivy plant hung over one of the windows with its goldenrod curtains. I had a very strong sense the plant was Miranda's doing.

"Gloves," I said, holding my hand out behind me.

Arthur went to the door and called out, "I need some gloves, people!"

It took about a minute for someone to appear with a box of gloves and a sack used for trash. One of the forensics guys with an ID badge that read Reeves appeared in the doorway. Arthur passed the box around. Even if forensics had found what evidence they could find, it'd be a bitch if we messed up the crime scene in the process of finding a potential clue. Every clue we could find or salvage from the scene counted.

I drew my sleeves up using my teeth and went to the bed, drawing in a deep, steeling breath before leaning over to search the comforter.

That's when another smell hit me. Something wasn't right.

"Arthur?"

"Yeah, Kass?" he asked from his post near the doorway. Reeves was quietly standing beside him. He was the only other man in the room besides Arthur who hadn't put on a pair of gloves. Which meant neither of the boys intended to get close to the evidence again.

"Your guys are testing the blood?" I asked Reeves.

He shook his head. "They had a runner take it back to the lab, but we haven't gotten the results."

"Lenorre?"

She moved up closer to me like some graceful shadow. "Yes?"

"Can you tell by smell if the blood is human or not?"

"Yes."

I touched the corner of the comforter where the blood hadn't managed to soak through.

"Wait," Reeves said. "Hang on a second..."

I waited. He returned with a small vial of swabs. Gently, he plucked one of the ends from the vial with his bare fingers and went to the wall. His brow furrowed in concentration as he retrieved a spray bottle from his pocket and sprayed the tip of the swab. He placed the swab against a line of blood that had dried seeping from the symbol, gave the stick an artful spin, and handed it to Lenorre.

"I doubt this will hold up in court," Reeves said, "but I'm curious to see if you're right when we get the results in."

She took it, waving it under her nose. Her pale nostrils flared slightly, and her dark eyelashes fluttered closed. "It is not human," she said, voice dripping with the damp coldness of sea fog.

"Can you tell what it is?" I asked.

She sniffed it again. "Unfortunately, no," she said.

"If it's not human, could it be animal?" I asked.

"It'd have to be a freaking horse for this much blood," Arthur said.

"You would be surprised, Detective," Lenorre said, pinning him with her silvery gaze. "I cannot determine what or who the blood belongs to by smell alone."

"What if you tasted it?" Arthur asked.

"Arthur!"

"What?" He shot me a confused look. "It's just a question."

"Possibly," Lenorre said, "However, I would rather not."

"Why not? It's just blood and you're a vampire."

"Arthur, your etiquette sucks worse than mine and that's saying something," I said.

"What's so rude about me asking her to taste the blood?"

Lenorre was growing more still by the minute.

I intercepted before she could give him an answer. "She's a Countess, Arthur."

"So?"

"Uh," Reeves dove into the conversation, and Arthur and I turned to look at him. "I think what she's trying to say is that what you're asking is like someone asking the Queen of England to eat a sandwich off the sidewalk."

"Yeah." I turned back to Arthur. "That."

He shook his head and raised his hands. "Fine. Sorry I asked. So if you don't think it's human, what is it?"

"There are numerous possibilities," Lenorre said calmly. "It could be human-like. It could be animal—"

"Wait, human-like?" Arthur asked.

"It could be a shape-shifter," Lenorre answered, "Elf, fey…"

Arthur actually grunted. "But you could find out what it is if you tasted the blood?"

I snatched the swab out of Lenorre's hands and held it in front of his face.

"You want to taste it?"

"No."

"Then stop it," I said. "You asked for help. I brought help. This"—I raised it closer and he took a step back—"is not a vampiric lollipop. Get off it, Arthur."

I dropped the swab in the trash sack.

There was a noise, a noise like someone was about to choke. I looked at Arthur. He laughed, loud and hard, laughed until he was clutching his sides. Reeves chuckled too, as if the laughter were contagious.

Lenorre met my gaze. The corner of her mouth curling slightly. "What?"

Arthur took a deep rasping breath, "Vampiric lollipop," he said. "I will never in my life forget that."

I frowned.

"Where are you going?" Arthur asked.

"Away," I said, pausing only briefly in the doorway.

He caught up with me in the hallway. "No, you're on a mission."

I looked at him, going wide around the bloodstain. "I want to see something."

I moved past the entertainment center with its Greek statues, past the onlooking cops and forensics team, through the dining room, and finally into the kitchen. Marble counter top, sink in one corner, dishwasher, fridge, gas stove…

I searched the pale green linoleum floor tile by tile. I opened a door that I thought led outside, but instead, the door led into a laundry room. A top load washer and dryer were placed beneath high cabinets. I moved around the washer and dryer, scanning the floor and opening the cabinets. Still, I found nothing. I opened another door, but this one led into the garage. My night vision took over as I scanned the wall, then I hit the light switch to my right. The garage was flooded in a soft yellow glow. There was a workbench on the far wall. A line of hooks on the wall held a shovel, weed-eater, what looked like a sprinkler, a broom, and a mop. I sensed more than saw Arthur and Lenorre standing in the doorway. They watched me in silence as I rounded the wooden workbench. A ladder hung on its own lone hooks on the opposite wall.

"Have they checked to see if anything is missing? Potential weapon?"

"They're looking into it," Arthur said.

The gray stone floor had a ghostly spot, like a faint memory that had been cleaned one too many times from a car that had leaked oil. I followed the walls, peeking behind boxes, an old stereo. There, in the corner between the door I'd come in and the door I was certain led into the backyard, was a large bag of dog food.

"That." I pointed.

Lenorre looked. Arthur kept staring at me.

"Arthur," I said.

He looked. "A bag of dog food?"

I went to the backyard door then unlocked and opened it. The locks worked fine, so I knew the killer hadn't used the back door, unless he had a key. "How do you think the perp got in? What's your entry point? Exit point?" I asked, peeking out the door and spotting an old chewed up green water dish. There was another black dish next to it. The dish had some food in it, but not much. It was hard to tell at a glance how long it'd been sitting there.

"There aren't any signs of forced entry at any of the doors or windows. We think the perp was let in," Arthur said.

"So probably someone the vics know," I mumbled.

Arthur peered out the door with me. I stared at the water dish just outside the square of concrete. "You think this case ties into the murder?"

"Yeah. The symbol on the body and above the bed is the signature."

I scanned the backyard. If I really wanted to see the backyard and all of the details, it would be best done during the day. I could tell there was a garden of some kind hugging the wooden fence at the far end of the yard and two smaller garden sections marked along the side of the house by the door, but with the season the gardens were barren. I leaned back in, flicking the switch for the back porch light. I stepped onto the concrete slab just outside the door. In the dried dirt, there were several unmistakable paw prints that belonged to a very large dog.

"You've got your work cut out for you."

He looked at the prints. "You think the blood belongs to a dog, their dog?"

"It's a possibility. I don't see any footprints. You should send your boys out with a cadaver dog or two and search the neighborhood."

Arthur glanced at Lenorre. "Is that your way of telling me we can't use Vampira?"

I intervened before Lenorre could speak. "Call me when forensics gets the test results back on the blood. Also, figure out where their car is. I didn't see a car in the driveway when we pulled up, and there's sure as hell not one in the garage. Find the car, find the dog. We'll go from there. Check the house again with a handful of cops and a few people from forensics," I said. "It wouldn't hurt. You should look for any addresses or phone numbers lying around." When Arthur gave me a questioning look I added, "We need to find out if they belonged to a coven. If they did, we need to bring them in for questioning."

Arthur closed the notebook he'd been scribbling in and grinned at me as he slipped it into his pocket. "Are you trying to get away?"

"It's getting late," I said blandly. "I'm fairly certain Lenorre and I have found everything we're going to find."

I glanced at her and she offered a confirming nod.

Arthur said, "I'll call you when we get the results back."

"Call me if you find their coven," I said. "They may be solitary. You need to find out."

"Solitary?"

"Witches that practice alone," Ackerman spoke from inside the garage.

Arthur held his hands out. "Give me your gloves," he said, "I'll toss 'em. It's not like you actually touched anything."

I peeled them off. "You sound disappointed."

"It's fun when you get grossed out." He smiled faintly.

"I don't get grossed out very often."

He laughed. "I could name a few times."

"If I remember correctly, you're the one who puked when we found that old man's body off of 104th two or three years ago."

"That's because it smelled like shit," he said. "And if I remember right, you were green in the face too."

"So," I said, walking through the door. "I held it down. That makes all the difference, Kingfisher."

He touched my shoulder on our way back through the house. I slowed my walk.

"One day, Kass, you're gonna toss your cookies at a crime scene."

"If I do, Arthur, I'll be sure to toss them on you."

Lenorre made a noise that I think was supposed to be a stifled laugh.

We left the scene in silence. I thought of a million questions to ask Lenorre and discarded them all. I leaned over and turned the radio on, letting my thoughts percolate. As far as crime scenes went, this was by far one of the strangest I've seen.

I stopped by my apartment on the way home to get a clean change of clothes. I was going to take a shower once Lenorre and I got back to her place. As a rule, I always shower after a crime scene, if only so I feel like I've washed the horror off myself. I packed an overnight bag and tossed it into the backseat. Lenorre watched me as I slid in behind the wheel.

"Kassandra," she said my name and I stopped buckling my seat belt in mid-motion.

"What is it?" I asked.

"Do you mind stopping by the club?"

I frowned, because in that moment all I wanted was a shower. At the look on my face she added, "It will not take long." I sighed, clicking my seat belt on. "Fine," I said, "But why?" I put the car in reverse and looked over my shoulder.

"There is a certain matter to which I must attend."

I put the car in drive. "That tells me a whole lot."

She gave a mysterious smile. "It tells you what you need to know."

The club Lenorre owned had once been a hotel. I don't know what it used to be called, but now it was The Two Points and the only vampire club in Oklahoma City. Lenorre and I walked through the lobby and the double doors that led to the converted ballroom. The song, "Vampyre Erotica," by Inkubus Sukkubus played over the sound system as we passed a small group of gothly clad folk chatting amongst themselves.

It was slow right now, but in an hour or two the place would be packed and difficult to walk through. Then again, I'd never noticed Lenorre having any difficulty navigating the floor, whether it was packed or not.

I recognized one of Lenorre's vampires whispering orders to a young blonde who was wearing a crimson satin vest cinched over a black blouse. The girl walked by on her way out of the ballroom and Stanley's blue, Siamese cat eyes met mine. It wasn't just his eyes that made him stand out. It was the outfit he wore—a black leather vest and a pair of white skinny jeans and boots. Unlike the other employees, Stanley didn't wear the red on black uniform.

His labret piercing caught the light, twinkling beneath his lower lip as he mouthed the words, "Evening, lovely," and blew me a kiss. If I didn't think he was batting for the boys' team, I would've raised my brows at him. As it was, I shook my head and silently thanked Lenorre for her presence. Had I been alone, I had a feeling Stanley would've approached, and I wasn't in the mood to socialize.

Lenorre led the way up the winding stairs, through the lounge area to one of the employee rooms where I could wait for her. The room was spacious, with candles on stands lining each of the four walls. Two couches created a small sitting area.

I made myself comfortable and tried not to feel irritated. I hate waiting for people, but after the crime scene, I took the opportunity to relax. You tend to miss a lot of sleep when you're dating a vampire. In an attempt to somewhat balance my schedule with Lenorre's, I didn't go into work until well after one in the afternoon on most days. The time of the year really depended on how late I was going to be up. Since Yule was quickly approaching, the nights were getting longer and the days shorter. Which meant I was going to be up later if I wanted to spend as much time as I could with her.

The arm of the couch had enough padding to use as a pillow. I curled my legs under me, rested my head in the bend of my elbow, and covered my face with my other arm. The room was completely silent; not even the sound of a heater whirred to life. The walls were blessedly soundproof. *Sleep,* my body said, and I didn't disagree with it.

❖

A massive black and white Great Dane gazed at me from where it lay in the grass. I reached out to pet the dog and it whimpered. Its fur was slick and wet where I touched it.

"It's okay," I murmured. "You're okay." The sky overhead was dark as I continued to pet the dog, trying to offer it some form of comfort. What was wrong? Why didn't this feel right?

The grass was high like it hadn't been cut in several months. The dog whimpered when I stroked its stomach.

Its furred body moved like some great hand was following mine from the inside, and I jerked my hand away.

There was so much blood it looked as if I had dipped my hand in red paint. Something rolled again beneath the dog's fur. I watched as it moved and pushed against the skin, threatening to break free.

The dog gave a loud cry of pain as its skin split with the thick sound of things that shouldn't be torn, tearing.

A wave of maggots, blood, and thicker things spilled out across the grassy ground. Horrified, I scrambled to my feet.

"Kassandra," a woman's voice rode the night breeze.

"No," I said, looking at my hand in horror and shaking my head. "No."

"Kassandra!"

The world wobbled in a dizzying spin. For a moment, the dream superimposed reality. The golden brown eyes of the wounded dog began to fade, replaced by a startling sea-green.

"Kassandra?" Eris's face was swimming in my view. Her sable hair fell around her pale skin in untamed waves down her body. Her fingers were digging a little too roughly into my shoulders.

"Are you awake now?" she asked.

I tried to move and realized she was sitting in my lap, pinning my legs with her weight.

"Yes."

Gently, she used her hands on my shoulders to guide me back down. The movement put her weight more solidly in other places.

"Eris." The breath caught in my throat, but I managed to say her name.

The last time I'd seen her, she hadn't understood why, if I was attracted to her, I wouldn't share blood with her. I thought my reasons were kind of sound, considering.

She touched the side of my face tenderly. "You were having a bad dream."

The dress she wore was black and covered in so many straps and buckles I probably would've gotten tangled up in it just trying to put the damn thing on. Two straps crisscrossed high on her chest, creating a black X and disappearing at the back of her neck like a halter. My gaze fell to the fitted bodice of the dress and the gleaming white mounds of her breasts.

"Eris," I tried again, making my voice a little firmer. Her skirts pooled around my lower body, bustled by tiny black buckles that extended, dangling from her hips. The buckles raised her skirt, leaving her slender thighs bare.

Eris's night job was as a dominatrix and she looked every inch the role.

She looked down at me and a smile tugged at the edges of her mouth. The expression seemed to say, "Go ahead; take a good look."

A little voice in my head said *Push her off*, and whether it was my conscience or the wolf, I didn't. I didn't want to touch her. Somehow, that seemed like a bad idea.

Eris watched me, smiling and calm, knowing the effect she had on me. She was a vampire; how could she not? Every subtle betrayal of my body, she caught. My pulse, the change in my breath, things I couldn't hide. I lay there, completely still, and utterly unsure what to do.

Eris didn't seem to want to climb off me anytime soon.

She gave a low laugh. "Oh, Kassandra," she said, cupping my jaw in such a delicate grip that one might not have thought she had the supernatural strength to inflict quite a bit of damage, even to a lycanthrope.

A little flicker of nervousness went through me.

"You're straddling me," I said, forcing my voice to sound smooth and even and less like she was unsettling me.

"So I am," she smiled softly, stroking my hair.

I wanted her to stop touching me.

I closed my eyes, because it was easier than looking at her. "Get off."

"Mmm, is that what you want me to do?" she asked.

The voice in my head went from saying *Push her* to *Oh shit.*

"You know what I mean, Eris. Get off of me."

She moved and I released the breath I'd been holding. Her hips swayed forward as she drew herself up the length of my thigh.

The movement brought her dress up high enough that I could see the edge of her black lace boy shorts. I thanked the Gods the slacks I wore were a thick material.

"You look a little uncertain, Kassandra."

"Eris," I tried for what seemed like the thirteenth time. "I'm serious."

Her mouth was suddenly close to my neck.

"Tell me you're not thinking about *it*," she whispered in my ear. "Tell me you don't want *it* and I'll stop."

"I don't want it, Eris. Get off me."

Her tongue traced the curve of my earlobe, sending tiny jolts of sensation down the back of my neck and arms.

She moved against me again and this time the muscles in my thigh went rigid.

There was *way* too little clothing between us.

Desire and fear made my throat tight. My heart gave a fierce thump against the side of my neck. I felt the pulse beating between my legs, a distant echo.

Not good, so not good.

Why was her smell so intoxicating?

I curled my hands into fists and dug my nails into my palms. The pain helped me to focus, but my entire body was thrumming with energy, her energy. The promise of it swept across my shields like something soft and gentle.

Where the hell was Lenorre?

Her hands moved, threatening to raise both my jacket and blouse.

"Say yes," she whispered, staring intensely at me. "I can smell your desire, Kassandra. Say yes to me. All you have to do is say yes."

I drew a slow breath, trying to steel myself against that coaxing breeze, against the weight of power and will in her gaze.

"Eris," I whispered, "stop."

Her hands slipped under my blouse. She splayed her fingers across my waist and her energy was stronger, like cool water. The muscles in my stomach jumped at her touch.

"Why do you fight your desire?" she asked, looking perplexed.

"Eris," Lenorre's voice dripped command.

Eris's hand flexed a second before she drove her nails into my skin.

I cried out, my spine bowing. Her energy hit me like a thrust, rough and sudden, pleasure and pain. A wave crashing against me and threatening to take me under.

Shit.

Her voice was as cool as her power. "Yes, Countess?"

"Leave Kassandra alone, Eris," Lenorre said, but instead of sounding angry she sounded tired.

I shuddered as Eris's nails tickled my skin.

"One day," she whispered, removing her hands from my stomach.

"Don't get your hopes up," I said.

"We don't have to do anything you consider to be cheating." She touched my cheek and I flinched.

Eris stood and I turned to meet Lenorre's silvery gaze. If there were any thoughts behind Lenorre's eyes, I couldn't read them. She was too contained.

Out of my peripheral vision, I saw Eris reach out to touch me.

I caught her wrist. The borrowed blood in her veins made her pulse leap against my fingertips.

"Stop it," I said. "Seriously, stop fucking with me." I meant it.

She frowned, shaking her head. "I do not understand you, Kassandra."

"No," I said, "you don't. So stop trying."

"I want to," she said and this time there wasn't any teasing to her tone.

I shook my head, letting go of her wrist. Her pulse beating against my fingers was distracting. "You've got a funny way of showing it."

"I show it in my own way," she said. "By the way." She smiled secretively. "You've forgotten all about your little nightmare now, haven't you?"

I tried to remember the nightmare, but all I could remember were bits and pieces. Too much of Eris overshadowed the remembrance.

"Next time, just slap me."

Eris made a noise in her throat. "And risk rousing an angry werewolf? I think not."

I gave her a narrow-eyed look to let her know she was already toeing that line.

"I don't like being played with, Eris."

Eris looked to an empty corner of the room. "I got carried away," she said, but not like she was happy about admitting it. "But should I apologize for something you felt as well?"

"Your little problem has been taken care of," Lenorre said with a vacant expression.

Eris inclined her head. "My thanks, Countess."

"I think it would be wise if you left."

Eris reached out like she was going to touch me again, and this time I growled. She tilted her head to the side, almost thoughtfully. "Consider my offer."

I opened my mouth to speak and she slipped past my guard, placing a finger against my lips. Her face hovered only a few inches from my own. "No, Kassandra. Do not decline just yet. I want you to consider what I offer. I will not cross the line if that is what you desire, but there may come a day when you are not so afraid. When you wish to explore your darker cravings more thoroughly, remember me."

"Don't hold your breath," I said.

"Even if I do," she said, rising to leave, "it will not hurt."

I watched her go. The back of her dress had a panel of fabric that covered her shoulders, leaving a small crescent of her back bare. As if she felt my gaze on her, she looked over her shoulder and offered one last dark and questioning look.

I blew out a deep breath.

"Are you well?" Lenorre asked, coming to me.

"Well enough."

She nodded and held out her hand and I took it, rising and letting her snake her arms around me.

"You do not wish to speak about this yet, do you?" she whispered the question against my hair.

"No," I said. "Not yet. Right now, I just want to go home."

Her lips met my forehead. "So, we shall."

"Thank you," I said.

Lenorre leaned back, looking down at me. "For what?"

"For being you. Most girlfriends would've had a conniption had they just walked in on...that."

"Ah well." She stroked my hair affectionately. "Most girlfriends do not understand the complexities of metaphysics."

"Half the time, I don't," I admitted. "Just remind me never to fall asleep here again."

"I could have told you that in the first place," she said with a hint of amusement.

"Apparently, I could've used the heads up."

Her lips met mine in a chaste kiss, warm and silky, her breath like sweet cinnamon against my mouth. "We should leave."

"I can't leave if you keep touching me."

She laughed and let me go.

"What?" I asked at the amused look on her face.

"Would you like me to drive?" There was a devious glint in her eyes.

"What are you thinking, Lenorre?"

Her shoulders gracefully rose and fell in response.

"Lenorre…"

"Let me put it this way, I do not think you should be driving after the, ah, energy exchange between you and Eris."

"Thanks," I said, "I appreciate your confidence in me."

The corner of her mouth twitched. "I have confidence in your head, Kassandra. Your groin, at the moment, is an entirely different matter."

I gaped at her. "What on earth is that supposed to mean?"

She cupped my face in her hands. "Oh, nothing as bad as you seem to be thinking. I know from experience you are not easy or casual by nature, but your groin does have a tendency to override all other mental processing."

"That's not a very nice thing to say, Lenorre."

"You think so, do you? I think it's very nice." Her expression darkened.

I dug the keys out of my pocket, holding them out to her. "Fine, drive."

She took them, looping her arm through mine. I leaned against her on our way out.

"Lenorre?"

"Yes, love?"

"Were you jealous at all?"

"We have discussed this before."

"I know," I said, "I just don't get it."

I don't like casual sex, as a rule. I'd slept with Rosalin before Lenorre and I had become a couple. What scared me with Eris was that she seemed to be trying to flip the same switch Rosalin had, the metaphysical one.

"Kassandra," Lenorre said once we hit the parking lot. I blinked up into the streetlights, coming back from the faraway place of my thoughts. "Let it go," she said.

"And how do you know I'm thinking about it?"

She smiled sweetly at me, opening the car door. She propped her arm on the door, emphasizing all of her delicious height. "Because I know you."

I shook my head and slid into the passenger seat. For as short a time as we'd been a couple, Lenorre did know me. Too well sometimes.

CHAPTER NINE

L enorre was quiet on the drive to her place. She guided the Tiburon onto I-40 when my cell phone rang from my coat pocket. I caught a glimpse of Rosalin's name on the caller ID before flipping the phone open to answer it. A bad feeling tugged at the pit of my stomach.

"Rosalin, what's wrong?"

"Kassandra, so nice to hear your voice again." My stomach dove unhappily.

"Sheila," I said. "Where's Rosalin?"

"She's here," Sheila said and her voice sounded distant, as if she were distracted by something on her end of the line.

"What do you want, Sheila? I get this feeling you don't want to sit down and talk over coffee."

"That would be an accurate assessment of the situation," she said, her voice too calm compared to the energy I was sensing. I felt a heat beneath her words that didn't match her tone.

"Great, glad to hear it. What do you want? Where's Rosalin?" So far, I was doing really well at controlling my temper. I took a steadying breath, counting silently in my head.

Sheila Morris, alpha female of the Blackthorne pack was no friend of mine. In fact, I kind of despised her. I'd only met her face-to-face once, but that one time was enough.

"We need to talk. You know where to meet me. If you're not here within the next thirty minutes," she slowed her words, making sure I got the full force of what she was saying, "you lay your wolf at the hands of my mercy. I suggest you hurry."

The phone clicked silent. Could this night get any better?

"This is so not my fucking night," I growled.

Lenorre gave me a sympathetic look before exiting the highway early to turn the car around.

"Reach into my pocket and use my phone to call Zaphara and Eris," she said, lifting her hip a little.

I leaned over and slipped my hand into the right pocket of her slacks. I retrieved her phone and stared at it.

"Lenorre…"

"What is it, Kassandra?"

"I have no fucking idea how to use this."

"Press the small button on the top of the phone."

The screen blazed to life, shining brightly in the dimly lit car.

"Touch the screen."

I touched the screen and looked at her, waiting for instructions before I resorted to a button-pressing fit.

Lenorre described a symbol on the phone and I found it, clicking on it and bringing up a very long list of contacts.

I was looking for a scroll button when Lenorre stopped at a red light. She laughed when I gave a rumbling growl of frustration. She held her hand out expectantly.

I frowned and dropped the phone in her hand, then watched as she scrolled through the contact list.

"You could have told me that was all I had to do," I said.

Lenorre tucked a curl behind her ear and held the phone up to it. She glanced at me before guiding the car back onto the highway. "This is easier."

I didn't disagree with her. She called Zaphara first and told her to pick up Eris and meet us in the clearing where the wolves met.

I sat back and tried to relax, though every muscle in my body was suddenly tense. It'd been a little over a month since I'd accidentally marked Rosalin as my wolf, since I'd accidentally psychically claimed her. It'd been a little longer than that since I'd executed Lukas Morris, Sheila's psychopathic serial killer brother.

Why had Sheila waited so long to throw this shit into the air?

❖

The parking area was littered with cars, letting me know that the rest of Sheila's pack was present. The area was dimly lit and would be dark until we reached the torches in the clearing. Zaphara and Eris approached as Lenorre and I got out of the car. Another figure was with them, a big, bulky figure with salt and pepper hair. Maddox greeted me with a nod. His eyes were pitch-black. Maddox had originally been among the vampires who came into town with the Count of Counts, a very bad vampire who had showed up seeking to claim Lenorre's territory as his own. Maddox had betrayed the Count of Counts and helped me to save Timothy Nelson.

Timothy had been turned into a vampire. His girlfriend Alyssa hadn't. Gwen Cunningham, Alyssa's mother, had finally left her abusive husband.

The Count of Counts had promised the teenagers power, power to protect them and to live forever. That power and protection had ultimately led Timothy to believe that becoming a vampire was his best chance of protecting Alyssa and her mother from Alyssa's abusive stepfather. For a boy of sixteen, Timothy seemed to genuinely love Alyssa.

Having been turned, he was one of Lenorre's vampires now, and though she'd given him the option of staying with her, Timothy had sought her permission to stay with Alyssa instead, in case Dennis Cunningham ever came back. Lenorre had agreed on two conditions. The first was that Timothy attend night school and graduate. The second was a stricter rule. He was not allowed to attempt to turn Alyssa, not until she was older. Lenorre had explained to him that it was not only because of Alyssa's age, but also because as newly *awakened* himself, Timothy did not yet have the power to turn anyone. Any attempts to do so would more than likely go terribly, terribly wrong. Lenorre had informed him that in time, if Alyssa still desired to be turned, the two could request an audience with her Primes.

Timothy had asked, "How old?"

Lenorre had responded, "When she is eighteen, Timothy, you may make a formal request."

He didn't exactly seem thrilled at the outcome of their conversation, but he acknowledged Lenorre as his Countess and didn't argue.

Timothy had grown close to Maddox during his time enduring the Count's torture, and Lenorre had stepped aside to allow Maddox to mentor him. Since I had been the one to rescue Timothy from the Count, he'd discovered my secret about being a werewolf. He promised not to tell anyone and I believe him, but every time I see him, he practically starts batting his big dark brown vampiric eyes at me and asking me to shift, just so he could see it happen. Unfortunately, his insatiable curiosity for the preternatural didn't miraculously vanish when he became one of us.

And no, I haven't shifted just to show him how *cool* it is.

"I thought you'd be with Timothy," I said.

"He has fed for the night," Maddox said in a deep voice that reminded me of rocks sliding against one another. I understood more than what he was saying. Timothy had fed, which meant he wouldn't need to feed for a while. So there was little chance of him going vampiric on Alyssa or her mother without Maddox there to chaperone.

Zaphara moved, catching my attention. The black trench coat she wore was shiny and reflective in the dim light. Her aubergine hair fell in a long braid down her back, bringing her triangular features out to stark perfection. Her lips were glossed and her eyes, the color of amethysts, were outlined in smoky shadow. I couldn't remember seeing Zaphara ever wear makeup. She was fey and beautiful in a way that didn't need it.

"You're wearing makeup," I said.

"I'm wearing a lot of things."

"She was on guard duty," Eris said smoothly, bringing my attention to her. She was still wearing the same dress she had been earlier, only now a flowing cloak graced her shoulders, spilling like a midnight waterfall to the ground.

"What does that have to do with Zaphara wearing makeup?"

"It's more attractive to Eris's clientele." The corner of her mouth rose in a dark smirk.

"So, you're what, eye candy?"

"Yes," Eris said with a devious smile "If she's to be present during a scene, oh yes. I want her to intrigue my clients, not send them running screaming from the room."

The two women shared a look I sensed had less to do with intimacy and more to do with some shared knowledge and experience. Rosalin had once told me that Zaphara had submitted to Eris. Looking at the two, it was hard to believe. If it came down to a fight, I'd have put my money on Zaphara. Oh, I'd seen them both fight and knew full well they were both lethal, but Zaphara was lethal in a very different way. If I woke in the middle of the night afraid the darkness would materialize and kick my ass, I wouldn't put it past Zaphara's magic.

Lenorre touched my shoulder and I put my hand over hers.

"Are you ready?" she asked.

"Do we have a plan?" Zaphara asked her.

"No," she said, "this we will play by ear. I think my presence alone will keep Sheila in check for the night."

"You're that confident you frighten her?" I asked.

"We are," Eris said. "Sheila does not like vampires."

Zaphara scoffed. "Sheila does not like anyone who is more powerful and secure than she is."

"You don't like Sheila?" I asked, genuinely curious.

"No, she is alpha only because she is the most dominant wolf in the territory."

"I didn't know you didn't like her personally."

"The wolves came to your call, Kassandra," she said, clearly trying to make a point I wasn't getting

"The wolves came to the call of another wolf…"

"Do you remember what I said when Trevor and Claire came to your call when you sought to comfort Rosalin on Thanksgiving?"

"The whole mark of the alpha thing? Yeah, I've been hearing a lot of that lately."

"Do you not think you are hearing it for a reason? Do you truly not understand why?"

"I understand where you're going with this," I said, "and at this point I'm not in the mood to agree or disagree. I just want to make sure Rosalin is safe."

"Sheila has not claimed any of the wolves in her pack, not like a true alpha would claim their wolves, not as you have claimed Rosalin. She doesn't have the metaphysical power or the mark to claim and dominate them with her energy. She dominates her wolves through fear and sadism, not because she's a true alpha. We dislike her because she requires submission but does not have the true authority to demand it." Eris took a step toward me. Lenorre stepped up against my back and I felt the cool line of her body through my clothes. I didn't need to see her face to understand she was warning Eris to keep her distance.

"Rosalin is the only wolf bound metaphysically to an alpha," she said, making no further move.

"Why are we talking about this?" I asked.

Lenorre's voice slid across my skin like cool silk. "You need to understand what we are about to walk into."

Zaphara said, "Sheila may make this a battle of dominance and physical strength, because those are her strengths. What are you going to do if she hurts Rosalin in front of you? Will you step up before the entire pack and protect your wolf?"

Lenorre's hand slipped around my waist from behind. She placed her palm flat over my stomach.

"I'll do what I have to, to keep my friend safe."

I sensed the wolf draw her ears back against her skull.

I took a step away from Lenorre and she let me go. A chorus of ragged howls sliced through the night air. To my human ears, they sounded like any other wolf howls, but to my wolf the call sounded like a challenge.

I walked away from our little group and opened myself to the night. I started at a run once I hit the edge of the woods, not waiting for my night vision to take over. I flung myself between the trees and trusted the earth to guide me but I didn't shift. I had a feeling that bursting onto the scene in wolf-form would be seen as a challenge, and having heard their howls, I knew Sheila had her whole pack with her.

I focused on the weight of the Kimber in its shoulder rig while I ran, thankful for the small comfort.

A black cat darted out in front of me and I knew it was Zaphara. I ducked a low hanging branch. My feet found a fallen tree trunk and I leapt off it. I didn't doubt. I didn't question. I threw my body between large trees and kept going. My vision tunneled on the soft glow of flickering torchlight ahead. Normally, I would've scolded myself for tunnel visioning, as it's a good way to lose your peripheral in a fight. But this wasn't a fight...yet.

The wolf and I were on a mission, and wherever the vampires had gone, we knew there was nothing in the woods waiting for us. What awaited us stood in the center of that clearing, calling with the heavy scent of pine and earth, with the sweet musk of fur and patchouli.

CHAPTER TEN

I sensed the wolves around me, their energy like mud on my skin. I focused on keeping the wolf within behind psychic bars.

Sheila sat on her carved throne, watching me as I made my way into the middle of the clearing. Her hands tensed where they rested on the arms.

She wore a white sweater with a pair of tight black pants tucked into dark leather ankle boots. Her long blond hair was pulled back into a neat French braid and she looked about as happy to see me as I was to see her.

Who'd have thought we'd have something in common.

"Kassandra," she said, inclining slightly. Out of the corner of my eye, I saw Trevor, a friend of Rosalin's, fidget uncomfortably.

"Where is she, Sheila?"

She leaned back, smiling with malice. "If you have truly claimed her, Kassandra, find her yourself."

"I didn't come here to play games with you." I forced myself to breathe past the agitation of my beast.

"But it seems you *are* playing games with me, Kassandra." The look she gave me was anything but friendly.

I crossed my arms over my chest. "And what gave you that idea, Sheila?"

"Stop saying my name like a curse," she said, eyes narrowing in hostility. "If you are not playing a game then set your cards on the table. Come and greet me as your alpha."

I didn't mean to laugh, but I did, and I wasn't sure if I was feeling the wolf's emotions at the idea or my own. Maybe it was a combination of both.

"You're not my alpha, Sheila. I'm sure as hell not going to greet you as such."

She stood and came toward me. The last time Sheila had touched me, I'd nearly lost my temper. I so didn't want her to touch me again. In the heels, she was taller, not as tall as Zaphara or Lenorre, but taller than me. As she moved toward me, she used all her height to try to make me feel smaller. Unfortunately, when you're petite like I am, you get used to people trying to do that.

A warning growl built and trickled out from between my half-parted lips.

She hesitated. "You would threaten me?"

"She's not threatening you, alpha." Carver, gamma of the Blackthorne pack moved from the large group and out into the open. His white blond hair fell over his blue and gold eyes. The white shirt he wore was only a shade lighter than his hair.

"I wouldn't be so quick to side with her, my third."

"I'm not siding with anyone," he said, showing no sign of fear while Sheila glared at him. "But you are threatening her with your body language."

One of the female wolves gasped. I wondered where Claire was, but didn't try to find her. I was too busy watching the alpha female in front of me.

Sheila shook with rage, her fingers curling into fists. Heat emitted off her. The anger of her beast brushed my skin, calling to mine in an unspoken challenge.

I took another deep breath, this time through my mouth.

"Then you come to me."

"Why?"

"I am the alpha of the Blackthrone pack. If you will not greet me as your alpha, you will greet me as one wolf greets another, Kassandra. If you don't..." She shook her head. She didn't need to finish her sentence to make the implied threat clear.

"You'll what?" I asked, tilting my head. "Sic your wolves on me?"

"You are a stray," she said nastily. "I am within my rights to punish a stray that has wandered into my territory."

A violent wind whipped through the clearing, extinguishing the torches. I shivered, suddenly cold. If it hadn't been for the fey blood in my veins, I would've chalked the gust up to the late December night. As it was, a tendril of power tainted that one breeze and I knew it was more, tasted it like candy on my tongue.

Zaphara's magic filled the clearing, making my breath fog on the air. She was one of the Daoine Maithe, a woman of the Sidhe and faerie people, and aside from shape-shifting, I didn't know what kind of powers she possessed, but I knew she was capable of some elemental control and manipulation, and I knew without a doubt that somewhere out of sight, she'd called her power.

A thin sheen of frost crackled across the ground.

The light of the crescent moon rendered some color to my night vision, though the colors were dull.

"On the contrary." It wasn't Zaphara's voice that whispered from the darkness. It was Lenorre's. "Kassandra is here at your request. You are the one who sent her the invitation."

Lenorre stepped into the clearing as if she had just materialized, but I knew she hadn't. It was either a trick of her power or Zaphara's that made it appear that way.

"Lenorre." Sheila made her name a growl. "This is wolf business."

"Ah." Lenorre smiled with distaste. "I am here only as a reminder."

"A reminder of what?"

"Of your allegiance to the vampires. Do not make this our business."

Sheila trembled with rage. Her hands clenched back into fists. If we were playing a game of seeing how many times we could piss Sheila off, I was pretty sure we were doing remarkably well.

"I'm not making this vampire business."

"Are you so sure? The wolf you hold in your custody is one employed by me." Lenorre's eyes burned liquid silver with power as she made her way toward Sheila. Eris and Maddox stepped out of the shelter of trees and entered the clearing. Eris's cloak swayed around her body. Her eyes burned with power like the crashing waves of angry green sea. Maddox's eyes were as deep and fathomless as empty space. That vampiric energy rode the breeze like the scent of cold stone and moist air.

Sheila glanced cautiously at the two vampires. Lenorre continued, her voice taking on a haunting and purring edge that caressed my senses like a flitting breeze. "Where is Rosalin, Sheila?"

"That's none of your business, vampire," she said the word *vampire* like it was supposed to be an insult.

Lenorre gave a cutting smile. "She no longer belongs to you, Sheila."

"Then have your *wolf* prove who she belongs to!" Her face contorted with rage.

"Kassandra," Lenorre said, "find Rosalin, seek out your wolf."

I stood there, wondering if I should go for my gun. The wolf reflected my emotions, pacing with agitation and uncertainty. A part of her just wanted to knock Sheila on her ass, but I ignored that part because logically, with Sheila's entire pack present, we were outnumbered.

Lenorre was flaunting her power. I didn't have a warrant to execute Sheila. I didn't have any evidence to back up drawing my gun and pumping her chest full of silver bullets.

I was about to confess that I didn't know how to find Rosalin, when a thought came to me. Surely, the wolf would know what to do? I lowered my shields slightly, like parting a curtain open. The night was suddenly more vibrant in my vision. I met Sheila's furious gaze and felt a responding anger.

Rosalin, I thought, inhaling through my nose, exhaling through my mouth. The smell of wolf called to the beast and I had to focus on exerting my will over hers. Where was Rosalin? Why couldn't I sense her?

Sheila said, "Calling your beast to your eyes doesn't prove anything, Kassandra."

Carver made a noise low in his throat and fell into a crouch. He crawled on his hands and knees toward me, his beast riding just beneath his skin. I knelt placing both palms on the ground, and when he was close enough to slide his cheek across mine and whisper in my ear, I didn't protest.

"Claim me as your wolf and I will tell you where she is." His voice was thick and rumbling with that edge of wolf. "It's a trap. You won't find her on your own."

The crisp scent of his aftershave and cologne burned my nostrils. Mingling with that scent was the smell of rich earth and fur. "How?"

Sheila yelled, "No!"

Her footfalls on the earthen floor seemed louder than they should've been. I blocked her path, standing in front of Carver.

She growled at me and though nothing physical about her changed, the heat of her beast brushed mine like a flame.

"He is *my wolf*, not yours!" She screamed the words into my face. "You will not stand between me and my wolves!"

"If you threaten to harm them, I will."

She stepped into my personal space, her energy biting my skin. "Will you protect them unto death, Kassandra? Each and every one of them? Do they mean that much to you?"

"They should mean that much to you."

Sheila put her hands on my shoulders and shoved. Carver caught me with an arm around my back and kept me from hitting the ground.

"You are siding with her." She stared at him when he caught me, surprise written across her features.

"Rosalin told you Kassandra didn't mean to claim her. She doesn't deserve to be punished and all you're doing is looking for a fight. You're antagonizing her, not the other way around."

"Do you feel antagonized, Kassandra?"

"Is that a yes or no question or are we talking on a scale of one to ten?"

"Fine," she said, "we'll do it your way." She went back to her throne, unnervingly calm. "Those of you who wish to be claimed by Kassandra"—she swept her hand out to gesture at me—"step forward."

I got to my feet. "Not only do I not trust your little offer, Sheila, but I didn't come here for your wolves. I came here for Rosalin, remember? If you don't want to lose Carver, to lose your gamma, tell me where the fuck she is."

"If she was truly your wolf you would be able to find her, to sense her. You bear the mark of an alpha, Kassandra, but you do not even know how to harness the power of it."

"You're a fucking bitch."

Sheila smiled, pleased with herself. I didn't think about what I was doing. One moment I was standing by Carver and the next I had my hand wrapped around Sheila's throat. I shoved her back against her throne and growled in her face.

"Where is Rosalin?"

Sheila continued to smile while I choked her, making no move to protect herself.

"I heard she fucked you before you hooked up with the Countess vampire. Is that true, Kassandra?"

I pushed harder. "That's none of your business."

Sheila laughed and her laugh thrummed against my fingertips. She moved in a blur, shoving my arm behind my back and pulling me in against her.

I hadn't truly known how Sheila had managed to dominate the rest of the pack, how she'd managed to put them in fear and to rule as their alpha. I had my answer. She was strong, a lot stronger than I'd expected. If the whole mark of the alpha thing was true, held against Sheila, I didn't feel it. The wolf paced somewhere inside me, considering.

"You'd be a lot of fun to play with." She jerked my arm up higher behind my back. I groaned. She whispered against my hair. "The energy raised between two powerful Lykos in the throes of passion is amazing, Kassandra."

Before I could move, someone grabbed Sheila and slammed her body unceremoniously back in her throne.

Eris stood above her, holding her down with a grip on her shoulder. She smiled at me and I had a feeling that the whole thing just amused the hell out of her.

"If anyone gets to play with Kassandra, it will be me, not you."

"Never you," Lenorre said, suddenly standing behind Sheila's throne. She touched Sheila's shoulder and Sheila flinched.

"I didn't make this your business."

"Actually, you did."

Eris leaned over to whisper in Sheila's ear. "You most certainly did."

Sheila glared at Lenorre like a sullen child. "How?"

Lenorre moved and held out a hand to me. I took it as she slipped her body behind mine, wrapping an arm loosely around my waist. She spoke over my shoulder. "As the humans say, you touched my girl."

A flicker of startled excitement went through me and I leaned back against her, reveling in the feel of her, in the cool energy kissing my skin.

"You can't mate her," Sheila said sourly. "You are a vampire. She is a wolf. It is not possible. If you plan on claiming her as your mate and setting yourself in a position to overtake my pack, it will not work. She does indeed bear the mark of an alpha, but she's yet to prove the power that comes with it. She can't even find her own wolf."

"She will," Lenorre said confidently. "Kassandra, call your wolf."

"I don't know that she's within hearing distance."

"Claim Carver," she said. "One way or another, we will find Rosalin."

"She has to find Rosalin," Sheila said. "You know the rules."

"Ah yes, and you broke them by punishing a wolf that does not belong to you."

At that, Sheila's lips pressed into a tight line.

"Carver," I said and he came to me. It took me by surprise when he dropped to his knees. "Yes, alpha?"

"Don't call me that," I said, glancing at Sheila to see the sour look on her face. "Do you want me to try and claim you, not just to find Rosalin?"

He glared at Sheila. "I made the offer," he said. "If I don't follow through with it she will punish me."

"Is that true?" I asked Sheila. "Would you punish him for protecting his beta?"

"I'd punish him for following you."

"Why?" I didn't understand it.

"She punished us when we rescued you from her brother," Carver said quietly.

A tidal wave of rage slammed into me so fast and hard that I shuddered where Lenorre held me.

"What sense of satisfaction do you gain from hurting them?" I asked. "They are your wolves. You are their alpha. You are supposed to protect them, not abuse them!"

"You don't tell me what to do."

"Stop taking what your uncle did to you and your brother out on them, Sheila. Don't become the monster whose eyes you've looked into."

She jerked her gaze away from mine as if I'd slapped her. "It's too late for that, Kassandra. Far, far too late."

"That's a weak and pathetic excuse to avoid taking personal responsibility for your actions. You are whatever and whoever you decide to be." I stepped out of the circle of Lenorre's arms and approached her. "Do you want to be a good alpha or a bad one?"

"And what will you do if I am a bad one? I am alpha, not you, Kassandra. Remember?"

"That can change."

The wolves behind us had mixed reactions. There were yips of encouragement and growls of protest, but a great many of them remained silent, as silent as the pack of meek puppies that Sheila had made them.

"Now you are threatening me."

"Yes, Sheila. Now I'm threatening you. If a hair on Rosalin's head is harmed, I will hunt you down and I will kill you."

"I can physically overpower you, Kassandra."

"I'll take my chances." I turned my back on her, trusting Eris to keep her from touching me again. I lowered my shields another fraction and said, "Carver, if you would be my wolf, come to me."

He came and took my hand. I didn't know how to claim him, but I remembered how I'd claimed Rosalin. I'd offered her my protection.

"You saved my life once. I don't think I ever said thank you. I will take you as my wolf, if you would be it."

"I will be it," he said and a shock of energy jumped between our clasped palms.

My skin grew warm.

"Kassandra." It was Claire's voice. She pushed through the meek crowd of wolves and approached me. She smiled awkwardly, her hazel eyes bright and confident. Her brown hair was pulled back in a low ponytail.

Claire held out her hand. "Had I known you were taking applications I would've put mine in when you guys picked me up from the station."

"This isn't something I planned," I said.

"If you don't want to become an alpha, Kassandra, why are you claiming them?"

I turned back to Sheila. "To protect them."

"From?"

"You."

"Will you claim every last one of them?"

"I will claim the ones that want it, Sheila."

She laughed, looking out over her wolves. "Not too many seem eager to join forces with you," she said.

"That is their decision."

Claire caught my hand in hers, skin against skin. "Will you have me?"

"If it is your will," I said.

"It is my will." As Carver had, she slipped to her jeaned knees on the dirty ground.

That same tingle of energy tapped my palm, sailing up my arm and warming my skin further.

I made eye contact with various wolves in the pack and only a few of them refused to meet my gaze. They would avert or lower their gazes for Sheila, because she was their alpha, but not me. I was an outsider. The wolf inside me understood that it wasn't a sign of disrespect.

I met Trevor's brown eyes through the eyes of my wolf. He, like so many of the others, stank of fear. Though Isabella, his girlfriend, was one of Lenorre's Prime vampires, there was something young and carefree about Trevor. Now his usual carelessness was gone. He looked like he wasn't sure what to do, and since he wasn't sure, the wolf and I turned away from him.

We would not take the uncertain.

Sheila's wolves parted, and Zaphara strutted up through the middle of them.

Her voice whispered through my mind. *I will help you find your wolf.*

I gave the slightest of nods, a nod that others might take only as an acknowledgement of her presence.

"Eris," Lenorre said. "Maddox."

"Yes?" Maddox grumbled, watching the pack carefully.

"See to it Sheila and none of her wolves interfere."

"I will take you to Rosalin," Carver said, raising his white T-shirt above his head and tossing it to the ground.

Claire removed the jean jacket she wore, letting it fall to the ground before following Carver and removing her shoes.

"Will you run with us?" she asked.

I unbuttoned the black coat and handed it to Lenorre with my gun and holster. She offered her arm and I braced myself, kicking off the boots. The wolf wanted to run with them, wanted to bond with them, wanted to find Rosalin.

I dropped my shields and flung open the doors that held the wolf inside. Generally, my shifts were slower and more careful. If they were fast, I still felt them, felt my bones popping, spine lengthening, felt every part of my body changing, but this…it was quick, so quick. One moment my body was changing, clothes tore, and the next I rose on all fours, white paws stark against the ground. Carver's blue and gold eyes met mine from the black mask of his wolf's face. Claire bumped up against me. Her fur was a rich brown with sprinkles of cream and white. Her eyes were the color of pine.

I pushed up against Carver, encouraging him to lead the way. He threw his head back and howled, turning on all fours like a horse about to charge into battle. He lowered his snout, and darted in the opposite direction that I'd entered. I followed him, the earth gliding under my paws, my nails ticking on twigs and bits of grass.

Someone grabbed my tail and I spun, growling a chastisement.

Claire gave a little whimper, but practically skipped around me.

I lowered my head and snapped at her ankle. She bolted ahead, catching up with Carver.

Carver led the group at a full out run. We darted through the trees, low enough we didn't have to worry about hanging branches.

I was passing a tall oak when something hit my side, slamming me up against the tree.

A furred body galloped past. I pushed off the earth and kept going, catching up to the black wolf that had collided into me. The wolf turned its head, amethyst eyes meeting mine with a look of mischief.

I knew Zaphara could shape-shift. It was one of her abilities as full-blooded fey, but I hadn't known she could choose the form of a wolf.

As if hearing my thoughts, her laughter rang in my head again.

Oh, you bitch. I projected the thought at her, knocking my body against hers, feeling our fur and muscles move together.

The wolf liked that.

Zaphara nipped at my ear and I ducked my head, making her miss.

I have my moments.

A few too many, I think.

At that, she laughed, offering a delighted and carefree yip to go along with the ringing in my head.

Carver made a sharp right and we followed through a break of tall, unkempt grass. Zaphara's furred body moved against mine, her paws hitting the ground in synchronicity with mine. I closed my eyes, mirroring the flow of her body.

Kassandra.

Hmm?

You're up my ass, witch.

I opened my eyes and backed off, pushing myself to catch up with Carver and Claire.

It didn't take long until I felt Zaphara's warm body flowing alongside mine again, until I felt her melding into me.

I thought I was up your ass?

Little did I realize you were keeping it warm.

The long grass ended and we erupted in another clearing. Carver stood over a body-sized mound of dirt and whimpered. He pawed at the dirt, starting to dig.

He looked at me and pointed his snout at the mound. Claire started frantically digging with him.

I didn't think. I didn't need to think. I just knew and started digging.

Sheila had buried Rosalin alive.

CHAPTER ELEVEN

We dug, dug until our paws were thick with dirt and soil. We dug with a frenzy, throwing showers of dirt like rain behind and on each other. Twice, I had to shake my head to keep the loose dirt from falling into my eyes. I averted my ears, feeling them flatten against my skull. Zaphara dug beside me, black paws as dark with soil as mine were.

Whoever had buried Rosalin had patted the soil down, making it tight and unyielding. Carver shook his head, dirt falling from his obsidian snout.

"Too deep," he said in a guttural voice, stepping back.

Claire followed Carver's lead and stopped digging. "We can't just leave her."

"We're not going to." I kept digging.

Someone touched my furred shoulder. I turned to see Zaphara, kneeling in her clothes, her trench coat trailing on the ground. "Get back, Kassandra."

It did not surprise me to see her fully clothed. She had once taught me how to emerge from a raven shift fully clothed. Returning from a shift was different with magic. Once, she had told me she could teach me how to return from wolf-form clothed, but I had not gotten the hang of it. From what I understood, it had to do with simultaneously summoning the fey magic in my veins and the beast. So far, I'd gotten the hang of it with the raven. That was it.

"What are you going to do?"

"Call the earth."

I didn't question her. Zaphara's power was elemental in nature, and earth was just another element. I moved back from the small crater we'd managed to create. Zaphara put her stark palms flat on the soil and closed her eyes. She whispered something, words I did not understand. A cool breeze picked up, tangling its fingers in my fur. The waist-length tresses of Zaphara's hair swayed in that breeze, dancing lightly. She had not wasted magic materializing the clasp that had secured her hair when it was braided.

The cool breeze grew warm to my pricked ears and I took another step back.

A tremor rumbled through the earth.

Zaphara sank her fingers into the dirt as if they were knives. Her eyes flew open and I didn't need to see them to know they were power-filled, to know they burned with the intensity of the gemstones they mimicked.

She closed her fists around the dirt and raised her hands.

The earth gave one last shudder, strong enough that I had to space my paws out to keep from losing my balance.

The dirt above Rosalin jumped. It hung in the air above the dark cavity, hung as if someone had slipped an invisible sheet beneath it and was holding it there. Carver and Claire sank low to the ground, backing off in a sign of submission. Neither seemed willing to brave Zaphara's magic and crawl into the hole to retrieve Rosalin.

I caught Zaphara's glance. The amethyst jewels of her eyes flickered with power in the moonlit night, a burst of color in my vision.

"Get your wolf, Kassandra. I cannot hold this forever."

I stood on my hind legs, a few inches taller than in my human form, and climbed down into the well-dug grave.

I jerked the dark pillowcase from the head of the body at my feet. Rosalin's features came into view, eyes closed, mouth slack.

My heart leapt erratically in my chest. Memories swam to the surface: Memories of Timothy's body naked and exposed to the cool October night. Memories of his tanned skin slightly paled, of his eyes opened wide in death, of his lips half-parted.

"No." She wasn't dead. She couldn't be dead. She was a werewolf, a shape-shifter. It took more than a little suffocation to kill us.

Timothy hadn't been dead, not truly. I tried to assure myself that's why my mind was reverting to that particular memory.

"Kassandra." Zaphara's voice was a distant reminder. I stopped thinking and scooped Rosalin's limp body into my arms, hauling her up. It was going to be difficult carrying her out, not because I couldn't carry her. I had the strength to carry her, but because even in wolf-form I wasn't exactly tall, not as tall as some of the others.

Carver was suddenly there, at the edge of the grave. He reached out with clawed fingers, grabbing the back of Rosalin's red T-shirt. I heard it tear as he pulled her to the ground above.

Someone wrapped an arm around my waist and jerked me unceremoniously from the grave. The earth fell in a shower of dirt and stones, making a sound unlike anything I'd ever heard. I wasn't so sure it liked Zaphara playing with it.

Since when did the earth have a mind to care?

Zaphara's arm slipped from around my waist. Dark blood glinted on her hands in the moonlight.

"Nature is two-edged," she explained, obviously understanding the question in my eyes, even if they were the wolf's.

Carver made a noise, almost a grunt and I moved, the night blurring for a moment in my vision. I knelt with him beside Rosalin. She was on her side. The jeans she wore were torn and dirty. Her red T-shirt had been torn by Carver's claws in the back, although he hadn't meant to.

Her hands had been bound behind her back. I trailed a claw along the diminutive leather straps that encircled her wrists, holding them together. The leather crawled up her arms, cinched tight at her elbows.

I knew those bindings. I'd had firsthand experience of those bindings, and it had taken Lenorre to get me out of them.

Sheila Morris had used the same leather bindings that Lukas Morris had used on me when he'd kidnapped me. I couldn't break them; neither Carver nor Claire could break them either, because underneath the leather, they were laced with silver chain.

I touched Rosalin's shoulder and laid my ear against her chest. Her heart wasn't beating.

"Zaphara," my voice sounded a hell of a lot calmer than I felt.

She came, kneeling with us. She looked at the bindings. "I will untie them."

I nodded.

"Shift while I remove them. Your wolf is not yet lost, Kassandra, but you're going to have to breathe life back into her lungs."

I was pretty sure she was telling me I was going to have to give Rosalin CPR and couldn't very well do it while in wolf form. Against all my modesty, I closed my eyes and drew the night air into my lungs. I held it there, along with the image of the wolf in my mind. I didn't lure her back into the center of my body, I jerked her into it, or maybe, understanding what I knew, she went willingly. I do not know, but it felt as if my body caved in on itself, skin replaced fur, claws sank to nails. My bones clicked and crunched together like shifting gears, sliding back into place.

The air was cold and my skin was sticky, sticky like I'd been running and sweating profusely, but I was warm with the aftermath of the shift.

Zaphara had removed the leather straps at Rosalin's arms and laid her on her back. I knelt over her body and tried to remember something I'd been taught way too many years ago. I found the notch where her breastbone met her ribs, pressing down just enough to make sure that was in fact where I wanted to pump the heel of my hand. I reminded myself to be calm and gentle. It wouldn't do any good to accidentally break something just because I was panicking and unaware of my strength. I folded my right hand over my left, leaned over my hands, then pumped while counting silently in my head.

I plugged Rosalin's small nose, tilted her head back, pressed my mouth against her half-parted lips, and breathed into her.

I leaned over and listened. Nothing.

Compressions. Breath. Compressions. Breath. I did it again and again. If the others were looking at me, if they were watching me, I did not care. I fell into a sort of trance, following the beat of remembered training and the flow of my body.

I pressed my mouth against Rosalin's soft and yielding lips and when I breathed, I shoved my will into her body.

Wake up, I thought calmly. Unnervingly calmly. *Damn it, Rosalin. Wake up.*

I turned, about to resume compressions when her body jerked.

A long, ragged gasp of breath cut through the night. Carver gave a satisfied rumble. Claire offered a triumphant yip. Rosalin looked up at me, panic in her eyes. Her nails dug into my skin where she clutched my shoulder.

I could suddenly taste cool ginger on my tongue.

"Kassandra?"

I licked my lips, closing my eyes and breathing a sigh of relief. I whispered a silent prayer to the Morrigan.

Rosalin's nails dug more fiercely into my shoulder, threatening to pierce my skin. I could feel her hand shaking, trembling.

A sob fell from her lips. I had only seen Rosalin cry once, and once was enough. I caught her arm and pulled her in against my body, wrapping my arms around her. Her body shook, trembling all over with the memory of Sheila's abuse. I didn't need to be inside her head. I could smell the fear and shock coming off her. Carver bumped up against her and Claire came to us, offering the balm of their furred bodies, offering the scent of family.

I stroked Rosalin's messy auburn hair. "It's okay," I whispered. "You're safe now. Rosalin, you're safe now."

Rosalin buried her face in the bend of my neck, crying and trembling.

I met Zaphara's eyes over Rosalin's shoulder. The look on her face was pure venom. The wolf growled through me, a shudder of rage suffusing my body.

Rosalin's hand slid down my back, following the curve of my spine.

Her fingers brushed the top of my buttocks and I stiffened.

"Rosalin," I said, warning.

She drew back, eyes wide, tears glistening on her cheeks. "Not that I mind you being nude right now, but where are your clothes?"

"I just pulled you out of a grave, gave you CPR, and you're worried about my clothes?"

Her eyes were haunted. "I've been through worse," she said plainly, no emotion, nothing.

Another shudder of rage sailed through me.

I stood, pulling Rosalin's hands off my body.

"Kassandra." She touched my leg, gazing up at me and searching my face. "What are you doing?" Her eyes were wide with surprise. "What are you going to do? You can't possibly..."

"Oh yes," I said, words dripping with heat and the wolf's power. "I can."

"Kassandra," Zaphara's amused voice made me turn. She held her hand out, trench coat dangling from her fingertips. Without the coat, the tight black long-sleeved T-shirt she wore and dark jeans looked glued over her long body.

"Thanks," I said, taking the trench and slipping it on over my bare skin. I buttoned the coat to my knees. It was a little long, but I didn't care. In fact, had she not offered, I probably wouldn't have even given the nudity a second thought until it was too late. Just the thought that in my anger, I'd completely overlooked that tidbit unnerved me, but I let it go. Pissed off sounded like a better state.

Rosalin said, "Kassandra, please, don't do this. Don't do what I think you're going to do."

I looked over my shoulder. "I told you once, if she laid a hand on you again, I'd break everyone of her Goddess-damned fingers. If there's one thing you should know about me, Rosalin, it's this: I keep my promises."

CHAPTER TWELVE

I made it to the edge of the clearing, and the wolves that had so readily parted for Zaphara did not part for me. They turned to look at me but made no move to get the hell out of my way.

Something about that pissed me off even more. I hadn't thought my wolf and I could get madder, hadn't thought there was a next bitch level. In fact, I'd been fairly certain I'd hit the max. I was wrong.

My skin burned hot, hotter than I'd ever felt it. The energy of the wolf unfurled from inside me and I felt my eyes bleed gold again. Her snowy fur brushed my insides, making my head feel thick and heavy. I moved and the ground felt faint and unreal beneath my feet.

I reached out to touch the wolf closest to me, a girl that looked much younger than the others. I touched her arm and she flinched a second before that hot wave of energy rolled from me and slammed into her. She fell to her knees, gasping.

As soon as she hit her knees, she averted her eyes.

It would be so easy to claim her, to take her from Sheila Morris. The wolf howled through me; she wanted to do it.

Girl. I reminded myself. She was only a girl, probably no more than eighteen or nineteen years of age.

"Go ahead and take her, Kassandra. I've no need of weaklings."

Sheila's voice carried to my ears and I turned, growling as the wolf's anger flared again. The wolves parted, giving me a clear line of sight to Sheila.

Lenorre and Eris stood by her throne, almost like they were guarding it, but I knew better.

I moved to stand, and fingers clutched my arm, nails digging frantically into my skin.

There was a look in her brown eyes that was pleading. I touched her brow, feeling the heat like something warm and sticky between us, feeling the energy of our wolves leap like a dancing flame.

Not now, I thought, getting to my feet, I turned away from the girl, heading for Sheila. I took my time about it, letting her see my anger. Sheila held my gaze unflinchingly as a satisfied smirk twisted her mouth. Her expression was cold and baiting.

I wanted to knock that look off her face and didn't try to hide it. The anger fueled the beast, giving her a longer leash to play with. I felt my canines lengthening.

When I got to Sheila, no one tried to stop me or to stand in my way. I paused in front of her, close enough to reach out and touch her. I drew my arm back and she didn't move to protect herself. For a moment, I think she didn't believe I'd actually do it.

I hit her, raking my nails across her face, tearing skin and sending blood flying.

"If you touch one of my wolves ever again I will destroy everything you are." I leaned in close, whispering.

Her eyes blazed with anger and I felt the heat of her beast threatening to swallow her. She licked the blood from her bottom lip.

"Will you, Kassandra? Are you that confident? How is Rosalin, by the way?"

I growled, grabbing her by the shoulders and yanking her out of her throne and to the ground.

Her wolves stepped forward and she raised a hand, stopping them.

"If you wanted to fight," she said, "all you had to do was say so."

She grabbed a handful of her shirt, tearing it down the middle.

A deafening shot shattered the silence.

Sheila's body jerked and she howled. The bullet knocked a spray of blood from her right shoulder. The wolves behind her scrambled and scattered, tripping over one another and their own feet.

Sheila made to move, but stopped, going completely still. Past the ringing in my ears, I heard Lenorre tsk softly.

"You do not want to challenge me, Sheila. I am much less merciful than Kassandra."

Lenorre moved up beside me and I knew from the strong ringing in my left ear that she hadn't been the one to fire the shot. Eris moved where I could see her, gun still aimed on Sheila.

Out of my peripheral vision, I saw her wink over the gun at me.

"This ends now," Lenorre said, calm and graceful as she walked to Sheila. "I am not only tired of your games, Sheila, but I am atrociously bored with them as well. Kassandra has not acted outside of Lykos' law. She has exacted blood payment and you know the repercussions if you lay hand on one of her wolves again. Do not seek to challenge her this night." She knelt and reached out to touch Sheila's hair.

Sheila jerked away from her.

"There is no way for you to win this, Sheila."

"Why not let your little wolf try me? Are you so scared you'll lose her, Lenorre? Are you so scared I'll break your precious toy alpha?"

Lenorre moved so quickly, all I saw was a blur of moonlit skin and her long onyx hair. She yanked Sheila's head back by her braid. "You know the rules, Sheila."

"I know the rules, Lenorre. Let Kassandra speak for herself." Lenorre let her go and stepped away from her. Sheila turned to look at me and moved toward me.

The wolves behind her took up a chorus of growls. The wolf within me paced, anxious and angry.

Sheila stopped moving, kneeling in her pants and torn shirt, the line of bra dark against her body.

"Challenge me, Kassandra."

"No!" It was Rosalin's voice. She entered the clearing with Zaphara, Carver and Claire still in wolf form behind her. "That's what she wants, Kassandra. She's trying to set you up to tear you down. Can't you see it? Don't challenge her, please. She can't hurt you, not by our laws, unless you challenge her."

I looked down at the alpha in front of me. I'd extracted blood payment, but if I touched her again, if I outright challenged her, it'd be a fight in earnest.

She spread her arms out, smiling. "All you have to do is challenge me, Kassandra, and we'll be on even ground. Your Countess has stepped aside and will not interfere. My wolves will not interfere. One on one," she whispered, and the coaxing tone in her voice made me laugh.

"Is that what you really want?" I asked.

"Oh yes."

I felt the dark smile that crept over my lips. "In that case, not only no, but hell no. This is done." I cast a glance to her bleeding shoulder. "Someone needs to look at your shoulder, Sheila. I only carry silver."

"It's not done, Kassandra, and you know it."

"Great, Sheila, but it's done for tonight. Remember my promise."

"Remember mine," she said.

"I'm really starting to regret not telling the cops about you."

"Why didn't you?"

"To protect you. And maybe to some extent it was about respect, having enough respect not to fuck with another Lykos's life, but if you start fucking with mine, Sheila, you'll pay for it. Trust me on that one."

"I'll keep that in mind," she said, but not like she cared.

"Good." I stood, ready to get the fuck away from her before I gave her exactly what she wanted—a fight. My hands were trembling with rage and the urge to strike her. "We're done here."

One of Sheila's wolves slipped from the group began probing at the hole in her shoulder. She watched me while he drew her shirt away and inspected the still bleeding wound.

Lenorre came to me, touching my wrist with her fingers. Rosalin breathed out a sigh of relief. I recoiled from Lenorre's touch, because in that moment, I didn't exactly feel like being touched by anyone or anything.

Eris came forward, holding out my clothes. I slipped the slacks on under Zaphara's coat, not bothering with the rest.

I just wanted to get the fuck away from Sheila and her wolves before I did something stupid.

Or really, really wise.

Chapter Thirteen

W e made it to the edge of the parking lot when I realized Rosalin's hands were trembling violently. If I hadn't been watching her like a hawk, I wouldn't have noticed. I reached out and brushed her palm with my fingers. She jumped, turning on me as if I'd just appeared.

"You okay?"

She let out a long breath, as if exhaling her pain. "I don't know," she whispered, eyes downcast and searching the gravel. It was kind of obvious by that one look that she wasn't okay.

I felt Lenorre move behind me. "Comfort your wolf, Kassandra. She needs you right now. I will drive."

I dug the keys out of the jacket I'd been wearing earlier and handed them to her. I slipped into the backseat, holding out a hand for Rosalin. She settled in against me and curled as much of her body around mine as space would allow.

I didn't bother trying to buckle my seat belt. Lenorre waited and before I could ask what we were waiting for, Zaphara eased into the passenger seat. She turned around, looked at Rosalin and me, got out again, then pushed the seat forward and climbed in back with us.

"She needs more warmth and comfort than you're going to be able to give her on your own, unless you shift," she said.

I nodded. It wasn't the first time Zaphara had helped me to comfort Rosalin. Wolves need touch, so I'd learned. When something bad has happened or we're stressed, we have a tendency to get snuggly. We're pack creatures, so it makes sense. Besides, shifting and tearing my upholstery didn't sound like the greatest plan. I imagine retractable claws come in very handy, but since I wasn't a shifter of the feline variety, I'd rather not tear up my car.

"Pity there's not more room," Eris said, shutting the door. She met my gaze with a beautiful smile.

Lenorre started the car.

"I thought you rode with Maddox?" I asked Zaphara and Eris.

Zaphara said, "Maddox is going over to Timothy's to check on him."

"Oh." I stroked a hand across Rosalin's shoulder. "Are you feeling better?"

She nodded.

"Not talking to me is kind of an indication that you're not feeling better, Ros."

That earned me a small laugh.

She nuzzled her face in the bend of my neck. "I was so scared you were going to challenge her."

"And give the bitch what she wanted?" I scoffed. "Not likely." Another shudder went through her. "Are you hungry?" I asked. I needed to eat and soon. We expend energy when we shift. Having shifted to wolf form and back to human, I needed some protein and iron to curb the fatigue that threatened to kick into high gear. My tremors weren't noticeable yet.

"I don't know if I could eat right now," she murmured.

"You should," Zaphara said, "as should the rest of us that eat solid food."

"I'd beg to argue that my food is quite solid," Eris said.

Zaphara raised her brows.

I stroked Rosalin's hair. "Does anything sound good?"

"Maybe some chili cheese fries?"

Zaphara said, "Meat is a good idea."

I agreed with her. Eris looked at us over her shoulder, scrunching her nose up slightly in distaste.

Lenorre stopped at a red light. "I need to know where I am going."

"Al's Diner," I said. "We'll go in and order. It'll give me a chance to scope someone out for a client."

"Very well then."

I looked at Rosalin again. "Anything else?"

"Maybe a salad too."

Zaphara and I both laughed.

"What? What's so funny about salad?"

"Nothing," Zaphara said, "nothing at all if you were a were-bunny."

"Fine," she said, playfully defensive. "A chicken salad. Happy?"

"Get whatever you want, Ros," I said.

She nodded, falling silent. Lenorre guided the car onto the highway heading north back toward the city.

"And maybe a small cheeseburger and a chocolate shake."

"You know, there is a zoo not too far from here. If you prefer, I am sure we could find some way to obtain a gazelle," Eris said in a musing voice.

"Oh!" Rosalin exclaimed, completely ignoring her. "And some fried pickles."

"You keep adding to that order and you're going to have to write it down," I said.

"I take it that was a no on the gazelle?" Eris asked.

I offered a slight nod. "Yeah, pretty sure that was a no."

Rosalin sat up straight in the seat. "Wait, gazelle? What? Someone said something about a gazelle?"

I put a hand on her shoulder and pulled her back into me. "Nothing, Ros. You're not getting a gazelle."

"That's a shame," she said, relaxing. "I've never had gazelle salad before."

❖

Al's Diner was one of those places that tried to pass as old-fashioned with black and white tiled floors; red, high-backed booths; and a jukebox that was purely for decorative purposes only. Zaphara and Lenorre stood next to me while I examined the menu, spouting off what I could remember of Rosalin's order to the blond teenager behind the counter. Her hair was pulled back in a ponytail, and the uniform shirt she wore was a little too dark for her, bringing out the pink undertones in her skin. Her eyes kept flicking between the three of us. Fortunately, I'd slipped my shirt and jacket on when everyone had gotten out of the car. And though Lenorre had tried to fuss with my hair on our way in, I was betting it was still a righteous mess.

I ordered a bacon cheeseburger, minus the herbivorous crap, and a large coffee to go. Protein and caffeine, the night was already beginning to look up. Zaphara finished her order and I handed the girl my card.

Al's Diner wasn't packed, but when I turned around my eyes confirmed what my senses had been telling me. Lenorre, Zaphara, and I were attracting attention. If it bothered either of them, they didn't show it.

I chose a booth where I could watch the servers and wait staff, in case Kamryn Sherman walked through.

Lenorre placed her hand on my thigh and I turned to look at her. She shifted her silvery gaze toward the restroom.

"Kamryn, you said?" she asked.

I nodded.

"A woman wearing that name tag just walked into the ladies' room."

The restroom was on the opposite side of the diner.

"You could read her name tag from here?"

Lenorre merely said, "Yes."

She stood so that I could slip out of the booth. I touched her arm lightly. "Thank you."

She bowed her head in acknowledgement of my thanks and I went, figuring I'd use the opportunity to my advantage and further try to tame my tangled hair. Shifting and running through the woods hadn't exactly done it justice.

Before I reached the mirror, I spied a pair of black sneakers under the second stall. I ran my fingers through my hair, trying to strategically place strands to hide the stickers stuck in it. I wouldn't be able to get them out without the aid of a brush.

I was washing my hands when Kamryn emerged, wearing the same matching black button-up dress shirt as the girl behind the register. The pants she wore were white. She tightened the matching belt at her hips and smiled at me.

"Hi."

"Evening," I said, casually glancing at her name tag and moving out of the way of the sink.

Kamryn Sherman was less androgynous than Hunter, with curly brown highlighted hair that brushed the tops of her shoulders. Her makeup was light and artfully done, the brown eye shadow bringing out the amber flecks in her dark brown eyes.

I held the door for Kamryn. She smiled at me.

"I like your hair."

"Thanks," I said, not really meaning it.

Lenorre and Zaphara were standing by the exit with bags of food in their hands. Lenorre was holding my cup of coffee and offered it to me as I approached.

"Did you find anything?" she asked as soon as we hit the open air.

"I know what she looks like now."

"But you don't know if she's cheating on her girlfriend?" Zaphara asked. I'd explained to everyone before we arrived that I was scoping someone out.

"Not yet."

Zaphara gave me a long look. Eris opened the passenger side door of my Tiburon and stepped out, holding it open for us.

"Why didn't you just make a pass at her and find out?"

I shook my head, switching my coffee cup to my right hand while taking the food from Lenorre in my left.

"It doesn't work like that."

"Why doesn't it? It's a simple thing to find out."

"It's disrespectful to my client, Zaphara. She didn't hire me to encourage her girlfriend to cheat; she asked me to find out if she *is* cheating."

It looked as though Zaphara was about to say something when Rosalin called my name from the backseat.

I peeked in. "Yes?"

"I'm starving. I can smell my chili cheese fries and I'm about to start chewing on your seats. Can't you two do that in the car?"

I handed her the bag I was holding and climbed into the backseat, careful that none of my coffee sloshed over the edge of the cup and went to waste.

CHAPTER FOURTEEN

When we made it back to Lenorre's I was exhausted, not only physically but mentally as well. Those of us that had ordered food had impatiently eaten it in the car on the way.

Everything seemed foggy and touched by that haze that tiredness will cast. I held Rosalin's hand, my other loosely resting at the bend in Lenorre's elbow as we made it to the basement levels. Zaphara opened the door into the lounge and I squinted, as always, waiting until my eyes adjusted to the spill of bright light. Once inside, I let go of Rosalin, figuring she'd find a room downstairs or return to her room upstairs. Lenorre stood still, and since she wasn't moving toward the bedroom, where I desperately wanted to go, I let go of her as well.

"Kassandra." Lenorre's voice made me turn. When I met her silvery eyes there was a look of expectation in her gaze. She tilted her head in Rosalin's direction.

Rosalin stood there staring at her feet as if she wasn't sure what to do.

"Ros."

She raised her honey eyes briefly.

"Rosalin," I tried again.

She crossed her arms and I got the vague sense she was trying to lock herself in her body.

Lenorre said, "Kassandra is speaking to you."

Eris, who had been quietly standing just inside the room, chose that moment to move. She snuck up behind Rosalin and wrapped her arms around her waist.

Rosalin's eyes went wide with panic. She tried to step away and Eris held her, whispering at her ear in a voice soft enough that I couldn't hear it, which meant she didn't want me to hear whatever she was saying.

Rosalin wriggled again, saying softly, "I don't want to be touched by you right now."

Eris still didn't let her go.

If she was trying to comfort her, it didn't look like it.

A spark of anger flared inside of me.

Zaphara was there. She placed a hand on Eris's shoulder. "Sheila is a sadist, Eris."

Eris stared at Zaphara as if Zaphara had just slapped her, her lips were half-parted in surprise. "I'm a dominatrix, Zaphara, not a sadist, and I am certainly not Sheila."

"What's the difference?" I asked, speaking before thinking.

Eris looked appalled. "That you would ask me that reveals how little you really know about the lifestyle. A *sadist* doesn't stop when asked, Kassandra, nor do they adhere to any code of ethics. A *sadist* doesn't care about the well-being of their submissive, only about their own selfish needs being met."

"Then let her go, Eris."

Reluctantly, she did.

I wasn't sure, but I had a feeling that both Rosalin and Zaphara had hurt Eris's feelings.

Lenorre touched my arm and I placed a hand over hers. "Rosalin," I tried again. This time she looked at me. "Do you want to come with us?"

She lowered her gaze again.

"Rosalin!"

Her head snapped up.

"Look," I said, "I'm exhausted. You either want to come with us or you don't, but make your needs known and stop caving in on yourself."

"I don't want to intrude," she said, voice small.

I sighed again. "Ros, I don't have the energy to expend right now on a pep talk, nor do I have the patience for it. If you were intruding, I wouldn't have offered. So yes or no?"

Lenorre remained silent behind me, her hand sliding down my side to my hip.

That one small touch made something in Rosalin's expression change. The hollowness that had been there was replaced by a look of yearning.

Eris said, "If you don't take them up on their offer, I will."

She put a sway in her walk, approaching while Rosalin refused to budge.

"Eris," Lenorre said.

Eris smiled beautifully. "Do not try to pretend it would be the first time we've been in bed together, Lenorre."

I tensed.

"Use your words carefully," Lenorre said. "Do not seek to play games with me by implying in front of Kassandra that we have slept together when we have not."

I relaxed a little, but not much, considering Eris was standing way too close for comfort.

Eris reached out, and with Lenorre behind me, I didn't have any room to back up. I went stock-still, forcing myself to stand my ground.

The tips of her fingers brushed my cheek, tracing my jaw, down my neck.

"Don't worry," she whispered, watching me with those intense eyes. "Lenorre speaks truth, but why did it trouble you to think we had slept together when the very woman you're inviting to your bed is one you have slept with?"

"Rosalin is my friend. The rest isn't any of your business."

Her fingers trailed lower down my throat, sending my pulse to humming in my ears.

Lenorre squeezed my hips. If she was trying to anchor me against Eris, her gesture had the opposite effect. I closed my eyes, exhaling a shuddering breath.

"And will you comfort your friend by sleeping with her?" Eris asked, tracing the line of my collarbone.

Lenorre's arms wrapped more solidly around me, pinning me to her as Eris had captured Rosalin. She buried her face in the bend of my neck, placing a kiss on my pulse that, despite its gentleness, made me flinch.

"No," I said. "I'm trying to be there for her, Eris, not get in her pants."

"And what do you think your little wolf wants?"

"What?"

"What do you think Rosalin wants, Kassandra?"

"I…I don't know."

Lenorre's lips parted against my skin, making my knees liquid. I whispered her name, trying to give her the hint to stop.

Eris took a step back so that I could see Rosalin.

Her face was blank, not as blank as Lenorre's went when she was trying to hide her feelings, but blank enough that I knew she was trying for neutral.

"Is that why you're hesitating?" I asked.

"I can't watch you and Lenorre," she said.

"Good Gods, I don't want you to watch us. Why would you think we would do that?"

"I don't know," she said, bowing her head again.

Lenorre's lips traced a spot on my neck and I said her name again, this time through clenched teeth.

"Yes, Kassandra?"

"I'm not sure what you're doing," I said, "but you're very distracting right now."

"I am very distracted right now," she whispered, murmuring against my hair, "I need to feed."

When I didn't say anything, she stepped away from me.

"Zaphara," she said.

I touched her arm. "Wait, you didn't ask me."

"And would asking you gain me anything other than your uncertainty and rejection?" Her words were harshly accented.

Eris chimed in. "I didn't know Kassandra wasn't sharing blood with you."

Lenorre and I both ignored her. I touched Lenorre's arm. "Fine," I said. "Point taken."

"Is that a yes or a no, Kassandra?"

"What do you want, Lenorre?"

"What do you mean, what do I want?"

"Tonight, what do *you* want? Do you have a problem with Rosalin coming to cuddle with us?" I asked. "You're the one that stopped and brought it to my attention. I figured you did so for a reason, or did I misread you?"

"You did not misread me. I understand that you need to comfort your wolf."

Was she jealous? Jealousy was never really Lenorre's style. At least, it hadn't been so far.

"What are you thinking, Kassandra?"

"Honestly, Lenorre, I'm trying to figure you out. Are you jealous? Is it the blood thing again? What's going on in that head of yours?"

"I can tell you what's going on in her head," Eris said.

"You think so, do you?" Lenorre asked, utterly calm.

"I know so and I know you, Lenorre."

"By all means, tell Kassandra what is going on in my head."

She looked at me. "By not sharing with her, you're hurting her and your relationship with her. Do you understand, Kassandra?"

"Okay, seriously, why is this such a big deal?"

"Well, for one, you're in a relationship with a vampire. What would make you think the sharing of blood wouldn't be a big deal? And for two," Eris said with a slight smile, "you're not with just any vampire. You're the lover of a Countess vampire, Kassandra. Not sharing blood with her makes her look weak."

"Is that true?"

"Partly," Lenorre said. "I care less about appearing weak. You know it frustrates me what you are trying to do by not sharing blood with me. You told me that you would try, Kassandra. That is all I am asking you to do."

"Kass." Rosalin's voice made me turn my attention to her. "Zaphara said she'll bunk with me tonight."

I looked at them both. "Are you sure?"

"Carver and Claire will be here soon," Zaphara said. "I will keep her company till they arrive."

"I told you," Rosalin said, "I don't want to intrude. Lenorre needs you, and Eris has a point."

"I do?" she asked, sounding surprised that Rosalin agreed with her.

"Yes."

"That would be?" I asked.

"You've obviously got ground to explore with each other. I don't think I can cuddle up with you and Lenorre tonight and not have my mind go *there* if she goes *there*. I'll take advantage of the distraction."

For a moment, Lenorre appeared just as confused as I felt.

"Are you saying it would hurt your feelings to see Kassandra and me together?" Lenorre asked.

"No, I don't think so. I don't think I can watch the whole biting thing without, you know. With our connection and my mood, I don't think I could keep my mind from going *there*."

Lenorre laughed, pure and genuine.

Rosalin offered a faint smile.

I didn't quite see the humor of the situation, so I stood there, frowning.

"Please tell me you're pouting because I won't be there to cuddle," Rosalin said and I shot her a look.

"I'm not pouting."

"Brooding, then."

"I'm not brooding either. I'm tired and I don't see what's funny."

"That's because you're tired," Rosalin said. She came to me, giving me a hug that I returned half-heartedly. "Normally, you'd be like, 'Gee, that's such a Rosalin statement,' but right now you're just too tired to roll your eyes at me."

"I'm confused. Ten minutes ago you were standing there staring at your feet, now you're okay?"

"I just want to curl up with someone and go to sleep." The fact that she hadn't answered yes or no let me know she was avoiding answering my question completely.

"All right," I said, feeling perplexed and irritated. "Do what you will."

Rosalin nodded as the room was enveloped by an awkward silence. I knew, despite her joking, that she wasn't *fine*. But if she was too busy worrying about intruding or getting worked up sexually, there wasn't a thing I could to do about it. Though I couldn't help but feel a small tendril of relief that Lenorre and I would have some privacy. I wasn't exactly looking forward to the prospect of opening a vein.

Lenorre said, "Kassandra, let's go to bed."

I caught her hand. "I'll try."

She paused, brushing my cheek with the back of her fingers just outside the doors to her room.

"I know."

CHAPTER FIFTEEN

I sat in the armchair in Lenorre's large bedroom and stripped off the boots I'd been wearing. I felt grimy after the damp sweat of shifting and frantic search through the woods to find Rosalin. I'd worked as much of the dirt as I could out from under my nails with the help of a napkin and antibacterial gel I kept in the glove compartment box. Still, I didn't feel clean.

Lenorre went to her closet and took our robes down off the hooks on the other side of the door.

"Would you prefer a bath or a shower?" she asked.

"Are you going to join me?"

"Do you want me to join you?"

"You grabbed your robe," I said with a slight smile.

One of her shoulders raised in a half-shrug. "I do not have to join you if you do not want me to." She reopened the closet door and I went to her. I placed a hand on her arm before she could hang the robe back on its hook.

"I'd like it if you joined me, Lenorre."

Her misty eyes caught the light, sparkling faintly. "So I thought. Shall I run a bath?"

I shook my head, lightly. "I probably still have twigs and stickers stuck in places they shouldn't be. A bath will not be conducive to getting clean when I'm this dirty."

Lenorre kissed my cheek. "I will start the shower when you are ready."

I nodded, retrieving my overnight bag from the couch and pulling out an oversized white shirt and a pair of black undies.

I heard the light click on in the bathroom and stepped onto the cool tiled floor.

Lenorre's bathroom was spacious. She sat on the edge of the tub with a brush in her lap.

"Take your shirt off and sit," she said, motioning with the brush to the tri-colored black, gray, and white marble step below her.

I unbuttoned the jacket and shoulder rig, hung the rig on the door handle, and draped the jacket over the cabinet. I had my back to Lenorre when I began unbuttoning the white blouse.

"Kassandra, I want to watch you."

I glanced over my shoulder and met the expectant look in her gaze. I turned and reclined against the cabinet as I freed the tiny pearlescent buttons. Lenorre watched intently, her metallic eyes darkening only slightly in the bright lighting of the bathroom. I pulled the shirt off and caught a glimpse of myself in the mirror. The white lace bra was almost as white as my skin, and the line of the slacks was a dark contrast. I went to Lenorre and perched on the step in front of her without argument or question. Try as we had, there were still stickers buried in the deep layers of my hair that only a skilled hand and brush would remove.

Lenorre's chilled fingers brushed the line of my shoulder as she swept my hair aside. She unhooked my bra and guided it down my arms before tossing it. The air nipped my skin, making my body tighten.

"You do not need that, my love."

"Sneaky," I said and was rewarded with a light laugh.

She set about searching through my hair for any errant stickers we'd missed earlier, working through the bottom layer that fell down my back and nearly to my waist. My hair still wasn't as long as Lenorre's, but in the few months that we'd been together it'd grown a few inches.

"Your hair is getting longer," she said as if she'd been reading my thoughts. Chances were, we'd both just been thinking the same thing.

"I know," I said. "It's always grown insanely fast."

"Even before you were infected with lycanthropy?" she asked. She found something at the base of my skull, fingers working gently to free it.

Whatever it was snagged in my hair and I took a quick breath that hissed through my teeth as Lenorre inadvertently pulled my hair while dragging the sticker out of it.

"My apologies," she said.

I raised my left arm, showing her the gooseflesh that had broken out across my skin. "That wasn't a pain response."

"Ah," she murmured, "your neck." She buried her fingers in my hair, drawing her nails lightly and intentionally from my hairline to the base of my neck in a way that made me shiver with visible pleasure.

"Don't do that." I breathed the words and was rewarded with a devious purring little chuckle that made me shudder all over again.

"Lenorre," I said in my best warning voice, "seriously."

"As you wish," she said, sounding thoroughly amused with me. "You never answered my question."

My thoughts raced frantically as she continued to search through my hair, working the brush through the handful of it that she held.

"About my hair and the lycanthropy?"

"Yes."

"Yeah, it's always grown quickly," I said, shuddering again as the bristles of the brush scraped my neck. When my insides stopped writhing, I turned my head to give her an accusatory look. "You did that on purpose."

She smiled wide enough to reveal the tips of her small fangs. "Mayhap." Her breath was suddenly hot against my ear. "But you seem to enjoy it."

The tip of tongue traced my earlobe and I groaned in response, aching.

"You know, the faster you comb through my hair, the faster we can ditch our clothes."

"Anticipation is the high point of desire."

"As glad as I am to be with a woman who holds foreplay in such high esteem, be careful of hitting the peak or I'll be tempted to take you on the floor."

I heard her put the brush down. A second later, her cool hands brushed my shoulders and traveled down the length of my arms.

"Is that what you want?"

I had a sudden image of Lenorre's pale body laid out on one of her large black towels, of my mouth between her legs as her body stretched and writhed.

The thought alone was enough to steal the breath from my lungs.

Lenorre laughed. "Well, that does indeed answer my question."

"Finish getting those damn stickers out of my hair," I spoke with gritted teeth. "Please."

She touched my hip and my muscles jumped like those of a skittish colt. She bent over me, dipping her fingers beneath the band of my slacks. Given the way I was sitting, the slacks had enough give that her fingers parted me, slipping through the wetness between my legs.

This time, Lenorre groaned. I fell back against her, my body going limp as her fingers explored me.

Without thinking, I threw my head back and met something solid. Pain, fiery and sharp burst out across the side of my skull. Lenorre hissed like a cat that had been thrown into water.

I reacted without thinking, with Lenorre's hand still in my pants. I tried to turn, albeit a little too quickly. Lenorre followed my movement, no longer touching me between the legs but turning her arm in such a way that it wasn't trapped painfully beneath the waistband.

A speck of blood decorated her bottom lip.

"Did I hurt you?" I asked.

She touched her tongue to her left canine, examining it. "I will let you know once the feeling returns," she said, but sounded more amused than angry.

I helped her work her hand out of my pants by unhooking them. I touched her bottom lip with my thumb. "Let me see."

She parted her lips and I touched the fang she'd been checking. I stupidly didn't think about pressure as I touched the tip of it and ended up hissing at the fiery prick.

I drew my hand away. "I hadn't expected them to be that sharp." And I honestly hadn't. Lenorre had teased me before with her fangs without breaking my skin. Had I truly pressed down that hard?

She caught my wrist, fingers like shackles around my skin. She stared at the drop of blood on my thumb very intently.

"Lenorre?" I asked, trying to pull away. Her hold tightened considerably.

She shook her head, almost violently, as if shooing away an unwanted flying pest.

"I am fine," she said.

"No, you're not," I said, watching as her cloudy eyes flicked back to my thumb with its trembling drop of blood. She still hadn't released me. "You need to feed."

"Are you offering?" Her dark brows arched exquisitely against her porcelain skin. Something flashed through her eyes. Impatience? Anger? I wasn't sure.

"I told you I would try," I said. "But if I'm going to try I'd rather you feed when you still have some control left. I've seen you without control, Lenorre. Charming isn't exactly the word I'd use to describe it." I remembered Rosalin's torn wrist, the arterial spray of her blood, Lenorre, driven by a wild hunger and not caring how she got it, only that she got it. Rosalin had damn near passed out. For a werewolf, that was pretty impressive.

Lenorre fell into the stillness that I'd only seen vampires capable of. I couldn't hear her heart beating, which meant it probably wasn't. In fact, she wasn't even breathing. Her fingers curled around my wrist trembled slightly.

"Your skin is cooler to the touch than it usually is, Lenorre."

She looked at me as if I'd just appeared.

"I'm fine, Kassandra."

"Liar," I said.

Her eyes darkened like a storm, narrowing slightly. Her grip tightened even more.

"Either let me go or take it," I said harshly.

She used the grip she had to jerk me up to her. I had to catch her shoulder with a hand to keep from spilling into her lap. Her eyes when she spoke were misty with power. Her voice dripped with it like a damp fog clinging to my skin. "Do you have any idea what I want to do to you, my little wolf?"

My pulse beat as if it were trying to jump out of my skin.

Lenorre watched me, gauging my reaction with that primordial hunger and power intermingling in her eyes.

"I can take a few guesses," I said, swallowing.

Lenorre tossed my hand away from her, sending the drop of blood spilling over the edge of my skin. I turned, finding her standing in the corner of the room, as far away from me as she could possibly get. Her arms were crossed beneath her breasts.

"Kassandra, get out."

She wasn't looking at me.

I stepped down the last few steps that led to the bath.

"No."

She jerked her head up then, searching my face. I'd seen her eyes lit with nothing but hunger. This wasn't it. Somewhere in there, Lenorre was still there, trying to place a steely resolve over her instincts and hunger. I saw myself in her in that moment, my struggle with my beast, and her struggle with her blood lust. I empathized with her.

"Kassandra, I do not want your pity. I asked you to leave."

"Tough," I said, crossing my own arms under my breasts. "I'm not going anywhere."

"I will not ask you again, Kassandra. I am trying to be courteous."

I swept my hair aside, exposing my neck. I stepped out of the slacks as they slid, unhooked, down my hips. I stopped when I stood in front of her.

Lenorre licked her lips, inspiring my stomach to sink.

"What are you doing?"

"What I promised I would. I'm trying to be your girlfriend." I touched her hands, tucking my fingers around them and easing her gently toward me, as if she were a startled animal that might shy away. I knew she wouldn't. It wasn't shying away that either of us was worried about.

It was the fear of losing control.

"I'm a lycanthrope, Lenorre," I said, sounding a hell of a lot braver and more certain than I felt.

Again, she refused to meet my eyes. "You are still frightened, Kassandra. I can smell your fear. I can taste it." A tremble went through her, echoing in the hands touching mine.

"I trust you," I said. "This is what we've been working toward. This is what you want…what you need."

"What do you want?" she asked, whispering.

"I want you to take your clothes off so I'm not the only one standing here naked." I stepped into her, our hands locked between our bodies. "You've seen my monster. Now show me yours."

Her gaze was intense, her eyes still vibrant with power. "Be careful what you ask for, Kassandra."

I tugged on her hands, guiding them down to her sides. I pushed my hands beneath the silken material of her blouse, stroking the coolness of her flat stomach. My skin burned hot against her, like fire and ice. Her power flitted across my skin, making me shudder, calling to the energy nestled within the heart of me. I sensed the wolf, her ears flattening against her white skull. She turned her face into the breeze of that power, closed her eyes as that icy wind sifted like fingers through her fur. She was an arctic wolf and at home in the wild cold. The energy of my beast burned with enough heat of her own to keep her safe from it.

We looked at the vampire in front of us, at the woman and lover in front of us, and offered the sheltering warmth of our power.

My arms were buried elbow deep beneath Lenorre's burgundy blouse.

"Do you feel that?" I asked in a breathy voice. A deep calm settled over me. The more I touched her, the warmer my skin grew.

"You feel like a hot summer night to chase away the cold," Lenorre said.

I stood on the tips of my toes. "And you feel like a blanket of snow that I want to roll and wrap myself in." I inched my arms higher, and the buttons strained to hold. So easily, I could tear them.

"Kiss me, Lenorre."

Lenorre locked her arms behind my back, bringing me up against her, trapping my arms between our bodies, beneath her blouse. I stayed raised on the tips of my toes as her mouth sought mine.

The coolness of her breath melted against my lips, as if I'd taken a handful of snow and brought it up to my mouth. I kissed her delicately, gently, teasing her lips open with the tip of my tongue. She opened to me, and I felt my warmth tumbling into her. She drank from my mouth as I drank from hers. The kiss became reckless and ardent, her hand moved to my hair, crushing a handful of it in her fist. If there were any stickers, neither one of us paid any attention to them. Her other arm snaked around my waist as she lifted me. I locked my thighs around her hips, our bodies molding together, our powers feeding each other. Her power felt so good, so incredibly good, and the wolf and I sought that, sinking into her, allowing her coolness to keep us from burning too hot. Distantly, I wondered if Lenorre felt what I was feeling, if the promise of my power, of my warmth, called to her as strongly as the coldness of hers called to me.

Temperance, I thought, two elements coming together in perfect union, balancing each other.

Somewhere in the middle, we met, feeding at each other, trying and struggling to become something more moderate.

I broke the kiss with a gasp, my mind reeling, my body hurting with the fierceness of desire.

I burned with a heat that only Lenorre could cool.

I kissed her cheek, sliding my mouth down the slope of her jaw and to her neck. "Take me to the bedroom," I whispered between kisses. "Take me and ride this."

She touched my cheek, turning my face to hers. Her hand slid to the back of my neck as she brought me close to her lips again. "The power?"

"The power," I said, "My body. All of it." I kissed her, tongues dancing. I caught the edge of her bra and tugged on the lace material. "I want this."

I felt drunk and light-headed. Strangely, I didn't care.

I caught her bottom lip between my teeth and a growl slipped out of me. "Give it to me."

The fist she'd balled in my hair slid down my spine, cradling my ass. "Remember when we are done that you asked for this," she said, carrying me to the bedroom.

I kissed her neck, sucking at her skin like it was candy. I clawed at her bra with my bare hands, trying to pull it down under her glorious breasts.

She spilled me onto the bed.

The glow from the frosty gray lamp cast a soft light through the room. She stood at the edge of the bed, watching me with shadows in her eyes.

"I'm having déjà vu," I said. "This is the part where you warn me, right?"

Lenorre smiled and it was almost predatory. Her blouse was in disarray due to my fondling. It appeared a few buttons were missing. I didn't remember tearing any of them.

"I've already warned you. Many times now."

"Ah," I said, leaning back on my elbows. "Then this is the part where you take those clothes off and put your body against mine."

The energy level dropped to something bearable between us, but the promise of it was still there, along with a sure knowledge that all we had to do was touch to send it spiking again.

Lenorre put one of her knees on the bed, towering over me. "You do realize," she said, "that if I come to bed with you right now, I will bite."

I sat up, placing the tips of my fingers against the hollow of her throat. "Stop trying to give me a way out," I said, lowering my hand and tearing through her blouse with nothing but my own strength. The fabric tore and buttons gave with a hiss.

The white skin of Lenorre's torso seemed to glow against the tattered material.

I raised the strip of silken fabric and waved it like a flimsy flag. "Oops," I said, knowing the grin I gave her was an impish one.

She put her hand on the mattress as she began lowering herself. I rolled out from under her and to my hands and knees. Lenorre reached for me and I pushed off the mattress. The tips of her fingers breezed past the skin of my ankle as I flung myself over the edge of the bed. My left shoulder hit the wall with a heavy thud as I used it to catch myself.

"Kassandra? Are you all right?" she asked, voice sounding somewhat strangled. I sat back on my heels, peeking over the edge at her.

Lenorre lay on her side, as if she were lounging and hadn't made a hurried grab for me. One arm was stretched out loosely in front of her, the other propped against the mound of pillows. It took me a second to realize she was laughing.

"I thought vampires were quick?"

"On the contrary," she said, "most vampires are a bit lazy. We prefer to compel and seduce our prey willingly as opposed to hunting and subduing them by using sheer force."

"Are you implying sheer force is a wolf thing?"

"I might be," she said, managing to keep a cool façade.

I laughed, getting to my feet. "Just for that, I'm going to make you work harder for this."

"You think so, do you?"

"Yeah, I d—oof," the word was knocked out of me as my back hit the wall.

Lenorre smiled triumphantly, one hand planted on the wall near my face.

"That"—I pushed at her chest—"was not fair!"

She stood, unyielding as marble. She reached for my hand still holding the piece of her torn shirt and I shoved my hand behind me, trapping it between the wall and my body with a defiant look.

"You're not going to give it up, aye?" Her soft accented voice tickled my cheek.

"Not easily, no. Wait, did you just *aye* me?"

Lenorre grinned, her fingers moving down my body and hooking on my undergarments. She caught the top of the white lace underwear and tugged, jerking my body toward hers. The warm air kissed my bare skin.

Lenorre raised her hand between us, lace spilling from her fingertips.

"Nay." She tossed the lace behind her with a flick of her wrist. "But that was fair," she said, hands sliding across my hips.

She picked me up and I wrapped my legs around her, my arms going instinctively to her neck. She kept my back pressed against the wall and lowered me. I kept my fist tight around the material as she held me, using her strength to move my body against the front of her slacks. The material at the band of her waist was slightly elevated due to the clasps underneath and I moaned at the friction it caused.

"You like that?" Amusement and something close to surprise mingled in her voice. I licked the line of her neck, tasting her skin like fresh snow on my tongue, colder with the need to feed. I caught the edge of her ear between my teeth, growling lightly.

She laughed and murmured, "Answer enough," without losing the slow and steady rhythm she'd found, making our bodies dance like two waves.

I gave myself to her, feeling the muscles in her arms work to hold me, her lean height sheltering me as her hips moved to a sensuous song that only she could hear.

"Take your clothes off."

"On one condition," she said, securing me against her with an arm under my ass. I held on to the back of her neck, moving my hand with the piece of her blouse in it to the front of her shoulder. She touched the back of my hand with her free one. "Hold on to that, Kassandra."

I snaked my hand up into the curls of hair at the base of her skull, pulling her head down to mine. "This and more," I murmured, kissing her and catching her bottom lip between my teeth and nibbling.

Lenorre carried me, laying me back in the middle of her great bed. In her slacks and ruined shirt, she sat back on her heels. "You do understand what is going to transpire here, Kassandra?"

I reclined against the pillows. "Why do you keep trying to give me a way out?"

Something flashed in her eyes, some flickering thought that I didn't quite understand.

"Are you nervous?" I asked.

She let out a deep and unnecessary breath. "Nervous?" she asked, shaking her head lightly, making her tresses dance. "No, I am hesitant, though."

"Why?"

When she was silent, I touched her arm. "Lenorre, why are you hesitant? This is what you want, isn't it?"

"Yes, but is it what you want?"

It took me too long to form a reply, and before I could say anything, Lenorre made to rise.

"Your lack of a response is answer enough," she said. "I am pushing you."

I caught her wrist, stopping her from getting out of the bed.

"I'm scared, okay?"

At my confession, she didn't look surprised, but asked, "Why?"

I shut my eyes. "I don't know."

"Yes, you do. Why are you so scared of being bitten? I've bitten you before, Kassandra. You were not so scared and apprehensive then."

I sat back against the pillows, releasing her wrist. "The times you've bitten me, Lenorre, I wasn't exactly in my right mind. I was wolf-ridden the first time you did it, and I'm fairly certain the second time didn't necessarily count as a bite, considering where your mouth was. I don't know what to expect. Should I expect it to hurt? Am I going to come close to fainting like Rosalin did the time you bit her?"

The corner of her mouth raised in a seductive half-smile. "Will it make you more comfortable if we lay out some ground rules?"

I shrugged. "It couldn't hurt. For one, stop giving me a way out. I can only not-chicken-out so many times. Seriously."

"As you wish," she said. "And may I note that when I fed from Rosalin I was consumed entirely by blood lust. I am not consumed by it now, nor will I be unless I go far longer than any vampire should."

"So, you're not close to it?"

"I behaved myself in the bathroom, did I not?"

I nodded.

She pulled her heels up under her, sitting back on them. "I am a Countess, Kassandra. I spent years learning to control my thirst and have acquired more control than most. I do need to feed, but I am not yet at that point where all of my senses will get swept away when I do. If we prolong this much longer, I will grow fatigued till I am nigh useless to you in the bedroom."

"I understand," I said. "Will it hurt?"

She looked a little surprised. "Will you give me permission to enchant you?"

I shook my head. "No." I remembered when she had enchanted Arthur once and the way his sight had glazed over like he had become an empty vessel for her power to command. "I need my control, Lenorre."

"Then it will hurt some."

"How much is some?" I asked.

The corner of her mouth twitched. "You are acting like a virgin about to be plucked on her wedding night."

I frowned at her. "Plucked," I said. "I think you mean *pricked*."

She leaned toward me, bringing her beautiful face close to mine. "Whichever," she said, trailing her nails down my stomach. "I will leave you your precious control." She kissed me gently, a brush of lips, before bending at the waist and kissing my breast. Her fingers swept across my nipple, making it stiffen. I sank back against the pillows, sighing at her touch. "As for this," she whispered against my skin, "this is mine."

She opened her mouth, sucking lightly. The tip of her tongue flicked against me and I moaned, touching her hair. She sucked harder, until I felt her fangs digging into me.

She bit down and I cried out at the fiery pain that shot down the front of my body. My fist cinched around the material as I tangled my fingers in her hair.

Lenorre looked up at me, her tongue following the crimson trail my blood had taken.

My heartbeat echoed between my legs.

"Dear Gods," I breathed. Lenorre laughed softly, raising my hand and placing a kiss against my knuckles. Gently, she used the loose hold her fingers had to turn and offer my wrist to her. She placed another small kiss against my skin, and this time, expecting to be bitten, I flinched.

But she didn't bite me. Instead, she traced the blue branch beneath my skin with the tip of her finger. "This is sacred, Kassandra. It is not simply a matter of food. You will be sharing the source of your life with me. What stronger tie exists than this? 'Tis as strong a bond as the wedding of flesh."

When I didn't say anything, she cupped my hand in hers and placed her mouth against my skin, opening and sealing her lips over the pulse beating there. She watched me, as if she were securing her mouth over more intimate and darker things.

Lenorre bit me, not a bite meant to tantalize and tease, not a bite meant to control or distract me, but a bite meant to draw blood, a bite meant to feed. Her fangs pierced my skin like needles, hot, burning, sending fireworks of pain shooting up my arm, making my muscles dance in protest.

I forced myself not to fight or pull away.

She bit down a little bit harder, her fangs gliding through skin and superficial muscle, puncturing the artery in my wrist. My heartbeat echoed down my arm, pushing my blood into her mouth.

A lot of movies make two major mistakes when depicting a vampire feeding. Yes, even in this modern day and age. The first mistake is showing that when a vampire bites, they just chomp down and go to town without releasing the wound. That is not true. Most vampires, in order to get a more effective feeding, unsheathe their fangs from the original wound. Their jaws are strong enough that if they do not release the wound, their fangs become stoppers, slowing the flow of blood despite the anticoagulant in their saliva.

Lenorre opened her mouth, slowly extracting her fangs from my skin. She caught the blood that threatened to spill over the edge of my wrist with her tongue, and sealed her mouth over the two dainty marks. Her tongue swept across my skin, over and over, as she licked the wounds. And though it was strangely sexual and intimate, I knew she did it because the Draculin, the anticoagulant in her saliva, would keep my blood flowing freely and my body from healing supernaturally quick.

The second mistake dear old Hollywood makes is by upping the gore factor of a vampire scene by showing more blood on the vampire than in the vampire. You know those scenes where there's an obscene amount of blood decorating a room? Unless a vampire is completely blinded by bloodlust and tearing arteries left and right, they're not going to let that much blood go to *waste*.

Lenorre certainly didn't. Cradling my wrist delicately to her mouth, she drank me. Her onyx lashes were long and feathery against her pale skin; her face was beautiful and serene, as she was lost in the moment.

This was indeed a sacred sharing. I felt it then, as I watched her. Her features were enveloped by a peaceful expression that made my heart light. Perhaps it was the effects of blood loss, but in that moment I felt I was beginning to better understand her nature and what exactly I'd been withholding.

As a lycanthrope, I didn't necessarily have to rely on anyone else for my survival but myself. Lenorre had to rely on someone. Every single night she woke, she had to rely on someone else to share their life with her to keep hers going.

When Lenorre drew away, she caught the last bit of blood that threatened to spill over before the wounds began healing. She raised her face to mine, her eyes shining with power like silver mist.

"Kassandra?" she said my name, reaching out to touch my cheek. "Why are you crying?"

I let go of the material still curled in my fist and used both hands to pull her to me.

"I'm sorry," I said. "I'm sorry I was being so selfish and afraid."

Lenorre laughed and her gaze was affectionate and sweet. "Well," she said lightly, almost teasingly, "now that we've overcome that hurdle…"

"I'll warn you, it's probably not the last."

"I don't expect it to be," she whispered the words against my mouth.

"You sure you can handle the others?"

"I told you once, I am a patient woman."

"And if all else fails you'll resort to shoving my ass over the next one?"

Lenorre leaned back, grinning deviously. "That is a thought, yes."

I playfully tugged on a curl of her hair and tilted my head. "Will you take your damn clothes off now?" I added, "Please?"

"For you to add the word please, you must be in dire need."

"Oh," I said, pulling at her torn blouse, "I'm positively aching."

Lenorre removed her clothing and crawled back to me. She lay back on the pillows beside me, placing a hand on my ass. "Come here," she said.

"Where's here?" I asked, rising to my knees.

"Put your leg over me," she said.

"You want me to straddle you?"

"Yes."

I flung a leg over her frame and began lowering myself. Lenorre's hands moved to my hips.

"Higher," she said, using her hands on my hips to encourage me to move up her body.

"How high?" I whispered.

One of Lenorre's dark brows arched beautifully. "I do believe you know what I am asking you to do."

I licked a wet line from her navel to her breasts. I slid my hands up her torso, cupping her breasts and lightly playing my nails across them.

"Tell me what you want."

"I want you to put your sex against my lips," she said. "I want to watch you writhe as I bring you."

I climbed her body, kissing her mouth, flicking my tongue against hers. I sat up, settling my knees to the side of her face, grabbing hold of the wooden beam at the head of the bed, and holding myself above her.

"All you had to do was ask."

Her hands moved up my thighs, squeezing my ass before she craned her neck and nestled her mouth between my legs. Her tongue found me, tracing the folds of me in a way that made my grip tighten on the smooth wooden beam. Lenorre licked me, a slow, broad stroke of her tongue that began at my entrance and ended with a suck at my clit. She found a rhythm, her velvet tongue tracing and enticing the slit between my legs, sealing over my clit and sending sparks of pleasure down to my toes. I threw my head back, riding the sweet waves.

CHAPTER SIXTEEN

I stood in a house similar to that of the victim's. I was looking at the same white covered bed. There were symbols on the walls. I was trying to figure out what each symbol meant, but they kept moving, changing. The lines flowed on the wall above the headboard like a kaleidoscope, making me dizzy.

Lenorre entered the room, her long hair free and unbound. She came to me, wearing a thin dress of black silk. Her cool fingers cupped my face in her hands. She said my name and lowered her head to kiss me.

The kiss began as something gentle and slow. Her hands moved on my body, tracing every curve hidden beneath my clothing.

Somewhere during the kiss, I remembered what I had been doing before she entered the room. I tried to draw away from her and her arms tightened around me. I tried to break the kiss and she pressed into it, kissing me more roughly than she ever had.

Her power became something thick in the air, too thick and heavy for me to draw a breath. I pushed at her chest. She wouldn't budge.

Lenorre tangled her hand in my hair, jerking her grip tight. I continued to struggle, to try to break away from her. I stopped struggling when I felt the points of very sharp nails against the back of my scalp.

No, not nails…

Claws.

Finally, she broke the kiss, laughing.

The expression on her face frightened me. Whatever it was, whoever it was, was not Lenorre.

I tried to speak, to command it to stop, but I couldn't. I was too aware. Every small movement that Lenorre made in the dream echoed through me. Every tiny brush of flesh seemed to be magnified, singing through my veins, making my skin twitch and ache to be touched.

She kissed me again and this time, I wanted her to do it. I didn't fight. I couldn't. I burned too hot. I threw myself into the flame of her power, hungry for it.

The thing that was not Lenorre rose above me, her nude body sliding across mine, and I couldn't remember when or how the dream had shifted. She rolled her hips across mine and the sensation of her wet, hot flesh against me sent my head back, my spine arching.

She caught the underside of my thighs and pushed my knees up, rubbing her body against mine. Her hands and body were slick, too slick.

I felt something wet, like water. It dripped onto the skin above my navel. I moved, trying to sit up. Lenorre put a hand on my chest, and, as if she were commanding my body, I froze.

I looked down to find that her hand was covered in blood, not only her hand, but patches of her body were covered in thick, wet blood. I felt it against my skin, soaking into my hair.

The sheets cradling us were no longer white. For a moment, I thought she had bled me, but then I realized she hadn't. The bed itself was bleeding.

Lenorre laughed again and a voice in my head said, *"Open your eyes."*

I tried to scream as she lowered her head to my body, but no sound came out. I don't know what made me think it, but I knew I did not want her to press her lips between my legs.

I stopped fighting, focusing instead on the fact that I had to wake up. I could feel myself floating, floating in that void between sleep and wakefulness.

A voice that was not Lenorre's screamed, "No!" and I was suddenly in the dream again, thrust back into my body and trapped by the weight of some unseen power. My throat grew tight, too tight to breathe.

Something was terribly fucking wrong. I was too coherent, too aware I was dreaming, and yet, I couldn't break the dream. I tried to call to the wolf, but it was as if I had become an empty vessel. She was not there to answer my call.

I tried to call to the raven, to the blood in my veins, and the choking hold around my throat tightened.

"Your magic will not save you from me!"

If I could've yelled back, I would have, but I couldn't. The hand around my throat threatened to crush my windpipe, made each breath feel like I was trying to breathe concrete into my lungs.

I felt the edge of heated energy, the brush of feathers against my skin, though I knew neither flame nor feather materialized in the dream. I heard the raven's call, a call to arms, a call to war.

Glass shattered, a window broke, a black mist slammed into the creature that had taken Lenorre's form and I could suddenly move again, breathe again.

The thing brought its arms up, shielding its face.

A hand touched mine and I turned my head. The hand was pulling me, pulling me out of the puddle of blood and sheets that had suctioned to my skin. The hand belonged to a cloaked figure, and though I could not tell who it was, I knew it was doing me a favor.

There were screams, screams that sounded more like the cries of an owl or a hawk than those of a human.

The cloaked figure jerked me free of the bed.

I drew a ragged and resounding breath. Someone was holding me, using their body like a shield around mine. I opened my eyes to find the shelter of Lenorre's dimly lit bedroom.

The figure holding me drew back, and I realized it was Zaphara.

"Are you all right?" With her body against mine, she looked down at me, her amethyst eyes concerned.

"What the hell was that?" I asked, shivering despite myself.

"You were being attacked," she said, drawing away.

For some reason, I didn't want her to let me go. I said her name, and as if she understood, she stopped drawing away. Her arms encircled me and I let her.

"Scare the werewolf piss out of you, did it?" she asked somewhat wryly.

"I'm freezing." My teeth were chattering when I spoke and I didn't understand why.

"It was feeding off of you, Kassandra."

I wasn't sure I believed her, but I was too cold and weak to protest.

"Is Lenorre awake yet?" I asked.

"She'll rise soon."

"How did you know?"

"Your raven sought aid," she said. "I answered its call when I felt the magic."

"I guess I should say thanks."

"I wouldn't say it yet." She rose from the bed and went to Lenorre's closet, grabbing a thick robe from the back of the closet door. Lenorre lay beside us, beautiful and still completely out of it. Zaphara returned, settling the robe about my shoulders.

"I could keep you warmer if you let me lay down beside you."

I curled up on my side, trembling with a cold that made no sense and feeling out of sorts. Zaphara used her long, lean body to spoon mine, bundling blankets and the robe around me.

I felt more tired than I had when I'd first fallen asleep.

As if Zaphara sensed it, she said, "Sleep, Kassandra. I'll stay and make sure you are safe."

I felt her magic like a warm glow, as if she'd drawn aside a curtain to let the light of the sun peek through. The warmth suffused my body, gradually calming my shivering limbs.

In time, with Zaphara's magic keeping me warm, I slept.

"Kassandra." It was Lenorre's voice that woke me but the smell of coffee that convinced me to sit up.

I gratefully accepted the mug she offered, mumbling thanks and hoping it would help clear the mists of sleep. I took a long drink, vaguely remembering the day's dream and Zaphara's presence, feeling surprisingly more comfortable in my skin than I had earlier.

"You died at dawn?" I asked after I drank half the cup's contents.

"Some hours after," she said, reclining beside me.

I raised my brows. "Thought I was powerful food?"

"You are," she said, smiling. "I drank Zaphara's blood then as well, and I believe that this time, because I needed to feed, it did not affect me as strongly."

Lenorre had drunk my blood during sex and the little bit she'd drunk had kept her alive and kicking through the entire day. Of course, she had fed from Zaphara earlier then too. I don't think any of us had really considered the fact that it could have been the combination of Zaphara's blood and my blood that had done the trick. I wondered when Lenorre had thought of it.

"What you mean is that because you went so long without feeding, because you needed to feed, that your body used it as fuel instead of an added boost?" I asked.

She dipped her head forward in response.

"So if you drink my blood when you've already fed, do you think it will work again?"

"I believe so, yes. Still, when I needed to feed, your blood shortened my death."

I took another swig of coffee, savoring its strong flavor softened with sugar and cream.

"Good evening, by the way."

Her lips curved again. "Good evening, love." She toyed with the ends of my hair. "Zaphara has told me some of what happened this afternoon, and though I wish to speak with you more of it, there is a certain matter which you must attend before we figure out what attacked you."

"What's wrong?"

"Rosalin seems to have taken to her bed," she said, tugging lightly on my hair before releasing it.

I swallowed a mouthful of coffee and lowered the cup.

"What do you mean?"

"She needs her alpha, Kassandra."

"I'm not her alpha, Lenorre."

"You are now," she said with an intense and serious expression. "You have claimed her as your wolf. She and the others."

When I didn't say anything, she asked, "Will you neglect them and your newfound responsibility to them?"

"I haven't had enough coffee for this conversation," I said, a bit sourly.

"Kassandra," she said.

I sighed. "I didn't want that responsibility."

"Can you look me in the eyes and tell me that you truly did not want them as your wolves last night? If you had not wanted them, if you had not agreed with your wolf, they would not be yours."

"I wanted to protect Rosalin. I really didn't want to sign up to be anyone's alpha."

She touched the white streak in my hair this time, letting it slide through her fingers. "Whether you desired it or no, it is what you are, Kassandra. The sooner you come to terms with that bit of knowledge, the better things will be."

Stubbornly, I shook my head and started sliding out of bed. I placed the mug of coffee on the nightstand by Lenorre's side.

"Where are you going?"

"I'm going to be honest when I say I'm not ready for this conversation," I said. "And I am going to get dressed and go check on my *friend*."

I went to Lenorre's closet and found a pair of black silk shorts that I'd left in case of emergencies. I stepped into them and settled the hem of the white shirt down over them. Lenorre reclined at ease on the bed, watching me as I shut the closet door.

"Being Rosalin's alpha does not make her any less of a friend. Why are you running from who you are?"

"I don't like the title. It implies ownership. I don't want ownership."

"No," she said, "it implies *leadership*, something Sheila Morris does not and will never understand. She sees her rank in the pack as means to possession. She does not lead them, Kassandra. A true alpha leads and protects. They do not possess. They do not force their wolves to give them submission. The submission is offered freely out of respect. Sheila has not given her wolves room to respect her. To fear her, yes, but respect…"

"Fear and respect are two different things," I said, agreeing. I pushed my hair out of my face, trying not to feel frustrated and failing. "Why are we talking about this?"

She came to me and I took a step back so that I could meet her gaze without tilting my head back at an awkward angle. "Rosalin has tasted what it means to be part of a pack. She knows what it is to live her life surrounded by a family of pack-mates. I know, because you are a lone wolf, you do not fully understand, but understand this," she stepped into me, "Rosalin lost the only family she knew, aside from her brother, when she was younger. She cannot return to Sheila's pack with your mark upon her, and now she has lost the only true family she knows. If she does not have someone to nurture and protect her, other wolves there for her, she will be a broken thing. The wolves have come to your call, whether you've willed it or no. Carver and Claire have defied Sheila. Will you deny them the leader they need because of your sensibilities to a title? Will you deny them the pack they need?"

"I don't know how to be an alpha, Lenorre."

"And you think I knew how to be a Countess? It is something you learn as you go, Kassandra. Consider yourself lucky that you have the wolf to guide you," she said, touching the white streak in my hair.

I licked my lips, shutting my eyes. "And what if the power goes to my head? Goes to the wolf's head?"

"Do you truly believe that will happen?"

"I don't know, Lenorre. I feel like I don't know anything right now."

Lenorre wrapped her arms around me, placing a kiss on my forehead. "Figure it out, Kassandra. For their sake, do not run from your power or rank, as it is the only thing that will help them right now."

I nodded. What else could I do? What was there to say? I felt the conflict between the wolf and me. In the clearing, I had agreed with her that we had to protect those we could from Sheila. But with the aftermath of the wolf's surety and power came a thread of insecurity.

I was scared to the bone that I didn't know how. The responsibility hanging over my head meant I would have to embrace my wolf even more, and though I had learned how to live with the wolf inside of me, as a part of me, that was all she was, a part. A piece. There was still a strong vein of fear that ran within me. If I embraced her too much, would I lose myself entirely? Would she take even more pieces of me until there was no Kassandra Lyall left, until there was only wolf?

CHAPTER SEVENTEEN

It wasn't until I emerged from the basement and into the main hall that branched off of it that I realized I didn't know exactly where Rosalin's room was. I knew it was upstairs, but aside from that, I'd never even seen her room. I strode barefoot past the life-size statues that lined the wall, rounding the corner and ascending the stairs that led to the upper level. Even if I specifically didn't know where her room was, I should've been able to find it by smell. I stopped to consider which way to go, left or right? I went down the hall to the right. I was sure I'd seen or heard Rosalin coming from that direction before.

As it was, Carver stood outside the second doorway on the right. He too, was barefoot, wearing a pair of light jeans. The white shirt he wore was dirty, probably the same one he'd been wearing last night.

"I see you haven't had a chance to shower, either," I said.

He shook his head. "Claire's in there trying to comfort her. We've been taking turns keeping guard outside the door."

I wondered why they were keeping guard. Lenorre's house should have been safe territory. Surely, Sheila wasn't crazy enough to try anything on Lenorre's property.

"She's still shaken?" I asked, keeping my voice soft even though Rosalin and Claire could hear us on the other side of the door.

Carver visibly relaxed in front of me, leaning against the wall, his shoulders dropping. "This is the worst I've seen her," he said. "She usually takes it better than the rest of us. As beta, she has to."

I understood what he meant, although I was anything but happy about it.

"After everything she's endured," I whispered, "the last thing she deserved was Sheila Morris."

"The last thing any of us wolves deserve is Sheila as alpha," he said.

I gave him a considering look. "Why?" I asked. "Why'd you help me yet again, Carver? I was an ass to you."

He smiled, but there was something sad in it. "I'm not strong enough to overthrow her," he said. "None of us are. I recognized your mark the moment you walked into my trailer with the police. I was angry about a stray walking onto my turf, accusing me of murder. How would you have felt? I realized when you visited the pack, that if we ever had any hope of getting rid of Sheila, you're it. Funny, huh?"

"I don't know that I'm you're hope, Carver."

He pinned me with a very serious expression. "You have to be, Kassandra. You stood up to Sheila last night. You're the only wolf I've ever seen stand up to her. Many of us have wanted to, but we didn't, we don't. If she doesn't punish us, she'll punish someone else within the pack that we care about. She finds a weak spot and drives her claws into it."

"I felt her strength, Carver. She's strong, stronger than even I anticipated."

"She is strong," he said, "but she's not powerful. Physical strength doesn't equal power, not always. You touched a wolf in the clearing and she fell to her knees in the face of your power."

"She was like, eighteen."

"She was the *epsilon,* the fifth strongest wolf in the pack and you dominated her with nothing more than a touch. Why do you think the wolves finally parted? You showed them power, the true power of an alpha."

I hadn't remembered Carver being behind me when I'd returned to the pack to confront Sheila. He must've followed me, but I didn't like it that I hadn't known that at the time.

"Why is it everyone's throwing this alpha thing in my face?" I grumbled, more to myself than to Carver.

"Why is it you're fighting it?" he asked, and because I'd already had that little conversation with Lenorre, I gave him an unhappy look.

"I'm not a fan of the title."

"Don't worry about the fucking title," he said. "Worry about fucking helping us."

"I can't worry about that right now, Carver. I'll do what I can, but right now I need to worry about Rosalin."

I reached for the doorknob, but it opened before I touched it. Claire stepped out of the room. Her eyes were red as if she hadn't gotten any sleep and as if she'd been crying.

She touched my shoulder. "I hope you have better luck than I did."

I nodded and with a heavy heart stepped into Rosalin's room.

"You're not going to accept it, are you?" Rosalin's voice came from under a mound of blankets on the bed.

"Accept what?" I asked, shutting the door quietly behind me.

"That mark in your hair and everything it means," she said.

"I'm a bit skeptical." I gave the mound a light push. "Move over."

Rosalin obliged, wiggling closer to the wall her bed was pressed against. I sat on the edge of her bed. Her room wasn't nearly as spacious as Lenorre's, but it was spacious, nonetheless. A painting hung on the wall by her closet doors. The painting was of a dark forest, here and there golden eyes peeked around bushes and the trunks of trees. In the middle of the painting, a wolf crouched low, skulking out of the shadows like darkness given form. The others seemed to watch, patiently waiting for that one lone wolf to guide the way.

My chest grew tight and I couldn't explain why.

"I see you're not holding up very well," I said.

"The bed is holding me just fine."

I reclined against the pillows. "So I see. Why are you hiding?"

"I don't know. Why are you skeptical?"

"I don't understand how a streak of white in my hair marks me as an alpha or how I'm supposed to be an alpha."

"You carry your wolf with you in human form," she said, "that marks you as an alpha."

I didn't want to bring up Lukas Morris, but something he had said to me crossed my mind. I decided to leave his name out of it. Morris was probably the last thing Rosalin wanted to be reminded of.

"I thought the mark of the alpha only happened with hereditary lycanthropy?"

She peeked over her blankets at me. "You actually know about hereditary lycanthropy?"

"Not a lot, but I've heard of it, yes." I was trying to remember Lukas's exact words, something about the virus taking a turn and mimicking hereditary lycanthropy in that regard. Honestly, I didn't understand either.

"Then you'd know that the lycanthropy virus actually branched off of hereditary lycanthropy."

"So you think it's a possibility because of that?"

"Don't you?"

I shrugged. "I don't know. I'm not a scientist."

"And lycanthropy is something that still baffles modern science."

I nodded.

"You want to know what I think?"

"I have a feeling you're going to tell me either way, so go ahead."

"I think you're questioning it to death because you don't want to accept it and if you keep questioning it, Kass, you're never going to accept it."

"Why is everyone ganging up on me today?"

"Sheila isn't going to let last night go."

"If we're going to have this conversation, can you at least come out from under the covers so I'm not talking to a pink cocoon?"

She pushed the covers down. Her honey eyes were as red and raw as Claire's had been, if not more.

"Don't try to change the subject," she said. "I can't tell if you're being arrogant and solitary or if you're really seriously just scared of being an alpha."

"I am scared, Ros. I'm not like you. I didn't come into this and find a pack to call home. I was infected and the only person there for me was Rupert, and he couldn't help me learn to control my beast because he's human. Everything I know, everything I've learned, I've learned fighting tooth and nail with this thing inside of me."

"Do you resent being what you are?"

"Every day? No. Sometimes, yes. The wolf and I are on much better terms, but there are still times when I don't understand her, don't understand this, this thing I am, this thing I'm supposed to be."

"I don't understand why you're scared, Kassandra. I really don't."

"Because, Rosalin, I'm not completely wolf. I'm human too and there are times when I'm afraid. Maybe, because of what I do for a living, I shouldn't be."

"Are you scared of Sheila?"

I had to think about my response for a moment. "I'm not scared of what she could do to me, because given the chance I'd pump several rounds of silver into her as fast as I could, but I'm scared of what she could do to those I love and care about. I'm supposed to be an alpha, and yet, I wasn't there for you when you needed me last night. I didn't even know what she'd done to you."

"How could you?" she asked. "It wasn't like I told you I was going to a pack meeting. I'm the one that idiotically tried to carry on as a member of the pack after you'd…"

"Go on," I said. "Say it. After I accidentally marked you. And look what that mark did, Rosalin. It brought you harm. It put you in danger. I promised to protect you and I failed at that. Some alpha I'm supposed to be."

"No." She stubbornly shook her head. "Sheila brought me harm, not you. You couldn't have known that she was going to punish me."

"But you did," I said. "You knew she'd punish you."

"I've been to a couple of meetings with the pack after you marked me. She didn't do anything then, so I thought she hadn't sensed it."

"She had, though?"

"Yes."

"Why did she wait?"

"I don't know. Sheila is unpredictable. She probably waited for that reason alone—unpredictability—to catch me when I'd finally let my guard down and stopped worrying about it."

"And now neither you nor Carver nor Claire can return to the pack."

"And you don't want to be our alpha."

"I didn't say I didn't want to, Rosalin. You're making it sound like I don't want to be your friend. Just because I don't want to pin a sticker on my shirt that says, 'Hello, my name is Alpha,' doesn't mean I don't care about you, any of you."

"It's the title?"

"And the responsibilities," I said. "As I said, if I'm supposed to be your alpha, I failed miserably last night."

"Kassandra," she said, and I looked at her.

"What?"

"Can I ask you a question?"

"Yes. Doesn't mean I'll have an answer though."

"Take out the title, and if the same thing happened to me last night, would you still feel the same?"

"What do you mean?"

"You're beating yourself up for not protecting me, though you did protect me. Hell," she said, "you knocked Sheila halfway across the clearing. If I was just your friend and you hadn't marked me, would you still have done that?"

I licked my lips.

"You would've killed her, wouldn't you? If you weren't a lycanthrope and didn't have to play by our rules, what would you have done? Lied to the cops, tell them I'd been attacked? Figure out a way to set it up so that the execution was done cleanly? What lengths would you have gone to to protect me, as a friend?"

"I don't understand whatever point you're trying to make," I said, "and murder is illegal. Being a lycanthrope isn't the only thing that stopped me last night."

"The rest of the pack?"

"That certainly crossed my mind."

"Well, aside from that. The point I'm trying to make is this, lycanthrope or no, metaphysical binding or no, would you still have protected me? Would you still have thought to avenge a wrong that was done to me just because I'm your friend?"

"Yes."

"How different is that from being an alpha?"

"I...I don't know," I said.

"Obviously, you get my drift," she said. "So stop questioning it."

I scoffed. "That's easier said than done."

"Kassandra Lyall, you can turn into a fucking bird. If you can accept that," she said, "I am pretty sure you can accept this."

I laughed.

"And," she said, "if it's any consolation, I don't think you'll botch the job as badly as Sheila."

"Thanks, Ros. I guess that's supposed to be comforting."

"I can make it more comforting," she said, raising the blanket between us. "Wanna come in and cuddle?"

"Um, no."

"Why?"

"I don't trust you."

"Why don't you trust me? I promise not to grope."

"Yeah, you say that now. You'll probably let a little werewolf biscuit slip and try to cover my head with the blankets."

Rosalin laughed then, the first genuine laugh I'd heard from her since I stepped into the room. I smiled hearing it.

"Oh my God," she said.

"You're considering it now, aren't you?"

"Well, now that you said something...yeah, a little bit."

I patted the blanket. "I think I'll stay out here then."

"So," she said, "did you feed Lenorre?"

I crossed my legs at the ankles, folding my hands over my stomach. "Actually, I did."

"And?"

"And what?"

"How was it?"

"It was...different," I said.

"Yeah, but did you enjoy it?"

I remembered the dark and intimate look on Lenorre's face, remembered her licking and biting down my body. Apparently, something showed on my face because Rosalin bolted upright.

"Oh my God," she said again. "You *totally* enjoyed it. You got all hot and bothered, didn't you?"

"Okay, how the hell did we end up having *this* conversation?" I asked, blinking.

"Don't you dare try and change the subject. I want details."

"Tough. You're not getting any."

"So Lenorre bit you and you thought it was hot, huh? Hot enough you don't want to share details." She grinned.

"You can go back under your covers now."

"Oh, hell no," she said. "I'm happy here where I can watch you blush."

"I'm not blushing."

"Yeah, you are. Do I need to get a mirror to prove it? Where'd she bite you?"

"That's none of your business."

"She gotcha in the nether bits, didn't she?"

I laughed, shaking my head. "No, no, she didn't get me in the nether bits last night."

"Then where'd she—wait, are you implying she's bit you in the nether bits before?"

"I didn't say that."

"You're blushing again. I'm going to take that as a yes. That's hot. Keep going…"

"You do realize Carver and Claire are right outside your door?"

"I can fix that," she said, and called Claire's name. The door opened and Claire peered into the room. It looked as though she'd been laughing.

"Yes?" she asked.

"Can you guys give us some privacy?" Rosalin asked.

"Sure thing," Claire said. She shot me a quick grin. "Don't protest too much, Kassandra. You know what they say about that."

"Oh, go," I said, shooing her out with a hand and trying not to laugh.

I waited until I sensed Carver and Claire leave their post outside the door.

"You know, Ros, I never pegged you for such a voyeur."

"This is what friends do, sweetheart. We share juicy details."

"Uh huh, like you were so keen on sharing juicy details when you fooled around with Eris?"

"Oh, that," she said. "Eris just bit my neck. When she bit me, I got off. Now, your turn."

"Fine," I said. "If you must know, Lenorre bit my wrist."

The excited expression she wore turned completely upside down. "What! She just bit your wrist? You made such a big deal out of it and all she did was bite your wrist?"

I pretentiously pouted at her. "Aww, you got your little voyeur hopes up, didn't you?"

"Yeah, and you're intentionally trying to spoil it! Seriously, that's all she did?"

"She's bitten other places."

"Better." She leaned back. "Much better. Keep going."

"Rosalin, I'm not going to divulge every single detail of my sex life."

"Did she enchant you?"

I shot her an impatient glance.

"No."

"Did it hurt much without the enchantment?"

"I can't exactly make a comparison, as I've asked her not to enchant me. It hurt a great deal less than I thought it would."

"I've heard there's a numbing agent in vampire spit."

"They have an anticoagulant in their saliva, but aside from that I haven't heard of a numbing agent. They share the same anticoagulant as vampire bats, and with vampire bites, their bite is less painful because of the sharpness of their fangs, not spit."

"Really?" she asked.

"I think so, but that's probably a question better aimed at Lenorre. She gave me some books to read."

Rosalin laughed. "You haven't read them, have you?"

I grinned. "Nope."

"Learn as you go?"

"Pretty much. I've flipped through them. They're thick," I said, emphasizing the size with my hands. "When am I going to find the time to sit down and actually read them? Especially when all I have to do is ask her if I have a question?"

"Still, if she lent them to you, she obviously wants you to read them."

I shrugged. "Probably. One of these days, maybe I'll get to them. So you let Eris enchant you?"

"Yes, that's how I was able to get off when she bit me."

"They don't have to enchant you to do that, though, do they?"

Lenorre had used her energy to bring me during sex and both times, she'd assured me she hadn't enchanted me.

"I don't know," she said, "I can tell you, that's where the thrill is."

"Being enchanted?"

"Yes."

"Lenorre's projected on me before. Does that count?"

"Yes and no. I think it would be a mild form of enchantment. The enchantment part is more where the vampire makes you feel what they want you to feel, but also to think what they want you to think."

"And how the hell do you know when a vampire has done that? If they're forcing their will on your thoughts…"

"There's fogginess afterwards. A feeling of weightlessness, drunkenness, a high. I don't know how to explain it, but you'd know. While it's happening, every sense heightens like that second before orgasm, and everything, every thought, every feeling, every worry, sadness, every emotion, just gets abandoned and washed away in this tide that carries you."

"And you're okay with that? With completely abandoning yourself?"

"Kass, some of us need that. We're not all the control freak that you are."

"I'll give you that," I said, because it was about control with me. I didn't like the idea of surrendering that completely to anyone or anything. I needed my ground to stand on.

"It'd probably be harder for a vampire to enchant you."

"Why do you say that?" I asked.

"It takes a strong vampire to enchant a lycanthrope as it is, throw a bit of fey blood into the mix and they've got their work cut out for them."

"Well, that's good to know."

"You would think that." She smiled.

I brushed a strand of auburn hair out of her face. "So," I said, "are you going to stay in bed and hide all day?"

"I'm feeling a little bit better."

"Only a little?" I asked. "I have an idea and I think it might be one that will make you feel even better."

"You're going to take your clothes off and get under the covers with me?"

I pulled her hair. "No, silly, but nice try. There's a wooded area around here, isn't there?"

"Yes, most of it's on Lenorre's land."

"Is it enough to provide cover?"

"Depends on what you need the cover for."

"Would you like to go run with me?"

Her lips parted in disbelief. "You're serious? I've asked you to go run with me and you always tell me no."

"I haven't showered. If you want to go run, now's the time to do it."

"I'd like that," she said, her expression tender.

"Then, get off your ass," I said, standing and offering my hand. Rosalin took it and I helped her out of her monstrous blankets.

When she got to her feet, she wrapped her arms around me. "Thank you, Kassandra. I appreciate the distraction."

She kissed my cheek and I touched her face. "You're welcome, Rosalin."

Truth be told, with the murder investigation, relationship dynamics, and bullshit with Sheila, I needed the distraction too.

CHAPTER EIGHTEEN

I told Lenorre where we were going, and even though the woods were on her land, she'd insisted Zaphara and the others accompany us. I had argued with her until she pointed out the fact that it would make Rosalin feel safer. I couldn't exactly argue with that. After what Rosalin had endured at Sheila's hands, I wanted her to feel safe. Rosalin, being more familiar with Lenorre's land, led the way to the woods. Closer to the house was a heated swimming pool and a beautiful gazebo, but this far away, there was only trees and the quiet murmur of night. Before heading into the dense coverage of trees that did not shed their garb for the winter, I'd managed to catch sight of the pond at the southern line, of the stars spread out across it.

I tried not to recall the Blevins's celestial sheets soaked in blood.

Tonight was a night to be free and wild and I was claiming it, not solely for myself, but for the others that needed it as well. For a long time, we ran with no clear destination. We used the trees as cover, circling back into their thick shelter when the woods threatened to end. The night was alive with its own music, with the song of crickets and other insects, of wind and leaves.

The dry grass crunched beneath my paws. My tail caught on something behind me and I turned, skittering to jerk it loose of the small patch of burs.

Great, now Lenorre's going to be picking stickers out of my ass.

I shook my tail in irritation, hoping to shake some of them out.

That's going to make it worse, witch.

Zaphara caught up with me, amethyst gaze framed by the black fur of her wolf form.

Someone gave a delightful yip that caught my attention. I cast my gaze to Rosalin's and Carver's large forms ahead. Claire threw her head back, let rip a tiny howl, and bounded through the trees.

Carver nipped at Rosalin's leg, signaling for her to move it.

Rosalin jumped, following after Claire.

I heard someone's paws skid in the dirt before they sounded like tiny drums again.

Claire came rushing back, chasing after a black-tailed jackrabbit like it was a bouncy ball she wanted to chew on. Rosalin pushed past her, cinnamon fur like gray ash in my night vision. She lunged forward, trying to get the rabbit's tail during an upspring, and missed. She shook her furry head, ears flapping as she blew dirt out of her nostrils.

This is a sad sight, Zaphara's voice flowed through my mind.

Claire and Rosalin didn't seem to think so.

They're playing, I thought to her. *It's not an actual hunt.*

Claire had taken over chasing the rabbit, which was conveniently heading toward Carver's direction. Rosalin had disappeared into the trees and I sensed her waiting, waiting for Carver and Claire to guide it through.

Carver sank as low to the ground as his massive body would allow, and the rabbit, heart hammering in its chest, veered away from him.

He joined the chase when it passed, encouraging it through the break in the trees ahead.

Rosalin got it, diving out from the behind the trees and catching it between her jaws. She skipped back to us, announcing her victory.

She lowered her snout, gently releasing the rabbit.

When it just lay there, frozen with fear, she gave it a push with her nose. Finally, it reacted, scurrying frantically away. Claire made to start chasing it again and I gave a low, warning growl.

Wolves in the wild probably would've eaten it, but we were not so desperate for food, and the rabbit had experienced enough torment. I headed toward the house, following the same path we'd come. My clothes were in the gazebo. Zaphara was still teaching me how to shift and call to the faerie magic in my blood. I'd stripped because I hadn't felt like another lesson when we came out to run.

Now, only two things sounded good: a shower and some food. Though I wasn't opening a vein for Lenorre, as Zaphara had fed her when I'd gone upstairs to see Rosalin, we would all need to eat something when we returned to the house. For a new wolf, Claire was doing surprisingly well and seemed to have gotten the hang of shifting at will. It was impressive. Carver and Rosalin didn't surprise me so much. I'd seen Rosalin come close to being able to hold a partial shift, but she couldn't do it for long. I wondered if I was the only one in the group who could call the beast to my eyes and hands without giving over entirely to her every single time. Did that also contribute to the role I was supposed to play, to the mark of being alpha?

We made it to the gazebo and shifted then quietly donned our clothes. When we finished dressing, the only one that wasn't covered in dirt and twigs was Zaphara. Carver's hands were as covered in dirt as mine and the others. Rosalin had a dirt mustache and Claire's hair was a windblown riot.

We made it to the dining room and Rosalin slipped into the kitchen, opening the fridge door and returning with what appeared to be about twenty bags of lunchmeat, turkey, beef, ham.

"Chow time," she said, dropping the bags on the table.

We ate in silence, all except for Zaphara, who'd slipped away as soon as we made it inside the house.

Claire reached for the bag of roast beef when Carver growled at her.

"Split it, you two."

Surprisingly, they listened to me.

I'd completely finished off two large Ziploc bags of meat when I heard Lenorre laugh from the doorway.

All of us turned to look at her. Claire quickly shoved the food dangling halfway out of her mouth, in it.

Lenorre's hair was still wet from her shower, marking damp spots on the red sweater she wore. A tight pair of black skinny jeans clung to her hips, tucked into knee-high boots.

"Did you have a good run?" Lenorre asked, directing the question at Rosalin.

Rosalin nodded. Lenorre affectionately tousled Rosalin's already messy hair.

"You had a phone call, Kassandra."

"Who was it?" I asked.

"Arthur," she said.

I pushed my chair back and stood. "I'll call him back before I get in the shower."

"No need," she said, walking around the table to me. She plucked a twig out of my hair. "I took his message and will relay it to you downstairs."

She stooped to kiss me and I stopped her with a hand high on her chest. "I'm dirty."

"So?"

"You're all clean."

"So?" she asked again, this time with a devious glint.

I turned on the pad of my foot, gracefully stepping out of her reach in a dance-like move. "I'm going to take a shower, Lenorre. This time, you're not going to distract me."

Of course, everyone at the table was staring at us, but I didn't care.

I left Lenorre standing there.

I was almost to the basement when the ground moved out from under me.

"Lenorre!"

She laughed.

"What the hell are you doing?"

"Carrying you, my love."

"I know that. Why?"

"Mmm, because I can."

At her mysterious smile, I shook my head.

"I'm serious. Don't you even think of dropping me on the bed once we get to the room, because sex right now is so *not* happening."

"Have no worries," she said, voice light. "I'll escort you to the shower and give you a most thorough scrubbing myself."

"With a washcloth, Lenorre. Trust me, you don't want what is on me in your mouth."

She laughed lightly.

"As you wish."

"And only if the message from Arthur isn't urgent. Was it?"

"It can wait," she said, descending the basement steps. "Afterward, we will sit and discuss Arthur's news and the psychic attack you experienced this afternoon. But for now," she mused, "I am going to get what I want."

"I didn't know you were so into dirty and wild," I said jokingly as the light of the lounge room left me momentarily blind from its brightness.

"Mmm," she murmured, burying her face in my hair, "only for you, my little forest nymph."

It was my turn to laugh.

Lenorre carried me past her room and into the bathroom. I'd thought she would put me down before turning on the shower, but she didn't. She opened the frosted glass door and stepped into the dim lighting.

She reached for the handle jutting out of the dark stone wall.

"Uh, Lenorre? You're going to get our clothes—" I closed my mouth when I got a face full of chilly water.

I coughed, laughing and wriggling in her arms. "You could at least have waited for the water to warm up!"

She used the arm she had behind my back to swing me upright and I instinctively wrapped my legs around her waist. She kissed me, stepping forward and guiding us out from beneath the harsh spray of water. My back met the wall.

I broke the kiss. "Lenorre?"

"Yes?"

"You're wearing your boots in the shower."

"So I am." She whispered the words against my mouth before gently nibbling on my bottom lip.

I groaned, sliding my hands down her wet body. She nibbled a bit harder and I tugged at the wet sweater clinging to her skin, raising it to unveil the incandescent beauty of her. Lenorre lowered me onto a small bench tucked into a corner. She pulled her sweater up over her head and discarded it to the floor. The bra she wore was the same blood red as the sweater. I caught the waistband of her jeans, pulling her to me.

Lenorre propped her foot on the bench and set about removing her boots. I removed my shirt and shorts and stood under the spray of water.

When I had completed the task of washing my hair and face, I reached for the bottle of soap sitting on the small shelf. Lenorre touched my arm, giving me pause. She was nude except for a small covering of shadowy lace at her mound. The onyx curls of her hair tumbled down the front of her body and to her hips, covering the mounds of her breasts.

"What are you doing?" I asked, curious, as she set the bottle aside. Of course, it was a bit obvious what she was doing. She put her hands flat against my stomach, spreading the sweet amber smelling soap on my skin, across my hips. Her fingers brushed downward, tracing the crevice between my thigh and groin in a way that made me nearly lose my balance.

Lenorre laughed softly, guiding me further away from the spray of water.

She touched my shoulder. "Turn around."

I did, placing my hands flat against the smooth marble wall.

She guided my hair over my shoulder, her hands gliding across my back, slick with soap and water, over the raven tattoo and its knot work.

True to her word, she was thorough. By the time she was done, I was panting and half tempted to set my nails in the wall. Her fingers played over my breasts and lower, low enough to encourage me to arch my spine and space my feet out. She parted me and I moaned. The tip of her finger moved against my clit, tracing it, sending little flits of ecstasy through me.

I felt her lips at my ear. "Yes or no?"

"Are you asking me if I want you to bring me right now?"

"I am."

"Gods, yes."

Lenorre obliged and brought me, shuddering and trying to keep my legs from going out from under me.

She snaked an arm around my waist, her hand cradling my hip as I fought not to collapse with the aftermath. "Mmm, that was not nigh as violent as it usually is."

I laughed. "That's because I was focusing on not falling on my face."

"A different position, then?"

I circled her wrists and I guided her arms close to her body. "Let me rinse," I said. "For now, keep those to yourself."

"As you wish," she said, not bothering to hide the devilish lilt in her tone.

I was about to step out of the shower when I ran into a vampiric speed bump. Lenorre barred the door. "You are done rinsing, Kassandra."

"So you're not going to let me get out and find a towel?"

"Not yet, no."

"If we do a repeat," I said, "I'm pretty sure this time I'm going to face-plant."

"Who said anything about an exact repeat?"

One second Lenorre was standing in front of me, and the next, she pushed my shoulders. The heel of her foot met mine and down I went. Lenorre caught me before I hit the hard floor as if the move had all been a dance she'd mapped out in her head. She lowered me gently.

I growled, unhappy about being caught off guard and unceremoniously tripped. Whether she'd caught me or not, I didn't like the fact that she'd put her speed and strength against me.

I was about to protest when she climbed my body, pressing her mouth against mine.

I growled again, but when her tongue teased my lips, I opened to her.

She kissed me, a deep and sensual dance of tongues that made my body melt from head to toe. Her breasts brushed mine and the growl turned into something closer to a moan. I curled my arms around her back, holding her close to me, tracing the curve of her figure with my hands.

Lenorre broke the kiss and her gaze was cloudy, but not with power, with that look a woman has when she knows you're hers. I sat up and used my body to push her onto her back. I removed her undergarments, dragging them down her thighs. I settled between her legs, pressing my lower body against hers. I shifted my hips, trying to find the position I wanted. Lenorre bent her knees, watching me with lips half-parted. I curled a leg around hers, angling my body.

Though it felt good, I feared there was too much of a height difference between us.

Lenorre laughed when I growled my frustration.

"If you are trying to do what I think you are trying to do"—she sat up, touching my cheek—"allow me."

I did so and Lenorre used her hands to push my knees apart. She bowed her body and set her mouth between my legs, sucking my clit. I cried out at the unexpected suddenness of it. She sucked harder, threatening to break my skin on the cusps of her fangs.

Lenorre worked me with lips and tongue, worked me until my breath was ragged and the waves of pleasure rocked my body. The hold of her lips broke before I came, the pulse between my legs thudding like a tiny touch. I could feel myself, wet and engorged.

I groaned and Lenorre pushed my arched leg up. She lowered her hands, leaving me to hold the position as she splayed me with the tips of her fingers and swung her hips forward to press her sex against mine. When our clits brushed, I thought I heard her gasp. She took hold of my leg like an anchor and began to move against me.

Lenorre mumbled something and I grabbed her arms before she could change the position.

"Don't stop," I said and the thrust of her hips became something less controlled and more urgent. I writhed, nails digging into her arms. "Gods! Don't you dare stop."

Goddess bless her, she didn't.

CHAPTER NINETEEN

I was sitting in Lenorre's bedroom with Zaphara, Lenorre, and Rosalin. Zaphara being present had been Lenorre's doing. When I'd asked what Arthur had called about, Lenorre had summoned Zaphara to be present during the conversation we'd yet to have. Rosalin was my doing, as I didn't want to see her fall back into her darkness and hide in her room.

Rosalin pulled her legs up under her, leaning into me and resting her head on my shoulder. She draped an arm loosely in my lap, across my waist, seeking comfort. I had a brief moment to wonder if Rosalin hanging all over me would bother Lenorre, before I caught sight of Lenorre's expression and realized her mind was elsewhere. I had no doubts that she'd noticed Rosalin cuddle into me, but I knew for sure in that moment, it really didn't bother her. Perhaps when it came down to it Lenorre knew more about wolves than I did, though I was slowly but surely beginning to learn more about them through myself.

It did make me wonder, however, if Eris's teasing at the club hadn't bothered Lenorre, what did? It was a strange experience for me, being with someone who was so confident and who didn't feel easily threatened.

If I'd spent over two hundred years watching the world and all its myriad relationships around me, would I have felt the same way? Would I have been able to sit here and withstand Zaphara taking comfort in Lenorre's arms? I shuddered at the thought, as it wasn't one

I liked, though it seemed Zaphara and I were on better terms. I wasn't sure how long that would last. Was it simply that Lenorre's and my natures were different in that regard? That she just wasn't the jealous type? When I thought about it, I wasn't sure I considered myself a jealous person. I didn't envy what another person had. I was protective and territorial about what I considered to be mine. Possessive, maybe. I wasn't worried someone would swoop in and steal Lenorre away from me. I didn't consider myself that insecure, and like me, I sensed Lenorre's loyalty was a deep and unwavering thing. I realized that perhaps it was selfish, but in a relationship I wanted the deepest and most intimate part of my significant other to belong to me. I didn't want tidbits or scraps from a lover, I wanted it all.

Lenorre was watching me as if she were trying to read my thoughts. I knew she couldn't, not unless I projected them to her, as we'd learned, and I was shielding too strongly for that.

"Are you going to tell me what Arthur called about or are we seeing who is going to break first?" I asked. If that was the case, I was pretty sure I'd just lost the quiet game.

Lenorre crossed her long legs. "The medical examiner completed her examination of the body," she said.

"And?"

"Do you remember the bruising you observed on the woman's neck?"

I gave a sharp nod.

"She could not withdraw any prints from the cadaver. She was able to recreate the size of the hand that had strangled the victim."

"Lenorre," I said, "stop drawing it out. Just tell me."

"The hand was not human."

"Okay," I said. "Do you have any guesses what it could have been?"

"Did Arthur send you the photographs of the sigil?" Lenorre asked.

I crossed the room to retrieve my cell phone from the nightstand. I went to the album on my phone, pulled up the first picture of the sigil, and handed the phone to her. Lenorre leaned over, offering it to Zaphara.

"What do you think?" she asked.

Zaphara gazed at the picture for a long moment.

"It's a summoning sigil," she said. "Though sloppy and homemade."

"What do you mean?" I asked.

"Each symbol corresponds to a piece of the summoning spell used," she said. "The symbol in the middle stands for sulfur, which corresponds to the element of that which the person summoned."

"Sulfur?"

"Demonic energy," she said. "Consider this symbol the key that goes into the slot and unlocks the door itself. The symbols around it build the room, the door. It all goes together, Kassandra."

"There were two symbols I recognized in that." I knelt on the floor in front of her, taking my phone and scrolling to the larger images of each smaller symbol that Arthur had been kind enough to provide me with. "Ceres?" I asked. "Why would Ceres be involved in this if it was used to summon a demon?"

"You do not believe it is demonic?" she asked, reading my tone and body language.

"I don't believe in demons, Zaphara. So it's kind of hard to."

"There's more to this world than meets the eye," she said. "You more than anyone else in this room should know that. I am not referring to the demons of Christian folklore."

"What are you referring to?"

"Merely a title for those beings of ill intent," she said.

"And what kind of spectrum does that cover?" I asked.

"A broad one, but given the psychic attack earlier this day, it's been greatly narrowed."

"You think what happened was more than a bad dream?"

"Yes, as well you know it was more than a bad dream."

I wasn't sure about that, but I nodded anyway.

"So what do you think it was? Specifically? What kind of... demon?"

"A night hag."

I felt my brows go up. "That doesn't tell me much."

"Perhaps this will. Whatever attacked you was an astral being of sex and desire."

"Like a succubus?" I asked.

"Yes, they have been called incubi and succubi, but they are also known as night hags. They appear to their dreaming victims and strangle them."

"Why would Ceres be a part of the sigil?" I asked.

"Ceres, as you know, corresponds to the mother and probably represents the summoner."

"What about the other symbol?"

"The full moon," she said. "You should know that one, little witch."

"Completion?"

"Or fertility."

Everyone in the room was quiet. I stood, leaving my phone in Zaphara's hands. If what she said was true, what would an astral being of ill intent, sex, and desire have to do with a mother and fertility? Something inside me clicked and shifted into place. It was a thought, an idea, and one that made me nauseous to even consider.

"You've thought of something," Zaphara said. "Have you figured it out?"

"It can't be possible," I said, surprise rendering my voice soft. "Is it?"

"That depends on what you are thinking."

"In folklore," I said thoughtfully, "incubi and succubi changed their gender to procreate," I said. "A succubus would lay with a man and steal his seed."

"And then," Zaphara added, "with his seed inside of her, the succubus would alter her shape to lie with a woman, to impregnate her."

"But," I said, "if they're astral beings, how is that possible? And wouldn't the succubus just act as a vessel, a fertility bank so to speak? How would they see the continuation of their species or whatever it is, if they're stealing human semen?"

"I do not know how to explain it in a way you will understand," she said. "The seed becomes hers. Their species, as you call it, are infertile, but once they steal from a human, she can change the seed inside her by altering her body, shifting her form at will. Her body alters the semen, taints it with her DNA to see the continuation of their kind."

"That's confusing," I said.

"And fascinating," Rosalin added. "Who needs a turkey baster? Order a succubus!"

"Horrible, Rosalin." I laughed. "You should probably steer clear of writing infomercials."

She smiled, but her eyes were still haunted.

"Zaphara, is that possible?"

"Is what possible?"

"Could the summoner have summoned a succubus to steal a man's seed for her? Ceres, the mother, the full moon, fertility. Could a succubus, or whatever it is, get a woman pregnant?"

"In spite of being none-too-fruitful themselves, it is possible. Once their bodies alter the fluid they've obtained, they're potent."

"Have to make it count, right?" Rosalin asked.

Zaphara nodded.

"What are you thinking, Kassandra?"

I turned to Lenorre. "Arthur said the neighbor knew the Blevins were looking to adopt. Obviously, as much as I hate to say it, the whole pagan thing opens the doorway to the possibility of one of them creating a spell to summon this kind of thing. What I don't understand though"—I turned to Zaphara—"is how this happens? Surely, if succubi can reach beyond the astral realm there would be more cases of this happening? How are they able to manifest, and can a human actually carry a succubus child to term?"

"With that title, it would be an incubus child," Zaphara said. "A succubus requires blood sacrifice to manifest. A human woman can carry a child to term, but she will not survive its birth."

I sat back down on the couch with a flop. I didn't want to ask her how or why a woman wouldn't survive giving birth to the child of an astral being. When I considered the possibilities, none of them were very comforting or pretty.

"In the dream," I said, "the creature wore Lenorre's guise. When I realized it wasn't Lenorre, it tried to kill me?"

"Yes," Zaphara said point-blank, not bothering to tender her words. "Though it was probably going to try and kill you anyway. Its intent was to seduce and destroy."

"Peachy," I said. "But why? How would it have known to attack me?"

"Because it knew you had seen what it had done."

"How could it have known that though?"

"In order to understand that you must first understand what I meant when I told you I am not speaking of the demons of Christian stories. The incubi and succubi are fey, albeit a much darker breed. Many years ago, they lived alongside the Daoine Maithe, until the rise of the current queen who saw them as the filth they are and cast them to the realm of Oíche, the land of eternal night. You are part fey and wherever you go, Kassandra, your energy leaves its mark to anyone else that is fey. That is how the night hag sensed you."

"I was shielding."

"Lenorre said there was some trouble between you and another police officer, a were-fox, if I remember correctly. She felt your shields slip, if Lenorre felt it, so did the succubus."

I sighed heavily. "If the succubus has murdered, there's no way in hell the cops can do anything about that. This becomes a cold case. It's unsolvable."

"Ah," Zaphara said, lips spreading into a cat-like grin. "It is not. You see, for the blood sacrifice, the succubus cannot reach beyond the realm of Oíche to kill. A human must do it."

"So in some way, it is officially a murder? Because a human had to make the kill?" I asked.

"Yes," she said, "It is a murder because your human had to make a kill, a sacrifice. He or she had to use a blood sacrifice to summon the hag in the first place to give her the ability to manifest in our realm."

"Okay," I said. "Let me see if I get this straight. What you're saying is that, initially, the witch summoned the succubus thing with a kill?"

"Yes."

"What about the crime scene where the woman was strangled? The odd prints around her neck, was that the succubus's doing?"

"Yes."

"I'm confused, Zaphara."

Zaphara made a frustrated noise. "The succubus was summoned the first time with a human or not so human sacrifice, Kassandra. If the sacrifice is large enough, then the succubus gains energy from the sacrifice to manifest. She grows in power each time she gains the gift of blood or life. If she can manifest, she can cause physical damage in this realm."

"But how do we prove that? Arthur obviously still hasn't found the Blevins's car or he would have told Lenorre. A dog was missing from the scene that I still haven't heard any word of."

"A dog?" she asked.

I nodded.

Zaphara shook her head. "If it did not happen to get out and run away, chances were the dog was used as a sacrifice. If the first sacrifice was large enough, the witch would only require a smaller sacrifice the next time he or she summons the succubus, in order to take the seed and create a child."

"A Great Dane being a smaller sacrifice?" I asked. She nodded. "How do we prove this? How do we find the summoner or succubus? And if we can prove this, how do you handcuff or hogtie a succubus that has a condo in the astral plane?" I was thinking aloud, asking myself more than Zaphara, but it was Zaphara who answered.

"I will rewrite the spell."

"And do what?"

"The succubus is a lesser fey," she said, a bit haughtily. "I will summon her and bend her to my will."

"Um, what?" I asked. Rosalin sat up beside me, and I didn't have to turn to her to know she was suddenly very focused on Zaphara.

"Are you confident in this, Zaphara?" Lenorre asked.

"I am," she said. "I will set about rewriting the spell to suit my needs."

"I'm not sure I'm too keen on this."

"I will use her to find your murderer, Kassandra. That is what you want, isn't it?"

"And what am I supposed to do, call Arthur and say, 'Hey, we used a succubus to track the killer. Go get 'em, boy?' I'm not sure that will fly."

"But if your forensics can prove there was indeed a victim and a human murderer at the initial scene, it will fly."

I still wasn't sure. "I guess we'll find out."

"We will," Zaphara said.

"Where are you going to summon this thing?" I asked. "And how do you feel about her summoning it under your roof?" I directed my second question at Lenorre.

"If she is confident she can control it, it might be worth the try. If we do not do anything, a killer goes free. Is not the risk worth taking?"

"It is if we can prove these things and actually bring justice to the victims and their families."

Zaphara said, "I will summon the creature in the woods nearby, where I am stronger and in my element. I will require your aid, Kassandra."

"Terrific," I said. "What will I need to do?"

"Combine your power with mine."

"You do realize I don't know how the fuck to do that, right?"

She placed a hand on my shoulder and her smile was dark and somewhat unnerving. It reminded me of Rupert, who was very adept at the cold and hard *I won't hesitate to kill you* look. The only difference was, Zaphara's seemed to add *and I'll probably enjoy it*.

I hated to admit it, but it gave me the serious heebies. In that moment, I wondered if maybe being her friend was in my best interest.

CHAPTER TWENTY

Zaphara left to begin working on rewriting the spell she thought had been used to summon the lesser fey. Rosalin was curled up on the couch beside me, her knees tucked close to her chest, head resting on her bent arm. She appeared to be asleep, or at least halfway there. Lenorre remained seated in her chair, quietly watching Rosalin.

My cell phone vibrated from its perch on the couch's arm. I felt Rosalin stir beside me before I retrieved it, and I walked into the bathroom for the illusion of privacy.

Arthur's number decorated the screen of my caller ID.

"What is it?" I asked, keeping my voice low and soft. It was probably the first little bit of sleep Rosalin had gotten. "Has there been another murder?" I asked, feeling something tighten uncomfortably at the pit of my stomach.

"Attempted," Arthur said. "You wanna come down to the station?"

"Attempted," I repeated the word, thinking furiously. "There's a witness?"

"Yep."

"Why don't you sound happy about that?"

"Because I don't know if I believe her."

I didn't ask any more questions. I didn't need to. If Arthur didn't believe her, chances were she might've had a real run in with what we were suspecting.

"I'll be there as soon as I can." I hung up the phone and emerged from the room. Rosalin was sitting up and though she was awake, she looked completely and utterly exhausted.

Lenorre stood and said, "I'll retrieve our coats."

There was something in Rosalin's expression that reminded me of a child, a vulnerability etched within the very contours of her features when she asked, "May I go?"

I didn't know where Carver and Claire had run off to and wasn't even sure they were still here at Lenorre's. Zaphara, I suspected, would be busy for some hours trying to recreate the spell to suit whatever her needs were. I hadn't seen Trevor or Isabella, and would've hesitated to leave Rosalin with them anyhow. Trevor wasn't dominant enough to make her feel safe, I knew that. Eris was nowhere in the vicinity, and even if she had been, Rosalin had shown last night that she wasn't exactly comfortable with her. When it came down to it, perhaps Lenorre and I were the only two capable of making her feel safe.

I didn't want to take that away from her, and so my reply, when it came was, "As long as you stay with Lenorre and don't get in the way."

"I won't," she said. "I promise."

Lenorre came back wearing an ankle length coat of ash gray darker than the color of her eyes. The coat had white fur lining at the wrists and hood. The back cinched artistically like the bodice of a corset. I brushed the fur with the tips of my fingers and knew it was real. If I had to guess, I would've said rabbit. Maybe the fur should have unnerved me a little, being pagan and a shape-shifter, but oddly, it didn't. The coat didn't look recent and for some reason I sensed it was something she'd had for a very long time, though it was in extraordinary condition.

I took my coat from her and shrugged it on over my black sweater and jeans. I didn't bother putting on the shoulder holster that still hung on the bathroom door. I doubted I'd need it in a room full of cops.

"Ready?" I asked.

"Let me grab my coat," Rosalin said.

Lenorre and I waited downstairs while Rosalin went to get her coat. In truth, we would've been fine without them because all three of us were less sensitive to the cold than humans, but people tend to give you a funny look when they're freezing their asses off and you're not. So for the sake of appearances and partly for comfort, we donned them and left, without question the best dressed people at the police station.

❖

Arthur opened the door to the interrogation room and ushered me inside. Astrid Meadows, and yes, that was her real name, was sitting in a chair closest to the door. There were two chairs on the opposite side of the table. I introduced myself, taking a seat as Arthur took his beside me.

Astrid's wrinkled eyes narrowed, not in malice, but as if she were sizing me up. "A preternatural investigator and a what?" she asked.

"Paranormal huntress," I said. "I work with the police on cases like this."

She turned to Arthur. "You called in a ghost chaser on me?"

I laughed, which brought her attention back to me. "Ms. Meadows, preternatural covers a broad spectrum, as does paranormal."

An impish twinkle sparkled in her gaze. Her brown hair was a mess of unruly curls that ended just above her shoulders. Given her age and the hint of gray at her roots, I knew she dyed it.

"And you think it has anything to do with this?"

Was she toying with me? I leaned back in my seat, folded my arms on the table, and said, "Why don't you tell me what happened to you and we'll go from there."

Something about the expression she gave me made me want to fidget and I didn't understand why. I didn't lower my shields so much as part them, like peeking out from behind the blinds of my soul. I didn't have a lot experience getting a taste for the energy of others, but something about Astrid intrigued me, lured me to check.

Her hand twitched slightly. I closed my eyes, focusing on drawing a breath in through my nose, tasting it at the back of my mouth. The smell of sage clung to her skin and hair, to the lavender shirt she wore. I reached out, metaphysically, feeling the edge of her shields like hard stone. There was a break in the stone, a crack. No, not a crack or a break, a small window opened in the line of her shields and I felt her energy brush mine like a gentle breeze caressing my skin. I smelled violets.

"Atta girl," the crone said, "a bit more gently, next time. Think less like a gust and more like a breeze. You're less likely to be noticed that way."

It was unnerving, the breeze of her energy moving unthreateningly but exploratively against mine. I wondered, since she had lowered her shields, should I lower mine more? Could I trust her?

I didn't realize I'd directed the thought at her until I heard her wizened voice crackling through my mind.

You can.

The smell of violets was thick, and though Arthur didn't seem to smell them, he asked, "What's going on? What is she talking about, Kass?"

I didn't answer him. I did as she had done, lowering my shields as little as I could for her to get a reciprocal taste of my energy.

Her energy came rushing in and the smell was almost a choking thing. I gasped, standing and grabbing onto the corner of the table. The chair I'd been sitting in was flung back against the wall. Arthur stood up.

"Kass? What the hell is happening?" he asked.

Astrid hobbled frantically around the table. I forced myself to try to breathe past that cloying smell, counting my breaths. She touched my arm and I heard her voice as if from a distance.

"Close the door," she was saying, her voice near frantic. "Focus and close the door, girl! You're a standing beacon!"

Was she mad? I could hear the breaths I was drawing and they were harsh and ragged. Something was going horribly wrong.

What the hell had she done to me?

A growl built in my chest, built and beat against my ribs as if the sound itself would drive away the threat. I closed my eyes and saw the wolf, hackles raised, teeth nearly bared.

Arthur said, "Shit," and scrambled away from the table.

I sank teeth into my bottom lip, stifling the growl as much as I could. Astrid hadn't removed her hand from my arm.

"Stop touching me," I said.

"I'm the only thing shielding you right now, girl! There's no way in Hades's realm I'm going to stop touching you."

Her energy was like a heavy wet cloak thrown over mine, stifling, suffocating, crushing.

The only thing I wanted to do was shake it off.

The fluorescent light above the table flickered.

I heard Arthur's gun slide free of the holster at his hip.

"What the hell is going on?" His voice was higher than it should have been, his words more hurried this time.

Astrid kept her hand on my arm, her energy blanketed over mine, but looked up at the flickering light and said, "It's coming."

The light burst and the room was swallowed by a darkness even I could not see in. Tiny shards of glass rained down upon the table. I heard Arthur click the safety off his gun.

"Arthur! Do not shoot!" I said. "You can't shoot this!"

"What the hell is it?" From the sound of his voice, I could tell he had pressed himself into the corner of the interrogation room.

Astrid answered, "Detective, you're about to come face to face with what I presume is your first demon."

"Is she kidding me?"

"'Fraid not," I said and turned, jerking my arm away from Astrid's touch.

As soon as I broke her hold, my shields fell away. The energy building in the room hit me so hard I went to my knees.

The wolf wanted out, but this was not her fight. Astrid was mumbling something in a language I didn't understand. A white light sprang to life in the cups of her hands. Arthur turned his gun on her and I rushed him, knocking the gun out of his hands and to the floor.

I stood in front of him.

"What's she doing, Kass?"

"She's trying to save our asses, Arthur. Don't fucking point the gun at her."

"What the hell is that?"

Unfortunately, I was short enough that Arthur was able to look over my shoulder. Astrid was facing the table, the surface of which rippled like a pool of water that a stone had dropped in.

There were sounds outside the interrogation room, sounds of someone trying to get in the door to no avail. I ignored it, taking a step forward and asking, "What can I do?"

"You can summon your magic," Astrid said. "Call to the blood in your veins and your Goddess."

I heard Arthur behind me ask, "Say what?"

I didn't question how Astrid knew what I was. Her gray eyes met mine and this time, they weren't gray. They were foggy like soft, shimmering crystals.

I knew in that moment, the strange language, the energy clasped between her palms—she was fey.

Darkness seemed to ooze from the surface of the table, spiraling in the air like a building vortex of energy.

"It's trying to manifest?" I asked.

"Yes."

"What in the name of all the Gods is it using to manifest?"

"It grows stronger, child. Lower your shields!"

I hesitated. I didn't know what to do if I lowered my shields all the way. The only thing that I'd dealt with that was even remotely close to a psychic attack was what Zaphara had once done to me. If I lowered my shields, I made myself vulnerable and defenseless.

Astrid's voice grew more urgent. "Trust your instincts!"

I didn't lower my shields; I shut my eyes and threw my shields down. When I opened my eyes, I saw the clawed hand that reached out of the black mist.

Astrid took the light she held, but instead of throwing it into the heart of the dark matter, she placed her hands flat on the table.

The light set the entire table aglow. Flickers of static electricity shot through the darkness like lightning. A creature screamed the same high-pitched scream I remembered in my dream.

Every sense within me heightened. Arthur's fear sent his pulse hammering loud enough it felt as though I could feel it against my skin.

I focused on Astrid, and with my shields down, I realized what she was doing.

Her parchment-like skin took on a luminous quality, the curls of her hair swaying in the breeze of power she called, strands clinging to her wrinkled cheeks. She summoned light, her hands flat on the table, her eyes narrowed as she gazed at the still growing darkness.

What magnified the light? For some reason, I remembered gazing out the window at Lenorre's, watching the sunlight dancing across the water of the pool outside.

Water.

I kept that vision in my mind, but larger, greater, a sea of rocking waves, violent waves, waves that did not hesitate to overturn ships or to slam themselves against rocks.

There was no energy in my hands that I could see, but my skin tingled with the rush of magic.

I put my hands flat on the table, mirroring Astrid. My energy spilled out from my skin in a rush, like a dam just lifted. I felt it connect with Astrid's and another scream sounded from the dark.

I raised my gaze to the mist and for a moment, I could've sworn I saw something looking out at me. The mist reached outward, a clawed hand beseeching.

When I raised my hand, Astrid screamed, "Don't!"

But it was too late. I took hold of the hand that stretched the mists and it felt sturdy and solid against mine. The creature's grip tightened, threatening to crush my bones, but I was fey and werewolf; it could crush my hand all it wanted.

I would heal.

Two carnelian eyes with slitted pupils pushed outward. The hand that held mine jerked roughly.

I curled my knees up, knocking them under the table as it literally picked me up.

Arthur's hands caught me at the waist and I heard him say, "Holy fucking—" over a loud wind that seemed to be coming from everywhere and nowhere.

The creature tried to pull me in again, and this time I pushed, but not with my body. I envisioned the waves that feared no stone, no high rock. Somewhere in my mind, I heard a raven cry, just as I had in the dream, but this time, it wasn't seeking aid.

We were at war.

I pushed the energy that built inside me into the vortex, into the crevice between the worlds the creature had torn open.

Wind whipped my hair like angry lashes against my cheek; dampness clung to my skin and soul. A foul smell permeated my senses like the smell in the air after fireworks have been set off.

Still, I shoved, trying to use the energy like a blade.

But something wasn't right.

Laughter rang throughout the room like a roll of thunder, making me wince.

Arthur still had his arms around my waist. "Kass!" he screamed, the wind threatening to swallow his words.

The wind whispered, *"Not strong enough."*

The table legs scraped across the floor, the screeching barely audible beneath the roaring in my ears.

I was doing something wrong. Every time I pushed outward, the wind picked up stronger than before.

I was feeding the creature energy.

With its hard grip still crushing my hand, there was too much contact for me to shield. I was too wide open.

I shut my eyes, tight, blocking out the ocular sensory and focusing on Arthur bear-hugging my hips.

Turn it around. I didn't know where the thought came from. I didn't know if it was my own. But suddenly, I understood. Or at least, I hoped I did.

I breathed, and on the heavy intake of breath, I drew that burning smell into my lungs.

"No!"

The creature lashed out and the energy hit me in the center of my chest, stealing my breath in a mind-numbing rush of pain.

If I had had the breath to scream, I would have.

The creature flung my hand from hers and I was suddenly airborne.

❖

I woke feeling the hard floor beneath me. Someone cradled my head in their lap and I looked up to see Lenorre.

Her cold fingers stroked the hair away from my face. I was about to ask her if everyone was all right, when a sharp pain like a knife wound blazed to life in my chest. I turned, coughing, my body heaving and rejecting something. I scrambled to my hands and Lenorre's arm circled my waist.

My body was thrust forward with the force of the heave. Something heavy and wet spilled from my mouth and I coughed, choking on some of it.

The taste of metal and ash coated my tongue.

Someone had brought a light of some kind into the room. The light illuminated the shiny liquid I'd vomited. Another fit seized me, and despite my best efforts not to, that stomach-turning noise emitted from my throat as I purged again.

I groaned, pressing my hand to my stomach as if that would help me. I hate vomiting. Worse yet, Lenorre was still trying to hold me, stroking my hair back from my face.

I opened my mouth to ask her to move when the urge hit me like another blow dealt to my midsection. I scrambled, not exactly sure what I was doing, but panicking and trying to move away from the growing puddle. My hand slipped in it and the only thing that kept me upright and not falling in my own vomit was Lenorre's arm around my waist.

The world spun as she helped me to get to my knees, pulling me back against her.

"Breathe, Kassandra," she said.

I tried, in through my nose and out through my mouth. Everything inside me felt raw and singed. The air stank of burning flesh, making my stomach turn.

Someone held a cup in front of my face. "Drink this, child."

I took the paper cup Astrid offered. My body jerked again, against my will, but this time I managed to hold it down. Point for me.

"Where's Arthur?" I asked. "Is he all right? What happened?"

"I'm fine," he said, moving around the table to kneel beside me. "You look like shit. It vanished after tossing you like a ragdoll."

"Thanks," I said. "It just left?"

"For telling you that you look like shit?"

"For grabbing me," I said.

"You're welcome," he said. "I didn't want Holbrook jumping down my throat for letting whatever that thing was gobble you up. And yeah, it apparently didn't like playing with you. After you went down, everything stopped."

"Your attack made it expend too much energy in defense. It couldn't hold its manifestation," Astrid said.

I tried to take a sip of the water she had given me, but my hands shook too badly. I ended up wearing most of it. Lenorre took the cup from me, but before she could help me, Rosalin was suddenly there. "Let me," she said.

Lenorre handed her the cup and I didn't protest when she helped me to take a drink from it, grateful to be washing out the vile taste in my mouth.

Rosalin said, "Lenorre and I tried to come in. The door wouldn't budge. I would have been here sooner if there hadn't been a line of police officers rushing to get in the way."

I nodded, taking another drink. My throat was raw, like I'd been screaming for days.

Lenorre gently moved me away from my vomit, easing me slowly down into her lap far enough away that the smell eased slightly. I rocked back against her until I was sitting, not wanting to move anymore than that.

"Well," I said, clearing my throat and looking at Astrid. "You're fey?"

Arthur distracted her by pulling a chair up for her to sit in.

"I believe you now," he said, offering a hand and helping her into the chair.

"What happened?" I asked, once she was comfortably seated.

"I'm part fey," Astrid said, "And it tried to attack my daughter."

"Who's your daughter?"

"She's the High Priestess of the Silver Crescent Coven."

"Does she know Miranda and Landon Blevins or Leana Davey?"

"Leana Davey is a member of her coven. Miranda and Landon, I do not know."

"Ackerman," Arthur said, "bring Ms. Meadows's daughter, Belinda, in."

Lenorre helped turn me to face the door. Astrid's daughter entered the room wearing a pair of faded jeans and turquoise turtleneck. She was a beautiful woman with light brown hair that fell straight almost to the crook of her arm. Her eyes were a reflection of her mother's, her lips full and brows high-arched. She spared the mess I'd left on the floor a glance. If she was startled or surprised by the current state of the interrogation room, she didn't show it. Point for her.

Why hadn't she been in the room when I'd come in to speak with Astrid?

I saw Astrid's hands moving fluidly in the air.

Her daughter nodded and signed back. She was still signing when Astrid spoke.

"Miranda and Landon had been to a few of the open circles, but they were not yet a part of the coven."

"Does she know anything more about them?" I asked.

Belinda came and knelt in front of me.

My mother tells me I can understand you.

I actually jumped where Lenorre held me.

Was telepathy a capability of all the fey? Did I really want to know?

What happened to you?

Belinda touched my hand lightly.

I was sleeping when the creature attacked. It tried to strangle me.

She pulled the turtleneck down to show me the bruises on her neck.

I did not think the cops would believe us.

Did you see anyone aside from the creature?

No, my mother and I guess that it attacked from a distance. It came to me as someone from the coven, someone I know well and am attracted to. I knew it was not her and it tried to kill me.

Been there, I thought.

My mother heard the dog barking outside. When she went to check, she found her with her belly cut from here—she put a finger at the top of her sternum—*to here.* The cut ended just below her navel. *Whoever summoned the creature used her familiar's blood to feed the magic. We think, because they killed the dog in the backyard, they were outside the house when they summoned it.*

Is the dog still there?

Yes, and we've notified the police. The detective said he sent someone out.

"Arthur?"

"Yeah, Kass?"

"Get Forensics out to their house. Stat. Don't pussyfoot about this."

"Kass, I trust you, but what the heck's going on?"

"We're talking. That thing you saw earlier is growing in strength. It requires blood sacrifice. Get a team out there and investigate. Find some shoeprints, something. Whoever summoned it used the dog as a sacrifice."

"Doesn't look like you're talking to me," he said, seeming to ignore everything else I'd just told him.

"I'll explain later, Arthur. Just do it. Now."

It was Ackerman who said, "I'm on it."

Do you know what it is? I asked Belinda.

Not really. My mother told me some of the stories that had been passed down to her when she was a child. The stories have been throughout our family for more decades than either of us can keep track of.

So you were raised aware of your fey blood?
Yes. She tilted her head. *But that's another story. The creature is some kind of spirit trapped in the astral realm. Do you know what it is?*

*I'm...friends...*I hesitated to use the word, but what the hell. *With one of the Daoine Maithe. She has informed me it's a type of lesser fey that was banished to the astral realm, a succubus or a night hag.*

Or an incubus?
That too.

She shook her head. *I am at a loss for why someone would summon such a thing to attack anyone.*

Are all the members of your coven like you are?
Fey?
I nodded.

No, but I know for a fact Miranda and Landon were. Only he, he was part elf. You look surprised.

A bit. What about Leana?

Leana is fey, though the blood in her is diluted. One of her ancestors allegedly was a siren.

I touched her hand where it rested over mine. I wouldn't bother telling them about Leana. That was Arthur's dirty work, not mine.

How did you stop it? I asked.
I didn't. My mother did.

Before I'd even asked the question, Astrid said, "I severed the link."

"How?"

Astrid smiled, her face crinkling. "You'd be surprised what a good ole sage bundle and a few choice words of banishment will do, girl."

I thought of something and she must've caught the thought over my features.

"Say it," she said.

"If that's all you had to do to get rid of it, do you really think it was trying that hard for your daughter?"

"What do you mean, girly?"

I ignored the "girly" bit.

"Shit," I said.

"Shit, what?" Rosalin asked. I'd almost forgotten she was in the room.

It was Lenorre who caught it first, who understood where I was going with the thought.

She whispered behind me, "It is tracking you, Kassandra."

"But how could it have known Astrid and her daughter would lead to me?"

Belinda was watching my lips with unnerving focus.

It is an astral being, she thought to me. *They see and know more than we do.*

"It's true," Astrid said. "The scope of their sight from the astral realm is wider than ours."

Peachy. Just fucking peachy. *Thank you, Belinda.*

Belinda bowed her head and stood, moving to help Astrid rise from her seat.

Astrid paused in front of me and pulled a chain out from under the collar of her shirt.

"Take this," she said. At the end of the chain dangled a small silver seven-pointed star. A gem of black onyx was fixed in the middle of the star. "I think it belongs with you, Child of Morrigan."

Before I could take the necklace from her, Lenorre took it.

Astrid chuckled. "It's not silver."

Regardless of her words, Lenorre stuffed the chain into her coat pocket.

"Either way," she murmured against my hair, "I'd prefer Zaphara check to make sure it is safe for you to wear."

"Good idea," I said. "I hope you're up for driving."

Rosalin moved in to help me to my feet and I let her. "So it's my turn to cuddle you in the back?"

"Sure, if the smell of brushfire is really your thing."

CHAPTER TWENTY-ONE

I didn't find out until I tried to leave that Arthur wasn't going to let me. He offered a few times to take me to the hospital, and every time, I told him no. Lenorre and Rosalin were with me as we sat in his office. Arthur had closed the door to give us some privacy. I didn't know where Dan Holbrook, my old boss was, and frankly, I didn't particularly care to find out. After much cajoling, I'd managed to talk the younger cop I'd met the other day into bringing me a cup of coffee. He'd brought Rosalin a soda from the vending machine.

Arthur was seated on the other side of his desk, his white dress shirt unbuttoned and his tie pulled loose.

"Arthur," I said. "Stop looking at me like that."

"Start talking, Kassandra."

"About?" I asked, tilting my head with the question.

"You know what," he said. "What the hell happened in there? What the hell were you and Ms. Meadows doing? What the fuck was that thing above the table and how is it you collapsed, woke up, painted the interrogation room floor with your blood, and are sitting there calmly in front of me as if nothing fucking happened?"

"Are you about to have hysterics?" I asked.

"Don't be a smartass, Kassandra. Not right now."

I pulled my legs up in the seat, nursing my cup of coffee since it seemed he wasn't going to let me leave any time soon. Neither Lenorre nor Rosalin spoke, but Arthur shot them both an expectant look and asked, "Either of you going to tell me?"

Rosalin shook her head, indicating she wasn't going to peep.

Lenorre said simply, "The answers to the questions you ask are not mine to tell."

"We told you what was happening, Arthur, as much as you needed to know. Astrid is part fey. She was using her energy to try and figure out what I am."

"That doesn't tell me anything, Kassandra. And no, you really didn't tell me what was happening. You knocked my gun out of my hands and told me not to shoot."

"If you had shot at it, Arthur, it wouldn't have done any good and someone in that room might've gotten seriously hurt. It was a battle of metaphysics, not weapons."

"What the hell was Ms. Meadows talking about *your magic?*"

"You know I'm a witch, Arthur."

He leaned back in his seat, shaking his head. "Kass, I saw you move. I saw your eyes."

"My eyes?" I asked. "What'd my eyes look like?"

"Unlike you," he said. "I don't know. They didn't look right. They shouldn't have been that bright. I'm going to ask you again, what happened?"

"You were in the room, Arthur. Astrid and her daughter are part fey. That's how they were able to protect themselves when they were attacked. When Astrid raised her energy to explore mine, it did something. I'm not sure what."

"The night hag is stalking Kassandra and when Astrid combined her energy with Kassandra's, even briefly, I believe that energy blazed like a light by which to guide the being to her," Lenorre said.

"Astrid said she was trying to shield me. Could you sense the energy?" I asked.

Lenorre offered a slow nod. "She tried to camouflage your energy as soon as she sensed the creature, I think, for fear that it would use your energy to try and manifest."

"But it didn't need my energy to manifest, Lenorre. It manifested even though she was shielding my energy."

"So I believe," she said.

"What are you two talking about?" Arthur leaned forward, and he looked more irritated and uncomfortable than I'd ever seen him.

"The thing that attacked us in the interrogation room is a being that lives in the astral realm, Arthur, and it put some kind of metaphysical tracking device on Astrid or me and when she and I raised energy, it found us. Lenorre suspects that Astrid tried to shield me so that it couldn't feed psychically off my energy and use my power to manifest in our reality. Are you following me?"

"Explain *power*."

"I'm using the words power and energy interchangeably. Every piece of life around you, from a plant to a person, has energy."

"The Chinese call it ch'i," Rosalin said. "Life force."

"Spirit?" Arthur asked.

I nodded. "Pretty much. It's the life energy that flows throughout everything living. The Druids themselves were animists believing that everything that was a part of the natural world and living had a spirit, a rock, a tree, a flower, et cetera," I said.

"What were you and Ms. Meadows doing to the table?"

I pushed my hair up and held it, wanting some air on my neck. The room was stifling and I suddenly wanted to be outside. The fact that Arthur wouldn't let me leave was making me feel trapped. Not a good feeling after I'd been attacked in the same building. "The creature had used its energy to create a portal, Arthur. We sought only to close it."

"Kass, the table was glowing as if you'd poured glow-in-the-dark paint all over it."

"We were using energy."

"I've never seen anything human use energy like that."

I released my hair with a heavy sigh. "I'm not human, Arthur. There, are you happy?"

"What are you? Are you like Ms. Meadows and her daughter?"

"Yes, Arthur. I'm part fey."

He looked as though he didn't believe me, but after a moment, he said, "That explains your height."

"It has little to do with my height," I said. "The fey, like humans, come in many different shapes and sizes. The creature you saw earlier was fey too."

"All these years," he said, "and you never told me. Why?"

"It doesn't change who I am, Arthur, and I didn't know myself until recently."

He pushed his chair back and stood, pacing the small area behind his desk. "That's how you're able to sense things and catch things we'd miss." He seemed to be talking to himself, so I didn't offer up a response. He stopped pacing. "What can you do?"

"That's a personal question, Arthur. I'd rather not answer it. I'm still human," I said.

"I can't tell if you're in denial or if you're trying not to creep me out," he said.

"What do you mean?"

"You were vomiting blood, Kassandra, and not just a little bit of it. Most humans wouldn't be standing after that."

"Trying to banish the creature came at a price for Kassandra." Lenorre swooped in, saving me from trying to explain something I didn't fully understand myself. "Her human body struggled to serve as the vessel for the energy she was trying to take in to sever the creature's link to our world. The fey blood in her veins merely makes her a bit stronger than a human, Detective, but she is no immortal."

It was partial truth and she told it well. I was certain the only thing that had kept me from being seriously injured or worse was the fact that I was a lycanthrope. There was no way I was going to tell Arthur that. Fey, he might've been able to handle, but finding out I could turn furry once a month, or whenever I wanted to, really would've changed his perspective more than I was willing to. Fey was the lesser of two evils when it came down to it, because although neither was evil, per se, our modern society was not exactly favorable to shape-shifters. In fact, the protection around us was finicky in and of itself. To kill a werewolf in human form was murder, but to kill a werewolf in wolf form, at worst, was animal cruelty. Nice, no? As vampires had been embraced and accepted into our modern society, so had been the fey and elves. All three had protection that lycanthropes and shape-shifters did not, despite the fact that some of the fey, like Zaphara, were capable of changing their shape at will.

Still, a lot of people believed that the fey and elves were benign. Mostly, that was thanks to the rise of modern fiction. But belief doesn't change the fact that good and bad come in a lot of different guises. Humans have their inner beasts as much as any lycanthrope.

"How much stronger than a human?" Arthur asked.

"Strong enough that the price I paid was only a little blood."

"Are you sure you're all right?"

"I'm fine," I said for what seemed the fifth or sixth time.

Arthur returned to his seat. "So how do we catch this?"

"We've already got a plan set in place. We're merely waiting to put it into action."

"A plan that you were going to go rogue on and leave me out of again?"

"If you didn't happen to notice, Arthur, it's a bit dangerous for you."

"Looked like it was a bit dangerous for you too, Kass."

"Fair enough," I said.

"What's your plan?"

"We're going to summon the creature and use it to track the initial summoner to find out who's really behind the murders."

"You're going to call that thing on purpose?"

"Yes."

"Kass, you know if this thing is behind the murders, there's nothing to prosecute."

"Actually," I said, "there is. The night hag was summoned by someone at the first scene. That, I believe, is where you will find your original murder and your murderer. Did the results on the blood work come back?"

"Inconclusive," he said. "Which is fucking weird, considering."

"Then the blood more than likely belonged to one of the Blevins," I said. "They cross-reference the DNA?"

"They did." He retrieved a folder from his desk and opened it. "They appeared to have a match, but there were too many doubts surrounding who or what the blood belonged to to know for sure."

I wondered if, though humans shared a similar DNA structure with the fey and elves, if something in elvish or fey blood would throw off the test entirely.

I asked Arthur as much. "Both of the Blevins were part human. Do you think being fey and elf would throw the test off completely?"

"I don't know," he said. "Their team doesn't have a specialist on site that's familiar with fey and elven blood. I don't think we have one in the entire state."

"For the sake of this case," I said. "They might want to bring one in."

Arthur scribbled a note on a piece of paper and slid it into the file. "I'll let them know. There's a guy in Kansas they can contact. What are you going to do when you find the murderer?"

"I think that's where you can come in. Last I checked, I can't be in two places at once. Can you put a team together?"

"You sure you can find this thing?"

"I'm sure a friend of mine can, yes. She's more experienced than I am."

"I'll put a team together," he said, no arguing, no more questions. It surprised me. Arthur was trusting me. I didn't expect that. "You call and tell me when and if you've tracked the killer's location. I'll send the team out to perform the arrest."

"May I leave?" I asked.

"Yes."

I stood and was almost to the door when he said, "And, Kass?"

"Yeah?"

"Be careful."

"You too, Arthur."

CHAPTER TWENTY-TWO

We made it back to Lenorre's and had just walked in when my legs went out from under me. Rosalin was there to catch me, slipping her arm around my back and hooking her hand under my armpit.

Lenorre touched my forehead, pushing the hair out of my face. "You're still not well," she said.

"I'm fine." I forced myself to stand straight and my legs quivered.

"Um, no, you're not," Rosalin grumbled, noticing the tremor of my muscles.

I heard a noise from the kitchen as a cabinet door closed. A moment later Zaphara emerged through the dining room with Eris trailing behind her.

"What happened?" she asked.

I closed my eyes and shook my head, trying to clear away the little black dots that obscured my vision.

"Kassandra was attacked again," Rosalin said.

Zaphara came closer. Close enough that for a second, I almost growled. She bowed her body and I heard the sharp intake of her breath close to my cheek.

"Your blood sugar and energy are low. You need to sit down."

Rosalin helped me into the parlor set off of the foyer. The room was done in shades of white and cream. She lowered me ever so gently onto the couch. Lenorre and Eris entered the room and were speaking in hushed voices by the door. I found myself incapable of focusing on their words. My stomach felt like it was going to rebel again. The light fixture hanging from the ceiling seemed to be swaying slightly in my view.

I put a hand over my face and groaned.

"Sit her up," Zaphara said. "Kassandra, drink this. It will help some."

Rosalin gently lifted me by my shoulders, sliding her body onto the couch behind mine. She propped me up against her almost the same way Lenorre had earlier at the police station. The glass was cold and the ice was clinking in my trembling hands. I sniffed it, its sweet and bitter smell telling me it was sweet tea.

I took a drink and as soon as the liquid hit my tongue, it was as if I'd been walking through a desert without water for days and hadn't realized how thirsty I was. I couldn't stop.

My focus sharpened slightly, and I was able to concentrate on Lenorre and Eris's conversation.

"If someone doesn't lend her energy, Lenorre, she's not going to be of much aid to Zaphara in this condition," Eris said.

Her words made me glance over to where she and Lenorre stood just inside the doorway. Eris's entire body was encased in a PVC catsuit that looked like she'd literally been dipped into the material. The glossy black material molded to her curves, bringing out every slope and arch to stark perfection. Her sable hair was pinned messily at the back of her head, leaving her neck bare with the exception of a few sprays of curls that had broken free. As if she felt me looking at her, she turned her head, revealing a dusting of obsidian eye shadow that made her sea-green depths more vibrant and alive.

The breath caught in my throat and I mentally cursed myself. Rosalin laughed above me, letting me know she'd heard it. No doubt so had Lenorre and Eris, as Eris smiled at me seductively.

Lenorre moved enough that she brought Eris's attention back to herself.

"I am not so certain Kassandra will be receptive to your proposition, Eris."

"I'm adept in this area and I've fed more than you have tonight. I've the energy to spare."

I rolled my head back on Rosalin's shoulder. "Do you have any fucking idea what they're talking about?"

"Eris is talking about giving you energy."

Zaphara returned with another glass of tea, though I couldn't remember her leaving. She gave the vampires an odd look when she entered, as if she too wondered what they were up to.

"Here," she said, but she wasn't looking at me. Her gaze was all for Lenorre and Eris as she tried to figure out what was going on.

"You can use me as your conduit, Eris. I am your Countess."

"No, Lenorre. The energy is best shared one-on-one, without interruption, and you know it."

"I give up," I said. "What are you talking about?"

"You can offer," Lenorre said.

It was Zaphara who answered my question. "Your energy is low, low enough that you need an outside source."

I turned to her and must have done it faster than I thought, because the room reeled and I actually put a hand out. "Oh, that was not good."

"And it's not going to subside until you find an energy source outside of yourself to regulate the energy you expended." Zaphara touched my forehead. "You're cool to the touch again, Kassandra, cooler than a lycanthrope should be."

Eris moved around the arm of the couch and closer to us. The outfit she wore was completed by a pair of modestly heeled boots that ended just below her knees. I thought the shimmer of silver on the boots were buckles, but upon closer inspection realized they weren't buckles but jewelry in the shape of small handcuffs, with chains stretching from one cuff to the other.

"I'm going to feed you energy," she said.

Lenorre said, "Eris."

Eris canted her head slightly. "Let me rephrase that," she said. "I'm going to feed you energy, if you consent. It will make you better."

"And if I don't consent?" I asked.

"You'll be useless this evening," Zaphara said. "It may take days, werewolf or no, for your energy to balance out and regulate itself after this kind of attack. Allowing Eris to feed you energy is a painless and quick solution if you can overcome your inner prude."

My mouth hung open at the guiltless honesty of her words. "What the hell is that supposed to mean? I'm not a prude, Zaphara."

Eris offered a smooth laugh. "By the definitions of one of the Daoine Maithe, you most certainly are. Never mind her definitions, though. Will you allow me to feed you?"

"Let me make sure I comprehend this. You want to give me energy like I'm some kind of psychic vampire?"

"Yes, precisely." There was an eagerness in her expression that made me suspicious of her motives.

"Lenorre, what is Eris not telling me?"

"The feeding will require close contact."

"What kind of close contact, exactly?"

Eris let out a harsh breath, as if she were becoming impatient. "My particular abilities lie in the exchange and manipulation of sexual energy. You are familiar with psychic vampires. Have you ever heard of an Eros vampire?"

"I'm familiar with some of the mythology of the God, Eros. He's a God of sexual lust and desire."

"Then you grasp somewhat of the meaning of an Eros vampire."

"So what you're telling me is that you're some kind of erotic vampire?"

"Quintessentially, yes. Why do you suppose I've chosen the profession of a pro-domme?" She smiled rather wickedly.

"You feed energetically off their desire?"

"Yes."

"And in order to give me energy, you need to get all hot and bothered?" I asked.

"I'd not put it as bluntly as that, but yes."

"Kassandra," Lenorre said, "before you decline, I am not opposed to this offer. I simply did not think you would be comfortable with it, but if you are, by all means"—her expression softened—"take it." She walked around Eris to kneel on the floor in front of the couch, touching my arm. "You need energy and Eris is in a position more fit to give it to you than I."

"Because she's fed more?" I asked, just to be sure.

Lenorre inclined her head. "I have not fed enough to give you the energy you need."

Rosalin shifted her hips, trying to get her legs out from underneath her.

I groaned as my stomach lurched. "Ros, stop doing that."

"Sorry," she murmured, "my legs went to sleep."

"Well?" Eris asked expectantly. "Have you an answer?"

"What happens again if I decline?"

Zaphara answered. "We put you on bed rest and don't catch your murderer."

That didn't sound like a thrilling prospect to me.

I'd forgotten the glass in my hand and wasn't aware it'd slipped until Lenorre caught it and placed it on the coffee table. My hand was still trembling slightly when she enfolded it in hers.

She said my name, prompting me for an answer.

"How much close contact?"

"A kiss should be sufficient to raise the energy needed," Eris said.

"And you're sure, absolutely sure, you're all right with this?"

Lenorre squeezed my hand. "I will be here by your side."

"Fine."

"That's a yes?" Eris asked.

"From Kassandra," Lenorre said, "it is."

I felt more than heard Rosalin's heart rate increase. "Do I get to stay?"

"No," I said.

"Why?" she asked. "I've kissed you. I've seen Lenorre kiss you."

Zaphara said, "Come, wolf, we'll leave them to it. You can help me with the spell."

"Kassandra?" Rosalin asked, her voice meek.

"Sorry, Rosalin. I'm more comfortable without an audience."

She let out a heavy sigh telegraphing her disappointment. I ignored it as Lenorre helped me to sit up so that Rosalin could get her legs and feet under her. She left the room with Zaphara, who paused in the doorway, glancing back before shaking her head and shutting the door behind her. Lenorre helped ease me down and though she did it slowly, it seemed every little movement sent my head spinning and that sick feeling rolling in my stomach.

The room was bathed in silence. It was a strange silence, and if I'd been feeling well, I would have found it uncomfortable. Lenorre was petting me, stroking the hair at my temples. Her fingers sifted through the strands, nails tickling my scalp tenderly.

The couch cushion dipped and I opened my eyes to find Eris crawling on top of me.

"I'm having déjà vu," she said, smiling beautifully.

"Keep the games to a minimum, Eris," Lenorre said, her tone cool and detached.

Eris straddled me and it was hard to keep my eyes open, hard not to focus on her weight pinning my body to the couch, hard not to think about the body beneath the slick PVC.

Hard not to remember her pale thighs and the line of dark lace near her groin.

Lenorre kept playing with my hair, offering a welcomed distraction.

"I need her to focus on me, Lenorre. She's distracted by you."

Lenorre inclined and I felt her breath ease out across the skin behind my ear. She pressed a kiss against my pulse, whispering, "This will only work if you let yourself desire her, Kassandra."

As soon as the words were delivered, as soon as the goose bumps broke out across my flesh, Lenorre withdrew, no longer serving as my distraction, my anchor, but leaving me alone and touched only by Eris.

Eris slid her body up my thighs and pressed her groin to mine. I gasped at the sudden contact and sunk my teeth into my bottom lip. The first flickering breeze of power flitted across my skin like the march of tiny moth wings.

"Don't fight me, Kassandra."

Her fingers stroked the line of my brow as she held herself above me, her body solid, heavy, and real against mine. Our clothes seemed too little barrier. She asked me not to fight her. As weak as I felt, I didn't think I could. Eris kept moving over me and I remained frozen beneath her gaze. The blood rushed like tiny rivers through my veins, disturbed by the slow trickling current of power.

Eris's lips were close enough a breath would bring our mouths together. "Don't fight me," she whispered again and pressed her mouth to mine. The energy became like a slow, lapping wave, washing swiftly over my body and caressing places that Eris wasn't physically touching.

The touch of her lips was soft and fleshy, like some forbidden and succulent fruit that I wanted to sink my teeth into and swallow. The fullness of her bottom lip teased mine in a kiss that was almost too light to be a kiss. The wood creaked beside my head and I knew she braced herself with a hand on the couch's arm. I sensed her struggle, her inner battle for restraint and determination to control the flow of energy between us. Her other hand found me, lifting my top as her fingers traced my skin underneath it.

The touch of her bare skin against mine made the energy spike. Her fingers tickled my side, her thumb playing along the highest arch of my hip.

That energy pulsed between my legs, throbbing and warm. I wanted Eris to kiss me, to finish that last push that would bring our mouths solidly together. I wanted to feel her lips open wide, to feel the first touch of her tongue as she delved into me.

I wanted more. I wanted her.

"So much desire," she said, sounding nearly breathless. "So much to drown in."

The sound of her voice alone nearly sent my head back. I needed to be touched, to be stroked, to be fucked. I could feel the energy spiraling in my sacral chakra like warm honey pooling between my legs, spreading outward, suffusing my limbs with its glow.

The sensation of it was strange and exhilarating, destroying my ability to think of anything else. I wanted to strip my clothes off and bring that power closer, to smear it, to spread her, all over my skin.

Eris's breath mingled with mine, but she held herself at bay. I wanted to cry with the fierceness of my need, to throw her back and pin her down, to take what my body craved from her like some kind of wild beast. But I didn't. Even the wolf within did not try to test her leash. I held my breath, waiting. I was afraid to move, afraid she would stop.

If I had thought Eris impatient, I had been wrong. Her eyes were closed, and her beauty was softened by pleasure, like an angel of love with skin as soft as dove's wings.

Eris placed her thigh between my legs and my will to remain still broke. I rubbed myself against her thigh, trying to find the friction and contact that my body craved.

She thrust her power into me and what had begun as too little clothing between us was suddenly too much.

Every fiber in my being ached beyond thought. I wanted her to bury her fingers in my wet and scorching flesh, to cool the fire she set within me. It was a heat that drowned out any thoughts of shape-shifting or magic. There was nothing but need.

She kissed me, hard and unexpected, molding her lips to mine as if my mouth were a chalice she would lick clean. I pressed into the kiss, and when her tongue spilled into me, I returned it fervently, every stroke etched with need, with little artistry, and the primal hunger that was threatening to sear me alive.

Her mouth fed at mine and I was vaguely aware of the sound of the wood still protesting under her harsh grip. Her thigh moved away from me and I nearly broke the kiss in a frantic effort to reconnect with it. But I didn't have to. Eris's thigh slapped down into me hard enough that my head fell back into the couch's arm. I cried out against her mouth, not in pain, but with a preternatural need.

She ate my cry, swallowing it with a moan that made my body buck up against hers. Her fangs dragged across my tongue and the coppery taste of blood welled between our locked lips. The blood seemed to encourage her as she kissed me harder, trying to obtain that sweet crimson flow.

A rush of adrenaline sang from the core of my being when she raised my wrists and pinned them to the couch above me. Some great chord felt like it had been hit, echoing a sound of desire that gripped me so completely I forgot everything but her and the fire she cast me in. I yanked my hands free and reached for her, craving her touch like a love-starved junkie, feeling the slick slide of the PVC against my palms. I swept my hands lower, discovering the hard, cold edge of a zipper and jerking it down. Her breasts spilled free of the tight material and I sank my hands greedily into the opening.

Her nipples stiffened against my skin as I cupped her breasts. Eris tore her mouth from mine, crying out, making my body jerk again. Her bottom lip was stained with my blood.

It took a moment for my mind to register that Eris hadn't torn her mouth from mine willingly. Someone had buried a hand in her hair and yanked her head back, forcing her spine to bow with the strength of their hold. Eris's pale breasts were exposed through the opened vee of her outfit, full and beautiful, with dainty nipples made for licking and sucking.

I felt a colder energy and a prickle of fear set in my throat like a thorn.

Lenorre stood beside the couch with a handful of Eris's hair in her grip and before I could stammer anything, an excuse, an apology, Lenorre brought her mouth down hard on Eris's, kissing her deeply and passionately.

Lenorre broke the kiss, a tremble of blood quivering on her bottom lip. I knew it was Eris's blood and not mine, knew Lenorre had set her fangs into her somewhere during their kiss. Her gaze was misty and crawling with power, the energy leaking from her was like moist stone, damp and cool.

A shudder went through me, anticipation, fear, or shame. I didn't know what. I didn't care.

Lenorre bent low and whispered in Eris's ear. "Do you want this?"

Eris's reply was breathy. "Yes."

"You want us both?"

Eris's eyes were filled with power too, like windblown waters, rippling. There was no mocking in her tone when she said, "Yes." There was only an unwavering certainty.

Lenorre straddled my legs, setting herself behind Eris. She snaked an arm around Eris's waist, her long fingers like moonlight against Eris's dark attire, her crimson painted nails vivid like a slash of blood.

She found the zipper and showed me that it unzipped a great deal more than I'd known, dragging it down between Eris's parted thighs.

"And you, Kassandra?" she asked, her voice sending an army of chills up my spine as she gazed at me over Eris's shoulder. She exposed Eris's shaven mound, playing the tip of her finger over the shadowed slit. "Do you want this?"

When I didn't answer, Lenorre parted her and slipped a finger down into her folds. The sight made me make a sound low in my throat. I could smell Eris's arousal; smell them both like immaculate snow and some crisp white wine. The wolf paced within me, curious and eager, but still not testing the bars of flesh. I knew Lenorre could use her energy to keep the wolf at bay, but if Eris or Lenorre were doing something in that regard, I couldn't tell. The wolf seemed content where she was, nestled in the back of my mind.

I sat up and pulled my legs out from under the vampires on top of me. I brought the line of my body closer to Eris and bowed my head, licking the top of her breast. Eris swayed back against Lenorre, releasing a sigh of pleasure that made my skin prickle. I kissed lower, flicking the tip of my tongue against her nipple and feeling it stiffen against my lips. I sank my mouth down on her, sucking gently, listening to the achingly slow rhythm Lenorre had set with her finger on Eris's clit. I knew from experience how expert that hand was, how much Lenorre could make of her touch a tantalizing tease that pushed one's body so close to the edge that a woman was left breathless and begging to be thrust the rest of the way into the oblivion of carnal pleasure.

Hands pulled at my sweater and I ducked my head as someone tugged it off, too filled with yearning to protest at the loss. Fingers slid between my breasts, grabbing hold of the bra I wore and yanking it off me. Eris's hands worked at my jeans and when her fingers fumbled with the button, she lost her patience and broke the button, as if she'd tear the jeans off me strip by strip.

Lenorre kissed her neck, watching me while she did it.

My pulse sped and Eris's hands swept upward. Her fingers played at my breasts, tugging and twisting lightly, making things low in my body writhe.

I pressed myself against her, against the back of Lenorre's hand. Eris shoved the torn jeans and undergarments I wore down my thighs. Her fingers sank into my yielding flesh. I cried out as she pushed them inside me. My body cinched around her, tightening in eternal hunger. Someone grabbed my hair, used it to pull me closer to Eris. I rose up on my knees, following the hand that led me.

Lenorre kissed me, trapping Eris between us tightly, leaving her so little room that Eris had to work her fingers out of me. I gasped against Lenorre's mouth at their withdrawal, but felt them again, teasing along the line of my buttocks.

Eris pulled me up into her lap with her hands under my ass, bringing my body more comfortably against her and Lenorre. Lenorre flicked her wrist, sending her knuckle and the back of her hand dancing against me while she stroked Eris. The feel of Eris's breasts against my bare skin made me claw at her shoulders. I thought I understood what it was to drown in pleasure, but I'd never felt anything like this.

Eris splayed her fingers over my ass, driving her nails into my skin. I cried out, moaning, pressing against Lenorre's mouth as if I'd crawl inside her. Eris's hands sank even lower, playing along the tuck of skin between my ass and thigh. Normally, I would've stopped to file a verbal complaint, as I don't like a woman playing too close to that intimate area, but this wasn't normally and I was too taken with power and senses to care.

Eris snaked her hand between my legs and I could feel her tracing me from an awkward angle. She found my entrance and pushed inside me again, easing in and out, making my body tighten as I rode the waves of sex and power. The back of Lenorre's hand flicked against my clit, making my hips twitch with pleasure. The orgasm built and I wasn't sure if it was because of Eris, Lenorre, or of the power enveloping us. The frantic inhale and exhale of Eris's breath fell into synch with mine.

Lenorre broke our kiss, opening her mouth wide and driving her fangs into the porcelain bend of Eris's neck.

Eris cried out, her fingers slamming into me and sending me spilling over the edge, bringing me with her as she came, piercing me with fingers as Lenorre pierced her with fang. My hands clawed her back, catching on Lenorre's clothes and tearing at them as if I'd climb through Eris to get to her. Eris's body bucked against mine, the energy hitting me hard and forcing me to cry out. Lenorre jerked her head back, grabbed me by the hair, and kissed me, pushing that sweet metallic taste into my mouth as another wave hit, drowning out the wolf, and sending me shuddering and moaning against her bloody lips.

When the orgasm passed, Eris and I collapsed on top of Lenorre. Eris started moving almost immediately. Before I could get my bearings to ask what she was doing, she slid down low on the couch. Even for a large couch, Eris and Lenorre were far too tall. Eris draped her legs over the couch's arm and used her hands to spread my thighs as she positioned her face between them. Lenorre stretched out under me, one leg completely flung off the couch while she took off her sweater. I grabbed hold of her pants, snapped off the button, and tugged them down to free her long legs.

Eris chose that moment to bury her face in my mound. Her lips sealed over my clit, sucking. I dug my nails into Lenorre's stomach as Eris seized my swollen flesh between her teeth. My ass arched, the sensation of her teeth stretching me made me cry out and bite Lenorre.

Lenorre moaned at the bite, closing her thighs slightly to indicate that she wanted me to move my face to her sex. I tried to lick her at first, to trace the folds of her, to flick my tongue lightly against the source of her pleasure, but Eris was like some kind of animal, licking, biting, sucking, and fucking me savagely with her mouth, killing my concentration.

I dug my nails in Lenorre's thighs, wanting to tell her that what she wanted wouldn't work with Eris doing what she was doing to me. With Eris holding my ass in her hands, feeding at my sex in a frenzy, I was afraid I'd hurt Lenorre, afraid there'd be no skill whatsoever left to me, only this senseless writhing thing driven feral at the command of another's mouth.

Lenorre didn't give me a chance to speak. She buried her hand in my hair and literally pushed me down into her. I opened my mouth, taking her between my lips, moaning and making small sounds against her while Eris's pace never faltered. When I was close to the edge, Lenorre pinned my face to her with her hands to ensure I didn't stop, her body tightening. The muscles in her legs went rigid over my shoulders as she cried out and spent herself against me.

Eris gave one last tug and suck, her fangs sheathing inside me, making me strongly aware of my body, of every pulse point. Eris tore the orgasm from my body, sending me screaming over the edge.

My hand rested on Lenorre's hip, my face cradled in the crook of her thigh. Eris gripped me by the hips and guided me to collapse beside her head. I could feel her face pressed against the skin just below my navel.

I was lying there, panting softly, groin still throbbing faintly while I tried to regain control over my breathing. A sharp stinging sensation and loud smack emitted from Eris's direction. I jumped, accidentally jabbing an elbow into Lenorre's thigh and making her hiss. Warmth spread out across my lower body.

Eris's laughter slowly trickled throughout the room. Her hand stroked my ass over the area she'd smacked. "I've been waiting to do that."

The shock and horror of what had just transpired hit me in the face and flooded my veins like ice.

I made to stand, to scramble off the couch, when Lenorre put a hand on my shoulder and pulled me back.

"What's done is done, Kassandra."

I covered my face and said, "Oh Gods, what have we done?"

"A ménage à trois," Eris said. "One that went exceptionally well, considering."

"Considering?" I asked. "Considering what?"

Was she teasing? How on earth could she be teasing me after what had just happened?

"Considering it was unexpected," she said, curling lazily against me.

"Most unexpected," Lenorre added, sounding calm and thoughtful and not at all like we'd just fucked.

"You," I said. "What the hell did you do?"

"I intervened," she said.

"Why?" I asked.

"Because," she said, still calm, "Eris was close to losing control. If you were going to be taken by her power, I couldn't sit back and watch idly."

Her words crushed my anger. How could I blame her when in truth, I was guilty. I felt guilty, guilty for wanting Eris as much as I had, for knowing that Eris could've taken me right there in front of Lenorre and I wouldn't have fought her.

Then again, I looked down at Eris. "You said just a kiss."

"I did," she said in a voice that made my stomach tighten. "But can you honestly say you regret it was so much more?"

"Was it an intentional loss of control on your part?"

Eris licked her lips, slowly, distractingly. "Yes and no."

"What does that mean?"

"It means she was as swept up in the tide of your desire as you were in hers," Lenorre said.

Eris made a sound that was relatively close to a snort. Her fingers kept sweeping across my ass, tracing distractive and fluent circles over the sensitive skin there. "You can blame us all you want, Kassandra, but you had just as much of a hand in this as we did."

I let out a deep sigh. "You're right," I said. "It takes two to tango."

"In this case, three," Eris said, continuing to stroke and pet me. I wanted to be angry with her. I wanted to protest. I wanted to want to tell her to take her hands off me, but I didn't. For some odd reason, I didn't mind that she was touching me. Was it because we'd just had sex?

"Why don't I want you to stop touching me?" I asked. "Better yet, why don't I feel guilty for admitting that out loud?"

Lenorre gave me a surprised look. "Why would you feel guilty?"

I blinked at her and leaned back, giving her a full view of Eris. "You did happen to see the dominatrix between my legs, right?"

"If you're going to look at it from that perspective, we're all guilty, Kassandra. Very, very guilty." Eris laughed again.

I turned to Lenorre. "What the hell is wrong with her?"

Lenorre's mouth twitched. "I think she's a bit knackered."

"Knackered," Eris repeated Lenorre's words, her laughter bubbling up unrestrained. Somehow, Lenorre and I got dragged into it, laughing as well.

When the laughter subsided, Lenorre toyed with my hair and asked, "How do you feel?"

"Better," I said. The tremors and nausea had passed and I felt less lethargic than I should have after what we'd done. "A lot better, actually."

Eris stood and zipped herself back up. "As much as I hate to leave," she said, "I need to go freshen up."

She paused in front of Lenorre and me and stooped to kiss me. "Kassandra," she said, stroking my cheek after pressing her lips chastely against mine, "it's been a pleasure."

The smile she offered was rather salacious. Her dark brow arched in Lenorre's direction. Lenorre softly shook her head.

Eris bowed hers and said, "Countess."

Lenorre mirrored the gesture respectfully. When Eris left, closing the door behind her, I asked, "What was that all about?"

"She was trying to be fair by offering to kiss me as she had you."

"It's probably a good thing you didn't take her up on that. I'm still processing. I'm not sure yet if I should be pissed off or not."

Lenorre laughed. "I think we've had our fair share of ravishing each other."

"Speaking of which," I said. "Where are your boots? I don't remember taking those off."

"I removed them before intervening," she said.

"Lenorre?"

"Yes, Kassandra?" As much as it made something in the pit of my stomach tense uncomfortably to even consider it, we needed to talk. I felt it was better we acknowledged the big pink elephant in the room rather than ignore it.

"How do you feel?" I asked.

"What do you mean?"

"About what just happened?"

Lenorre pulled me into the circle of her arms and still, she remained calm, as if untouched by the night's events. The whole thing didn't seem to unsettle her. It did me, whether I wanted it to or not, whether what was done was done or not. There was a flicker of fear inside me. How had taking Eris to our bed, seduced by power, changed us? I rested my head on Lenorre's shoulder, thinking.

"Kassandra," she said at some length, "it was not my first ménage à trois."

At that, I raised my brows. "Do I want to know?"

"More than likely not."

"But it was your first time with Eris?"

"Yes," she said, and I didn't understand why she sounded amused.

"Eris implied you'd been in bed together before…"

"I've watched her feed," Lenorre said. "I've known Eris for many years, and when she wanted to work at the club, I was not going to hire her without learning of her control. And no, before you ask, there was no physical sex involved. I've seen her dominate. I needed to be sure she could do it without crossing any boundaries."

"Like she crossed mine?" I asked a bit snidely.

"An exception," Lenorre said. "And fortunately not one that happened at the club." Her expression was drawn into seriousness. "Eris does not lose control. Never once have I known her to lose it, but she did tonight, for you."

"Because she wanted to," I said.

"More than likely," she said, "It is hard to remain in control when the very thing you want is within arm's reach."

"How does what happened with Eris change things between us? How does what happened change us?" I asked.

"It doesn't," Lenorre said. "Why should it? The only thing I ask of you, is that, if something happens again with Eris, do not do it behind my back."

"I don't want anyone but you, Lenorre."

"I know you do not *want* to want anyone but me, but that could very well be beyond your control, Kassandra."

"What do you mean?" I asked.

"Eris is an Eros and a Prime," she said, "and you have tasted both her flesh and her power. I think you may find she may be a difficult thing to refuse."

I sat up. "What are you saying, Lenorre?"

"The touch of an erotic vampire can be an addictive thing, Kassandra."

"You slept with her too."

"Yes," she said, that one word empty of any feeling.

"Does that mean we might both become addicted to her touch?"

"I can refuse her," Lenorre said. "Her power was not directed at me and I am her Countess. I fear you may find it a more difficult challenge to refuse her, not because you are weak, but because her body called to yours even before this night. I tried to shield you from it by drawing your attention to me, but I do not know how well that worked."

"Then don't leave me in a room alone with her."

She laughed lightly. "I assure you, I'll apply my best efforts to be present."

I glanced up at her and the expression she wore. "You really did enjoy it."

"Vampires make lousy lovers with each other," Lenorre said. "Watching you with Eris was somewhat…moving."

And because I remembered Lenorre kissing Eris, her hand sliding down Eris's body, I shuddered and said, "I have to disagree. There was *nothing* lousy about that."

"You are not jealous?"

"I don't know," I said, "It seems silly to be jealous when I was obviously all hot and bothered. Whether that was Eris's power at work or no, it's still truth. If you did something behind my back with her, oh yes. I'd be furious." I paused and finally asked, "This doesn't make us non-monogamous, does it? I was serious when I told you I'm monogamous, Lenorre."

"My heart is yours and yours alone, Kassandra, always."

I was quiet. She had answered my question and I was sure she was trying to be comforting, but she hadn't exactly said, *"Yes, we're still monogamous."*

Lenorre put a finger under my chin and turned me to look at her.

"You are uneasy." Her silvery eyes searched my face.

"I'm worried."

"You do not have to fear losing me, Kassandra."

"I don't want to have to fear sharing you either, Lenorre. I don't do that very well."

"And you think I do? The fact that I joined should tell you otherwise."

I raised my brows at her, letting her know I wasn't grasping what she meant.

"Ask me why I joined," she said.

"Why did you join?"

"If it was going to happen, I figured it'd bloody well happen with me rather than without me. So I say again," she whispered, pressing her lips against my temple, "you do not have to fear losing me, ever."

"Do you swear it?" I asked.

She cupped my face in her hands and I tried to blink away the tear that threatened to spill down my cheek. "Yes, Kassandra, I swear it. A thousand times, a million times, if I must."

Lenorre kissed me gently before drawing back an inch. "You have been cheated on?"

Slowly, reluctantly, I nodded.

Lenorre wrapped her arms around me and said, "What a fool was she."

Unfortunately, fool or no, it didn't erase the reminder of that pain. I was older and wiser. I understood things better than I had in the past. It'd taken time, but I had finally realized that my ex's infidelity had less to do with me and more to do with her. Most people simply are what they are and by being what they are, they just don't fit, no matter how hard they try.

I hadn't realized until later how I had expected her to conform to my idea of what I thought a partner should be. In ways, she had done the same thing to me. There was still a small pool of resentment in me, a part of myself that still felt had we just been honest with each other and with ourselves, we would've dodged a lot of pain. It was part of the reason I was such a stickler on honesty and full disclosure. I'd seen the dark side of love in more ways than one and I didn't particularly care to ever tread that ground again. If the light of honesty would keep us safe, I would use it as my guide.

Lenorre had said nothing between us had changed and yet, I felt changed. I'd walked through my entire life never thinking that I'd do what I'd done with Lenorre and Eris, especially when in a committed relationship. How was I supposed to feel? I sure as hell wasn't sure.

Why did it seem that the preternatural complicated everything?

Fucking lust and metaphysics, it was enough to make me want to scream.

CHAPTER TWENTY-THREE

I could still feel the faint impression of Eris's fangs. The memory of her body clung to my hair and skin, to my lips and hands like a sin no soap or water could wash away. I could smell her and Lenorre, as if I'd bathed in their respective scents. Lenorre's clothes were not so destroyed that she couldn't put them back on. I picked up my shredded jeans and dropped them. The jeans, the bra, and my underwear were completely useless, torn by Eris's greedy hands. The button of Lenorre's jeans was broken, but she was still able to pull them on and hide the broken button by pulling her sweater down over them. She handed me a soft green throw from the back of the armchair in front of the fireplace.

"I will go find some clothes for you," she said, kissing me before she left the room.

I wrapped the blanket around me, sitting back on the couch and sighing heavily. My mind still reeled.

I thought Lenorre was already returning with clothes when the door opened. I turned to find it wasn't Lenorre who stood in the doorway.

Rosalin's gaze settled on my face after sweeping the room, her hand unmoving on the doorknob.

"Ros?"

She turned and walked out, but not before I'd caught the look on her face. I scrambled off the couch, holding the throw around my body.

"Rosalin!" I called after her, hearing her hurried footsteps as she climbed the stairs. I stumbled up behind her, speaking to her back. "Rosalin! Wait." I dove forward, catching her wrist. Rosalin turned on me with preternatural quickness. She jerked her arm away from my touch, recoiling as if I had burned her.

"You smell like her," she said. "You smell like them both." Her face was drawn in tight, painful lines, lines of hurt and disgust I didn't understand.

"Rosalin," I said, voice small and soft. I reached for her and she put a hand up to ward me off.

"Don't touch me, Kassandra. Don't fucking touch me right now."

I felt my surprised expression. My lips seemed frozen in their half-parted state. That old familiar fire returned to my veins.

"Excuse me? Where the hell is this coming from? What is your problem?"

"All this time you've sworn unbending loyalty and monogamy to Lenorre and"—she gestured at me with a hand—"this? Kassandra…really?"

"It just happened, Rosalin."

"What? You *just happened* to slip and impale yourself on Eris's fangs? Don't give me that bullshit, Kassandra. The least you could do is be honest with me."

"I am fucking being honest with you, Ros! What the hell? Why are you angry?"

"I could hear you," Rosalin said. "I could hear all of you."

"Maybe you shouldn't have eavesdropped." As soon as I said it, I wished I hadn't. Rosalin flinched as my words struck her and hit home. I took a step toward her. "I'm sorry, Rosalin. I didn't mean that."

"Yeah," she said. "You did."

I didn't know what to do. I understood she was angry with me, but I didn't really understand why. I took a deep breath, trying to release the defensiveness I felt, trying to let go of the anger that threatened to rise in me.

"I didn't mean to hurt you," I said. "I don't know why you're so upset or how I've hurt you, but I didn't mean to."

"Well," she said. "You did. Thanks, Kassandra. Thanks for letting me know how much you care about me."

"I do care about you, Rosalin," I said. "I care about you more than you know. Is that what this is about?"

"But you don't love me," she said.

Those were not words I'd expected.

"Romantically, no," I stammered. "And you know that. I'm in love with Lenorre, Rosalin. Why is this bothering you so much? What is that supposed to mean?"

"You chose Eris over me," she said. "You could have had me. You could have taken me to your bed, and you chose her."

"If you don't remember, Rosalin, we *have* slept together. I didn't choose anyone. I told you, it just happened. Eris offered me energy that Lenorre couldn't, and even though things got a little out of hand, she did help to heal me, Rosalin."

She shook her head. "Kassandra, the one time we slept together, I was the one doing all the work. I pursued you. I fucked you. I was fully clothed and you didn't even touch me."

"So what? I wounded your pride? What the hell, Rosalin?"

"You really never thought for a second that might have hurt my feelings, just a little bit?"

"I didn't know you, Rosalin!"

"But you do now, Kassandra. The woman you don't know is Eris, and from what I heard, the fucking was reciprocated."

I took a deep breath, counting to ten.

"You kicked me out, like you knew it was going to happen and didn't want me around to see it."

Surprisingly, my voice when it came was calm. "No, Rosalin. I didn't know it *was going* to happen. But I'd had a taste of Eris's power before, and if things had gotten out of hand with you in the room, I don't think my sensibilities could've taken it. You know me, Rosalin."

"I thought I did," she said, sounding as if there was something sour in her mouth. "Now I'm just starting to think you have a preference for vampires like everyone else."

"What is that supposed to mean? You've let Eris bite you. You readily admit to having gotten off on her fangs. What right do you have to throw this in my face and why on the Goddess's green earth are you acting like this?"

"Because!" she yelled that one word, as she stepped in close, "I want someone to look at me the way you look at them. I want someone to desire me the way you desire them. I want someone to hold me the way you and Lenorre hold each other, as if you can't get enough, as if you could never get enough. I don't get that. I get to see it prancing around me on a daily fucking basis, but I don't get it, not even a scrap of it. Every day, I get to remember that when you could've had me, you turned around and chose Lenorre. And you know what? I don't blame you, Kassandra. I really don't, but the fact that you never even really fucking considered me, another wolf, yes, that fucking hurts."

"I'm sorry, Rosalin. I'm sorry I couldn't be that woman for you."

I knew in that moment it wasn't me she wanted, not really. It was an idea that she craved, something her heart longed to find in a person. We'd talked about our friendship. Rosalin wasn't in love with me and I wasn't in love with her. We knew that about each other. If I offered her sex, I knew she would've taken it, not for a one-night stand or just to get off, but because she was seeking comfort and a connection. Something I knew in my heart I couldn't give her, not the way she wanted it.

"What I want, it doesn't exist. Not for me."

"Yes, it does, Rosalin. Love requires faith."

"I'm out of faith," she said. "I'm dry, Kassandra. I'm out of faith, out of hope. I'm just…empty. I'm empty and I'm sick and tired of waiting for some woman to come along and fill me, to want me."

"You're not empty, Rosalin. There's love all around you and if you can't see that, I can't open your eyes and make you see it. It may not be the kind of passionate love or soul connection you're looking for, but it's love nonetheless, and that should be worth something."

"Do you love me, even a little?" she asked and there was something close to fear in her honey gaze.

"Love comes in many forms," I said. "Yes, I love you, just not the way you seem to want me to. I'm sorry, Ros. I really am, but I'm being honest with you when I tell you, you don't choose who you fall in love with. It just happens."

"Do you mean that?" she asked.

"You know she means it," Lenorre said, standing at the top of the stairs with a bundle of clothes in her hands. "We both love you, Rosalin. It may not be in the way you wish, but we do."

I could smell the sweet salt-tang of Rosalin's tears, though she'd turned and hidden her face from us. I went to her, touching her shoulder, and when she didn't protest or shrug me off, I wrapped an arm around her waist. Rosalin folded her arms around me, holding on to me as if I were her anchor or life preserver. I brushed my cheek across hers, feeling the longing of the wolf within to comfort and soothe. Though we both wanted to ease her pain, a cold stone of knowledge dropped to the pit of my stomach. I knew that we could not.

What her soul screamed for, I couldn't give her. It just wasn't there inside of me to give. It was true, I loved Rosalin. She was beautiful inside and out, but whatever ingredient it was that set the foundation for Lenorre's and my relationship wasn't there between Rosalin and me.

I felt safe with Lenorre, but with Rosalin, I felt like I needed to protect her.

Was that what it was?

Rosalin backed away and hit the wall. She slid down it, burying her face in her hands and sobbing as if she couldn't stop herself. I knelt and touched her hair. I looked at the young woman in front of me and saw pain, so much pain. An immense well of it that had accumulated drop by drop, filling her skin to near bursting, from the loss of her parents when she was twenty-one to the abuse she'd been subjected to as beta of the Blackthorne Pack. How could I help her? I couldn't erase her past. I couldn't reach in and miraculously heal her and I couldn't love her the way she needed to be loved, the way she deserved to be loved.

The pain in my chest made it feel as though a piece of my soul were breaking. Rosalin's sobs grew heavier. She was whispering over and over, "Make it stop. Just make it stop."

Every word was ragged with a desperation that raked its claws at my heart. I couldn't make it stop. I didn't know how.

Rosalin howled her sorrow, throwing her head back against the wall hard enough that she knocked a hole in it.

"Rosalin!" I grabbed her by the shoulders, pulling her body into mine, ignoring the blood trickling down her back. I locked my arms around her like shackles, trying to pull her away from the wall. "Rosalin!"

She continued fighting me, wiggling and trying to shake off my hold.

"Let me go!"

"No," I said, crying. "No, Rosalin. I'm not going to let you go."

"I just want it to stop, Kassandra. Don't you understand? I can't live like this," she sobbed, choking on the words.

I seized her face between my hands. "Rosalin," I said, "breathe. I know you're in pain. I know your heart hurts. Just breathe."

Rosalin shook her head too fast, too sharp, her movements jerky and frantic. She tried to pull away from me again and I could feel the fine thread she hung from, so frail it was close to snapping. If I didn't do something, it would break, and in her panic, I didn't know what she would do.

I didn't think; there wasn't enough time to ponder my next move. I lowered my shields, summoning the wolf within as if calling her from a distance. The wolf came running, running toward my call, her energy spilling and drifting through me. I held Rosalin's face in my hands and put my forehead against hers.

The first spark of wolf energy kindled between us, and for a moment, I thought she would be receptive to it, thought she would stop fighting. But she didn't. Rosalin's entire body went rigid. She shoved me hard enough that I had to put a hand back on the carpet to catch myself while she clambered to her feet. Her eyes were wild, searching for an escape route.

The wall shuddered and Lenorre was there, holding Rosalin back against it with an arm like a bar of steel across her chest. Rosalin struggled in an effort to get away, but it was in vain. Lenorre was too strong, even for her.

"Please," she pleaded.

"You want the pain to stop?"

"Yes," she cried. "Yes! Please!"

The hallway crackled with Lenorre's energy like a rumble of thunder. Pinpricks of ice marched up and down my skin. In the face of Lenorre's power, Rosalin went completely still.

"Please," she whispered. "Make it go away. Make it stop."

Lenorre's skin was luminous. Her power crept over every inch of my skin, brushed every tiny hair on my arms.

Lenorre didn't say anything. She used no words to control and direct her power, but I felt it, felt it narrowing down on the wolf before her, felt her pushing that cool energy into the center of Rosalin's body.

Rosalin turned her face into Lenorre's power like a blossom turns to a kiss of sunlight. Only this was not sunlight, and nowhere near as harsh the glare. Lenorre shaped her power into a gentle thing and pushed it into Rosalin's body, into her soul. Rosalin's features went slack, her lips parting, and her breath easing out in a sigh. Every muscle in her body unclenched; relaxed to the point that Lenorre had to hold her or she would've crumpled, uncaring.

Aside from the soft whisper of our breathing, the hallway was enveloped in silence. I got to my feet, wiping the tears from my face with a corner of the blanket. Lenorre withdrew her power and I shuddered as I felt it like a serpent slithering past my skin.

She gracefully scooped Rosalin into her arms and said, "Kassandra, the door."

I opened the door to Rosalin's room and Lenorre laid her on the bed. "She will sleep for a time."

I stood there, unsure what to do, knowing that I couldn't leave Rosalin but desperately wanting to be anywhere else. I felt guilty all over again; guilty that I hadn't realized how close to the edge she had been. Guilty that my actions had driven her damn near over it.

Lenorre touched my cheek tenderly, bringing me back to myself. "I will get your clothes from the hall," she said, pulling me close and kissing the top of my head. I wrapped my arms around her, trying to relax.

"This isn't just about me, is it?" I asked her.

I felt Lenorre softly shake her head. "No, my love, it is not."

And it wasn't. It may have initially been about the sex accident and Rosalin's loneliness, but it was so much more than that. How had I not seen it before it happened? Carver himself had said that Rosalin had endured worse at Sheila's hands than this. I knew there was a well of sorrow inside Rosalin that she didn't show anyone. I'd seen it back around Thanksgiving when she'd broken down over the loss of her parents and admitted that the holidays depressed her.

And when we'd first met, I'd seen the scars on her back, scars I knew had been Sheila Morris's doing, though Rosalin never told me truthfully what happened.

She never talked about Sheila torturing her.

I rarely hate, but standing in Rosalin's room with her induced in a sort of vampiric coma, I felt hatred. I felt hatred toward Sheila for taking this beautiful woman that life had already been unkind to and showing her ugliness and cruelty; hatred toward an alpha that took her own history of abuse out on the innocents in her pack.

There was light in Rosalin, a beautiful light. I saw it when she laughed and when she smiled, and though she'd broken down in November, something had changed in her since then, something I hadn't seen until it was too late.

Sheila had buried Rosalin alive, but what else she may have said or done remained a mystery to me.

I had an image then of Sheila, so strong that it superimposed Rosalin's bedroom. I saw her face close to mine and her mouth shaping lies, disgusting, cruel lies.

"No one wants you."

I reached out, bracing a hand on the wall.

"Kassandra." It was Zaphara's voice. I turned to find her in the doorway. "What were you looking at?"

"Nothing."

She came to me, reaching up to touch my face. "Liar. You saw something."

I looked back toward the bed and Rosalin's sleeping form. "I don't know if it was real or not."

"Tell me."

"I saw Sheila Morris. She was abusing Rosalin."

"You had an impression," Zaphara said. "Chances are it is true."

When Lenorre returned, I put my slacks on as if in a daze, tugging the Two Points T-shirt down over them. The slacks smelled as if they'd been washed, which wouldn't have surprised me.

"What happened?" Eris asked from the doorway.

"You didn't hear it?" I asked.

"I was down in the basement," Eris said. "Is she all right?"

"No," I said, trying to keep my voice steady. "No, she's not."

"I've finished the spell," Zaphara said.

"We have not the time to perform the summoning," Lenorre said. "It will be dawn soon and I want to be present when it happens."

Zaphara nodded.

"I'll call Arthur and let him know it's been postponed until tomorrow," I said. If he had a problem, well, he could kiss my ass.

Lenorre shook her head, curls swaying at her waist. "I will contact the detective. Stay here with your wolf."

I touched her wrist. Lenorre came to a halt and met my gaze. There was a sorrow in her that I hadn't seen.

"Will you come back?" I asked.

The back of her fingers swept across my cheek. "I will come lay with you and your wolf until sunrise," she said.

"Thank you."

"There's a hole in the wall," Eris said. "Rosalin's doing?"

"Yes."

"Poor thing."

I shot her a disapproving glance. "She doesn't need pity, Eris. She needs compassion."

Eris shrugged as if to say, *I'm not going to argue with you.* It was probably a wise decision, considering my current temperament.

I crawled into bed beside Rosalin, nestling my body in against hers. Zaphara surprised me by climbing in between Rosalin and the wall.

Lenorre returned, and closed my cell phone then placed it on top of Rosalin's dresser. She placed herself beside me, wrapping an arm around my waist and spooning me while I held Rosalin.

"I see there isn't any room left for me," Eris said, sounding more amused than disappointed. "I'll bid you good night and claim one of the rooms downstairs for the morning."

Zaphara sat up, a trickle of energy rising in the form of a dark mist. When the mist lowered, Zaphara shook her furry head, as if shaking it off her. She rose to her paws in wolf form and moved to the foot of the bed where she settled down across our feet. The warmth of her fur was a welcoming thing and so I slipped my feet up under her, kicking her lightly. Zaphara grumbled her protest, but didn't make a move to stop me from using her as a foot warmer. Eris had changed her clothes and let her hair down. A loose white tunic covered her torso, falling just below her waist over a pair of dark leggings. She lowered herself into the spot Zaphara had left for grabs, her arm finding a place over Rosalin's still form.

Lenorre buried her face against the back of my neck. The rhythm of her breath lulled me to sleep.

CHAPTER TWENTY-FOUR

I woke to a cold, wet nose. A low rumble sounded and a snout bumped my face again. I put a hand out, lightly covering that persistent snout with my palm.

I pushed and Zaphara's furry weight hit the floor beside the bed. I rolled over, shoved my arm back under the pillow and tried to cling to sleep. The next thing I knew, I was clawing at the pillow, trying to find something to hold on to while Zaphara forcefully yanked me out of bed by my pant leg.

My hands slapped down on the carpet and I turned and growled. Zaphara had a mouthful of my slacks and was literally dragging me across the floor.

"Zaphara! I'm up! Good Gods!"

She shook her head, growling over the mouthful of my pants she had just about pulled off me. I rolled, grabbing the material at my waist and holding my pants up while Zaphara continued to drag me.

I yelled her name again and she didn't stop, continuing to drag me toward Rosalin's bedroom door.

"Carpet burn!" I exclaimed, my elbows taking the brunt of the abuse. "Zaphara, fucking stop! I'm awake!"

She stopped in front of the door, releasing me and sitting back.

Her ears went back against her skull. "*Must I drag you the rest of the way? Get up.*"

"You're a pushy bitch in the morning."

She snapped at me and I snapped back, whether it looked strange on my human face or no.

I got to my feet, pulling the waist of my pants back where they belonged.

"Where's Rosalin?" I asked, spotting the empty bed. I was sure Eris and Lenorre had retreated to the protection of the lower levels of the house to die when the sun rose. I went to the curtained window and peeked out. The gold, crimson, and orange sky let me know that I'd slept all day and that the sun was beginning to set.

"She's in the dining room downstairs."

So she was, sitting at the table with a mug of hot tea between her hands. The curtains over the windows in the dining room were drawn, blocking out any remaining threads of sunlight. I followed the smell of coffee into the kitchen and found a mug hanging on a rack above the coffee maker. I added a careless teaspoon of demerara sugar and milk.

"When did you wake up?" I asked, leaning against the frame of the doorway that was usually curtained off between the kitchen and dining room.

"Not long ago," she said.

"How are you?" I asked.

"All right, I guess. What happened last night?"

I sat in the seat beside her and took a long drink of coffee. "You don't remember?"

"Bits and pieces," she said.

I wasn't sure what Lenorre had done to her. I didn't think she'd done to Rosalin what she'd once done to Arthur, taking any memory of his interaction with her. But I didn't know if she had used her powers to cloud any of Rosalin's memories.

"What do you remember?"

"You," she said. "I was upset with you. You still smell like Eris and Lenorre, so I'm guessing that's why."

"So you remember the fight we had in the hallway?"

"Vaguely."

I put my hand over hers on the table, noticing that she was being cold toward me and not liking it. Rosalin looked down at my hand.

"Are you still upset with me?"

"No," she said. "What you do with your personal life isn't my business."

What the hell had Lenorre done to her? This was not the Rosalin I knew. Her eyes seemed shadowed, making them darker than they normally were. Her face was blank and emptier than I'd ever seen it. I couldn't recall ever seeing Rosalin with a blank expression. Her face was always alive with whatever she was feeling or thinking. But this...was it Lenorre's doing, or had something in her just closed down? Shut off?

I drew a long breath, trying to put a hand over my emotions. "Rosalin, what can I do?"

"You can't do anything, Kassandra. You can't fix me."

"Rosalin," my voice was soft, "there isn't anything about you that needs to be fixed. You're perfect just the way you are. You've been through a lot. I just want to help you through it."

"I woke with your head on my shoulder," she said.

"Does it bother you that I slept with you?"

She was silent for several moments before she shook her head and said, "No, I'm thankful for it. There's a hole in the wall outside my bedroom door. Did I do that?"

"Yeah."

"And Lenorre," she said. "I remember her. I remember begging her to take my pain. She took it, didn't she?"

"You asked her to help you and she did what she could."

"She should've taken that memory."

"Which one? The one where you threw your head against the wall?"

"No." She sighed heavily, her shoulders rounding forward as she hunched over her tea. "I went down to the library to help Zaphara, but she didn't really need my help. So I came back up and waited on the steps outside the parlor."

"You'd said you heard everything. I'm sorry, Ros. I didn't do it to hurt you."

"I know," she said. "I was just..." A tremble of a breath emitted from her, shaking her shoulders. "I need, Kassandra. I feel so lonely.

My heart aches, and I'm not sure anymore that I know what it aches for. I don't want to lose you. I don't want to push you away, but I feel like I'm losing my grip. I didn't stay with the pack because I had to. I stayed with them because it fills something inside of me that needs to be filled, Kassandra, and I'm lost without it."

"I'm not going anywhere, Ros. I'm right here."

"I need you to accept me as your wolf. If I can't be your lover, then please, Kassandra, accept me as your beta. Accept the fact that you're an alpha and stop running from this. I can't fight this many internal battles. I've fought this blackness inside of me for years and I can't do it alone. I can't do it without some semblance of a pack and a place where I belong. Just when I think the light's returning, something eclipses it."

"An eclipse doesn't last forever," I said. "It'll shine again if you let it, but you can't feed the beast of darkness and expect to conquer it with sympathy."

"Kassandra," she said, searching my face. "Can you do this?"

"Be your alpha?"

"Accept yourself. Accept those of us you've claimed."

I thought about Sheila. I thought about the vision I'd had of her and all the harm she'd inflicted on those around her. I especially thought about the harm I didn't know about. The secrets hushed within the pack.

"Yes."

"Give me your oath."

"You have it."

The muscles in her shoulders went slack as she slumped with relief over her tea. She whispered the words, "Thank you."

"May I hug you without landing on my ass?"

Rosalin raised her head, giving me a smile that was both sad and sweet. "How do you do that?"

"Do what?"

She rose from her chair and folded her arms around my neck. I slipped mine around her waist, holding her close and feeling the fall of her hair against my cheek, feeling her heart beating against mine through our chests. "How can you make me smile when I feel like I don't have any left?"

"It's something friends do," I said, stepping back. "At the risk of potentially ruining the moment, can I ask you something?"

The look she gave me was wary. "I guess..."

Goddess knows, I didn't want to ask the question I was about to, but in some part of me, I knew I had to.

"You're really not in love with me, are you?"

Rosalin was quiet for several moments, long enough that it unsettled me, long enough that I was afraid of her answer, afraid I had been wrong in thinking she was just looking for something in the wrong place.

"No, no, I don't think so," she said at last. "I mean, I love you, but *in* love?" She shook her head, auburn strands clinging to her cheeks. She raised a hand and pushed the hair out of her face. "No, and I think that's what frightens me the most."

At that, I raised my brows. "That you're not in love with me?" Surely, that was a good thing?

"That I'm not in love with someone," she said.

An awkward silence wrapped around us. I really didn't know what to say. What was there to say? Hey, I hope you find someone? It seemed a bit cold, even to me.

I sighed. "I don't know what to tell you, Ros. You know I want to see you happy."

"I know," she said, her voice soft. After another awkward pause, she changed the subject, "Lenorre should be waking. Are you going to feed her?"

"Maybe. If Zaphara hasn't already. I'm still not sure leaving you alone is a good idea."

"You don't need to babysit me."

"I'm not," I said. "Well, not in the way you're probably thinking. I'm feeling protective, that's all."

"So you're inviting me to tag along?"

I didn't know how I felt about Rosalin going downstairs with me when Lenorre had just woken for the night, especially if I was going to be the one offering to open a vein, but I really didn't want to leave her alone again. Something in the pit of my stomach, especially after this morning's display, told me it wasn't the brightest idea.

"Would you like to accompany me?"

She made a sound that was almost a laugh. "That sounds more like something Lenorre would say," she said. "Next you'll have matching T-shirts."

"What do you mean?"

Rosalin smiled. "You're starting to sound like her. *Would you like to accompany me, daaaah-ling?*" She said that last bit in a horrible impersonation of Lenorre's accent.

I shook my head, trying not to laugh. "You're a little heavy on that *dah-ling*," I said.

"Darling," Lenorre's voice sounded behind me and I about jumped out of my pants, sloshing coffee onto the tiled floor. "Kassandra is correct. I don't drawl."

She stepped into the room wearing a pair of slinky red silk pajamas. Her long hair was secured with a black ribbon. She placed a light kiss against my temple. "Good evening, love."

"Good evening," I said, reaching out to play a hand over her hip. I withdrew, remembering that Rosalin was still in the room with us and not wanting to feel like I was flaunting or throwing my relationship with Lenorre in her face. I wouldn't stifle myself, but Rosalin's wounds were too fresh and I didn't want to feel like I was throwing salt in them. I'm not a sadist, after all.

Lenorre seemed to understand, remaining close to me but not being overly touchy-feely or affectionate.

"Have you fed?" I asked.

"I was waiting for you."

Apparently, Zaphara wasn't on the menu. For her to have been waiting, she must've woken very recently. There were times when she woke riding the lust for blood, but those were few and far between. As there were certain triggers that flipped on my literal bitch switch, there were triggers that awakened Lenorre's hunger. Foreplay before she died at dawn was one of those. The bodily lust not being slaked channeled into the bloody kind when she woke.

"Where is Zaphara?" I asked. "I haven't seen her since she literally dragged me out of bed."

"She is in the library making sure all is in order."

I'd almost forgotten about the necklace Astrid had given me at the police station. I still couldn't really fathom why she'd given it to me and Lenorre hadn't let me handle it to find out. If Astrid and her daughter were part fey, I wasn't opposed to Zaphara checking it. Which, I presumed, Lenorre had given the necklace to Zaphara for that reason. Jewelry, like the symbol on the wall at the Blevins's, could be charged and spelled.

I felt Lenorre watching me and knew that she needed to feed.

"Do you know if Carver and Claire are still here?" I asked Rosalin.

"You'd sense them if they were," she said.

"With or without trying? I haven't tried to sense them."

"More like a gut instinct kind of thing, but you'd sense it more if you tried."

"So they're not here," I said as she raised her cup to her lips and took a drink.

I went into the kitchen to get a washcloth to wipe my spilled coffee off the floor, wondering what to do with Rosalin.

"Trevor and Isabella are here," Lenorre said.

"Trying to find someone to babysit me?" Rosalin asked. "I told you, I don't need a sitter."

"With everything that's been going on, Rosalin, we're just being protective. Will you let us?"

"Fine," she said.

"I'm not confident in Trevor, and I don't really know Isabella." Trevor also still belonged to Sheila, which made me feel rather distrusting of him. My goal was to keep Rosalin safe and feeling safe. Trevor helped neither of those causes. He was too weak, and although Isabella was one of Lenorre's Prime vampires, I didn't know her well enough to trust her.

"Would it bother you if Rosalin came downstairs with us?" I asked Lenorre.

"I am more worried about it bothering you."

"Will it bother you?" I asked Ros.

"No, not unless you start doing the hanky-panky and even then—"

I held up a hand. "Please don't finish that last bit."

We made it to Lenorre's bedroom and I sat at the foot of the bed. Rosalin chose to sit at the head of the bed, reclining back against the pillows.

"Just make yourself comfortable, Ros."

She smiled at me widely enough to reveal her perfectly white teeth. "Oh, I am."

Something about the way she made herself comfortable and just sat there watching Lenorre and me made it feel as though we were about to put on a show. I didn't like the feeling, and when the discomfort rose in me, Lenorre must've sensed it, reaching out a hand and sweeping my hair past my shoulder. The tip of her finger traced the vein in my throat.

Lenorre murmured, "This would be a great deal easier if you were in my lap or lying on your back."

"Which do you want?" I asked.

Lenorre sat and guided me into her lap. I curled my legs around her as her arms sealed over my waist. The line of her torso against mine and the feel of her beneath me was a distracting thing.

She kept one long arm locked around my waist, gently lowering me ever so slightly so that she could get the angle she wanted when she went in for the bite. Her lips traced the vein in my neck as much as her fingertip had.

"You have to relax," Rosalin said, noticing the tension that had strung through my body. "The tenser you are, the more it'll hurt."

"Ros," I said, "you're not exactly helping here."

I felt Lenorre's lips part over my skin, her tongue tracing a wet line that made me sigh. She sucked lightly at my skin, her fangs teasing the delicate and sensitive flesh of my neck. The pleasure helped ease the tension that knotted my back, forced me to relax one muscle at a time. Lenorre's jaw tightened as she bit down harder, easing her fangs into me in a way that made me feel every sensation, every tiny bit of teeth. I gripped her shoulders, nails digging in at that first painful kiss. The muscles in my body protested, clenching tight in immediate response to the surge of pain. I forced myself to go limp, shutting my eyes tight. The more I fought the pain, the more it hurt. Lenorre opened her mouth wider, unsheathing her fangs. I gasped as her lips sealed over the wound, her mouth working me in ways that seemed far, far more intimate. Too intimate, making my body go slack at the sensation. It felt as if a cord was directly attached to the pulse in my neck, coursing through the rest of my body, nestled between my legs. Lenorre sucked at the two dainty puncture wounds and things low inside of me tightened and jerked, making my breath come short.

I didn't know how long she'd been drinking from me when I felt the bed move. Rosalin was on her knees and for a moment, I thought she was crawling toward us. But when she raised her hands, lifting her hair and sweeping it aside, I realized she wasn't.

She was offering her neck to Eris, who in her long tunic and skintight leggings, crawled toward her with a dark and predatory hunger.

Lenorre's hands moved at my back, raising my shirt and slipping under to touch my skin. My body remained slack with pleasure as I rode the small tides that ebbed and flowed from the wound to my groin. The sensation was not so strong that I'd climax, though Lenorre was certainly capable of such a feat, considering past experience. It was like falling naked into a bed of fur and silk and feeling that smoothness slide and shelter every inch of my body, sensual and inviting.

Rosalin gasped and the bed rocked slightly. That cool vampiric energy rose in the air, like the scent of night and cold stone. I could feel it spreading outward like a growing vine, seeking, searching, and stretching. It made my skin flush and prickle when it found me.

I must've let go of Lenorre, for she stood, cradling me, not once breaking the hold of her mouth on my neck. My back met the mattress and I opened to her. She crawled between my legs, the very essence of my life flowing into her.

Someone was making small pleased noises. They were practically whimpering with it as the sound became less controlled and more urgent. I turned my head where I laid, trapped beneath the weight of Lenorre's long body, trapped under her crimson kiss.

Eris had her knees between Rosalin's parted thighs, holding her in her lap. She fed at her neck and her hips rose and fell, as if dancing to some seductive tune I couldn't hear. Rosalin's hips twitched, echoing Eris's movements. Her head fell back and Eris followed her, keeping her hold as Lenorre had done to me.

Lenorre licked my neck, her tongue dancing over the bite marks to encourage the flow of my blood. Something low in my body writhed as if her flicking tongue had commanded it to do a trick.

Eris was blurry in my vision, but I could make out the shape of her outline as she rose high on her knees, still feeding at Rosalin's neck. The wolf inside me lazily perked her ears at the smell of blood and desire.

Eris cradled Rosalin against her body, moving her hips and forcing Rosalin's to follow that unheard song.

Rosalin clung to Eris. Her breath was louder than it should've been, coming quicker, shuddering from her lips every time Eris's hips rose to meet hers.

Rosalin cried out. I grabbed two handfuls of Lenorre's hair, covering my face with it, drawing in the wintry and sultry scent of her, trying to block out the smell of blood and sex. Rosalin's whimpers turned to soft moans and I knew she was close, close to falling on Eris's power as if it were a sword. She gave a strangled cry and I had a moment to be thankful that Eris was directing her energy at Rosalin and Rosalin alone.

Lenorre found my lips with hers and I opened to her as she pushed the taste of sin and metal inside me. Her tongue was wet and hot with life. She held herself above me and when she drew away, I released her hair. It swung over our faces like a curtain.

I kissed her softly, tenderly, using only my lips to tease her mouth.

I felt Rosalin's body collapse back against the mattress.

Lenorre murmured, "Seems we are the ones that received the show." She sat back on the bed, lifting me against her. I couldn't exactly disagree. Rosalin was flat on her back, staring at the ceiling as if she wasn't really seeing it.

Eris met my gaze, her eyes still rich with power.

There was a knock on the door and I jumped. Lenorre went to it and allowed Zaphara to enter the room. Zaphara took in the scene in the bedroom but didn't make any verbal note of it. Rosalin appeared to be off in her own little world and I wondered just how much power Eris had really been focusing on her. Eris stroked Rosalin's hair in a gesture that was tender and almost done with something close to affection. One thing I was certain of, Eris cared about Rosalin. They might not have been lovers or truthfully even friends, and I don't know why in that moment I saw some kind of compassion in Eris, but I did. I saw a strength in her that did not arise out of harshness or cruelty or thirst for selfish gain, but something more akin to how a dark Goddess must feel about her charges, sheltering, protective, while remaining unopposed to laying out the challenge and seeing what they're made of.

I also realized Eris wasn't embracing all her power. There was too much control behind her energy. It was like standing at the foot of a mountain waiting for an avalanche.

It was hard to meet her gaze when she raised it from Rosalin's form, something about her expression made the memories of last night heavier. Her mouth was an inviting thing that stirred so many thoughts, namely of what she had done to my body.

I wanted to block out the sight of her, but knew I couldn't. I could cover my face with my hands, but I could still feel her, sense her, smell her…

"Kassandra?" Lenorre was talking to me.

"Huh?"

"Are you well?"

"Yeah," I said, and my voice sounded distant even to me. "I think so."

"Zaphara asked me to inform you that she is ready when you are."

I gave a sharp nod. "I'll give Arthur a call and see if he's put together a unit." I pushed myself from the bed and to my feet. "I need a shower first," I said. *Preferably,* I thought, *a cold one.*

Rosalin appeared more at ease than I'd seen her in the past couple of days. I was happy to see her settle down, even if it was Eris's vampiric mind tricks at play. Lenorre's words in my head haunted me to the bathroom.

The touch of an erotic vampire can be an addictive thing, Kassandra. I fear you may find it a more difficult challenge to refuse her.

I undressed and stepped under the hot spray of water, praying it was not true, praying that I could scrub the memory of Eris off my skin.

CHAPTER TWENTY-FIVE

The shower helped a little, but some thoughts kept buzzing around like a persistent fly that wouldn't go away. I struggled with those thoughts. When Rosalin had pursued me before Lenorre and I had began our relationship, the energy of our beasts had fanned the fire between us and I'd relented to that energy, surrendered myself to the magic of it. I'd come to grips with what had happened between Rosalin and me. Yes, I'd had casual sex, sex inspired by years of pent up desire and metaphysical seduction. I didn't regret it. Why should I when I am a woman and it is my decision what I do and do not do with my body? In its own strange way, perhaps the experience had in fact, actually helped us forge some of the bond of friendship that we had. We'd both spiraled headlong into desire, and then, when it was done, it was done.

Of course we'd talked about it. We expressed our feelings. I'd been honest with her about what I wanted and what I didn't want. I didn't feel the kind of heart and soul magnetism that I felt with Lenorre.

I didn't feel it with Eris, either, even though the aftertaste of her power clung to me like a silken web. That was what unnerved me. Perhaps some part of me would've been able to say to myself *it was all lust and metaphysics,* and I would have been able to put it behind me as I had done with Rosalin. But I feared I couldn't, that I wouldn't be able to put it behind me. One, I hadn't been in a relationship when things had gotten out of hand with Rosalin, and it certainly hadn't been a ménage à trois. Lenorre hadn't played any role in it whatsoever. She had with Eris; she'd even been the one guiding the ship. Could she have stopped it? Had I really been that taken by Eris? Is that what Lenorre meant when she once told me she was intrigued by the way Eris called to me? That she wanted to watch Eris make love to me? As soon as I thought it, the words didn't sound right. *Fuck*, seemed more appropriate. Eris had fucked me. And as all women know, there's a difference between fucking and making love. Not that I'm opposed to either under the right circumstances.

I shook my head, raking a hand through my wet hair. I didn't entirely comprehend Lenorre's lack of jealousy. I remembered her comment about the threesome not being her first. It made me wonder what kind of vampiric debauchery Lenorre had been exposed to and participated in.

If I wasn't afraid I'd run screaming or that it'd alter my view of Lenorre as the woman I knew and loved, I might've had the courage to ask.

But in truth, we are the pages of our history, and like books, where we begin is not always where we end. We may leave the past behind us, but every love, every touch, every page and experience along the way goes into the making of who we are. It's how we choose to deal with those experiences that make us who we become. I was learning that, albeit slowly, with every day I spent in my life as a non-human. Lucky me.

I hunched over the cabinet in front of the mirror, deciding in that moment I would never love Lenorre any less for whatever shadows lingered in her past. Every light and darkness contributed to the whole of the woman, of the vampire, that I loved.

To deny an aspect of a lover is to cheat them. You cannot say, *I will love only this in you and deny all the rest*, and truly love someone. For some unusual reason, I recalled a scripture from the bible about love being patient, kind, enduring, and not jealous or boastful. If I'd ever met a woman that embodied those characteristics, it was Lenorre. Okay, so most Christians would look aghast at the fact that Lenorre had shared me with another woman, let alone another vampire, and the simple fact that I'm lesbian. The whole "aghast" thing wasn't hard to come by. But in truth, none of us had been particularly jealous or boastful last night. It might've been a bit of a play on words, but let's face it, fanatics of so many different flavors have been twisting the meaning of religious texts to suit their own ends since the beginning of time.

As a Pagan, I didn't view what had transpired between us as a sin, and I didn't feel the need to repent for it. I still wasn't thrilled that it had happened, or delighted at the fact that yet again, metaphysics seemed to be complicating my life. But metaphysics or no, we'd all had our hands in the cookie jar and there wasn't a damn thing I could do about it now.

I found a pair of charcoal slacks I'd left at Lenorre's for work and paired them with a white T-shirt. I was running out of clothes and would have to make a trip back to my abandoned apartment soon. I thought of Rupert, whom I hadn't seen or heard from in nearly a week. I guessed he was busy, either working at his shop, Guns Unlimited, or maybe he'd taken an out of state gig, as he too was a licensed paranormal hunter.

It wasn't anything out of the ordinary to not hear from him for weeks. Rupert wasn't really a call-you-up-and-chat-about-how's-your-day kind of guy. No, break-into-your-house-to-see-what's-up was more Rupert's style. Though, to my relief, he'd only done that once when Lenorre and I had first started seeing each other.

I rang Arthur after dressing and let him know Zaphara's spell was most definitely a go tonight. We briefly discussed our plan of action. Zaphara would use the spell to summon the astral being and bend it to her will. She was confident she could force it to track down the witch that had summoned it and assured me she could pry a location from it. If we got a location, I would call Arthur and let him know where the killer was hiding and what to look for. When I'd asked Zaphara why she was sure she could find the murderer, she seemed annoyed with me and so I'd stopped asking questions, figuring the Daoine Maithe knew what she was doing. Chasing down astral spirits was a completely new area to me. However, I was sure of one thing: if it didn't work, we were screwed. We couldn't exactly catch it and haul it down to the station.

I'd also just gotten off the phone with Hunter Kinsley to let her know I was still working on the case but hadn't yet put it to a close, when Zaphara placed a book back on one of the shelves. We stood in Lenorre's library, and I knew each and every book belonged to Lenorre and could tell by that musky paper scent that some were very old. Shelves lined each of the four walls from floor to ceiling. The highest shelf was tall enough that even Zaphara and Lenorre would need to step on something to reach it. The books were well kept and dust free. I didn't know if it was Lenorre's doing or if one of the other residents maintained it, but it was cozy.

Zaphara picked something up off the table and handed it to me.

"The necklace has not been spelled although it has been blessed," she said. "It will not harm you to wear it. It may actually serve as beneficial."

I held the necklace up, inspecting it. "Do you think that's why Astrid gave it to me?"

"For protection?" Zaphara asked with an expression that told me she was only partially listening.

I nodded and she must've caught it out of her peripheral vision, because she wasn't watching me when she said, "Yes. Onyx is a particularly good stone at helping one shield against astral spirits. The septagram is also a good symbol to focus on when calling to the faerie magic in your veins."

I put the necklace on, feeling a barely noticeable rush of warmth where it rested over my shirt. For a moment, I panicked, catching the septagram and holding it away from my body.

"That's the blessing you're feeling, Kassandra. You're not likely to burst into flames."

I felt more than saw Lenorre enter the library, and I let go of the charm, assuring myself that it wasn't silver. No, silver wouldn't burst into flame when I touch it, but it does itch and burn like fuck, and the rash that accompanies it is just *not* sexy.

The rich and seductive smell of Lenorre's perfume permeated my senses, making me turn to find her as if she had a collar set about my neck. She'd changed into a pair of skinny jeans that were tucked into a pair of cuffed boots. A black velvet waistcoat cinched at her waist, white lace blossomed at her wrists and throat, though the collar of the shirt had been left opened, offering glimpses of the flesh beneath it that was nearly as white.

Lenorre's delicious lips curved in a mysterious smile, letting me know she acknowledged and appreciated the attention I gave. She came to me, burying her fingers in my hair and kissing my cheek. I touched her hand, twining my fingers with hers, feeling the coolness of her energy tangling with my warmth, setting my soul and the beast within at ease.

"Is all prepared?" she asked Zaphara.

"It is. I'm ready when you two are."

"Kassandra?" Lenorre asked.

"Zaphara, would you leave the room for a moment?"

Zaphara didn't answer me with words, but she did leave the library. Lenorre waited until the door clicked closed to ask, "Kassandra, what is it?"

If her hair had been unbound, I would've buried my fingers in it to bring her mouth down to mine. As it was, it spilled down her back in a cascade of curls held captive by the same ribbon she'd been wearing earlier. I stood high on my toes, lacing my fingers behind her neck. Her lips found mine and I kissed her, putting my entire body into it.

I pulled away, rather reluctantly, feeling the quiet murmur and sweet hum of my blood.

"Is that all?" she asked.

I brushed her cheek with the tips of my fingers, before lowering myself flat on my feet. "And I love you," I said.

Lenorre didn't say it back. She didn't need to. I was almost to the door when her hand caught my wrist. She used the grip she had to spin me around and pull me up against her body.

She kissed me slowly, sensually, as if savoring the taste of me.

When she drew back, her breath tickled my skin and my throat burned. "And I love you."

We left the library holding hands, our fingers laced together, anchoring us to each other and mirroring the bond in our hearts. Lady only knew what kind of darkness we were about to walk into, but Lenorre let me know with tender devotion that we walked into it together.

Zaphara was waiting outside the door. Eris and Rosalin were approaching from the end of the hall closest to Lenorre's room. They walked apart, but Rosalin looked more like herself than she had when I'd found her in the dining room. Relief flooded through me and I tried to hold on to the hope all around me.

I really didn't like the idea of facing the night hag again. I liked the idea of everyone risking their lives even less. They were some of the bravest, most interesting people—preternaturals—I'd ever known. I didn't like the idea of anything bad happening to any of them, to any of us. Even Zaphara and her weirdness.

I found it oddly touching.

I swallowed a little too loudly over the stitch in my throat.

"What's wrong with you?" Rosalin asked as she approached.

"Nothing," I said, trying to blink away my blurred vision.

"Are you…are you about to cry?"

"No," I said. Clearly, she didn't believe me, but she didn't bother pressing me about it.

Lenorre's hand squeezed mine, a comforting reminder that she was there and hadn't failed to catch whatever expression or thoughts flickered across my face. I returned the gesture as we made our way to the upper levels, trying to focus on the task ahead and to ignore the whole kick-ass paranormal huntress turned sappy werewolf moment.

Zaphara made it clear when we entered the wooded area behind Lenorre's house that she was going to be the ringleader. She'd brought a bag with her that I assumed she'd used to carry whatever supplies she needed. She picked an area that had a small break in the trees and walked an observational circle.

"This will work," she said, coming to me and kneeling to begin pulling supplies out of the bag. "I'll need your help casting the circle."

"I know how to cast a circle by pagan definitions," I said, "is that what you're asking me to do?"

"Your pagan practices are based off ours," she said. "So it is similar, with a few minor differences. I don't want you to call any quarters, not with words." She handed me a small vial of what appeared to be water and a seashell that was slightly larger than my hand. "We will use the elemental representations to attract the elements and create a barrier."

I thought I understood what she meant. In a pagan or Wiccan ritual, the elemental representations usually went on a witch's altar. When a witch cast a circle, she would go to each of the four corners and use words of invocation to summon the guardians of each element. Zaphara wanted to use the elements to anchor the spell, so to speak. Each corner, or direction, corresponds with an element. I went to the eastern edge of the circle, placed the shell on its back, removed the tiny cork stopper, and poured the water into it.

I turned to find Zaphara placing a large crystal at the northern point, symbolizing the earth element. I was about to stand when she, without turning to look at me, said, "Visualize, Kassandra. Do not be hasty."

"What do you mean?"

She shook her head, murmuring something about *witches* and *sloppy*. She knelt beside me, touching my shoulder. "Lower your shields," she said.

I drew in a deep breath and lowered my shields when I exhaled. The night became more vibrant, thrumming against my skin.

Zaphara shut her eyes, lips parting slightly. I watched as she breathed, slow and steady, hearing her breath like lapping waves.

The water in the shell rippled as if she'd dipped a finger into it.

"Call the element," she said. She put a hand over her heart. "Feel it here, in your body, your breath, your blood. When it comes to your aid"—she swept her hand high above the shell of water, and a tiny wave splashed some of it over the edge—"you'll feel it…like a quiet click."

A quiet click was a good description. With my shields lowered, I felt the small energy that unfurled as if someone had traced wet fingers across my skin.

Lenorre, Rosalin, and Eris stood off to the side and I could feel them silently observing. Zaphara handed me a bowl made of some kind of stone and a piece of charcoal. When she headed back toward the northern edge, I asked, "What am I supposed to light this with, exactly?"

"Consider it a test of sorts." She knelt in front of the crystal. "Use your will." She touched the crystal and it seemed to come to life beneath her fingers, glowing ever so faintly. I realized if I looked at it straight on, it looked like nothing more than a crystal, but when I caught it out of my peripheral vision, I could see the faint amethyst light of her energy igniting it. It was definitely weird, but then again, I'd seen her bless a wooden stake and draw a faerie star in the air above it like it was a neon sign. The gift of sight, she'd called it. Rosalin had been in the room and though she admitted she couldn't actually see anything, she was a lycanthrope and she'd felt it. I had no doubts that she and the vampires standing outside the circle could feel what we were doing.

I sighed. Perhaps Zaphara was merely amusing herself or maybe she was trying to prove a point…that she could do things I couldn't.

I placed the items on the ground at the southern corner and sat back on my heels. I'd had years to practice visualization and working with the raven energy and the wolf within over the last few months had given me even more practice to fine-tune it. But when I visualized fire, the images had their way with me, coming to me without much of a conscious thought. I saw Lenorre's moonlight skin, kissed by firelight, the flicker of it darkening her stormy eyes, sketching shadows across her features.

The heat was low in my belly, spilling outward toward my limbs. Desire, passion, a dancing fire. I forced myself to hold the image, to make it clearer.

Hold the coal, Zaphara's voice in my mind was smooth and flowing. *Push your magic into it.*

The vision was so vivid that I didn't dare open my eyes, for risk of losing it entirely. I placed my hand over the coal and curled my fingers around it.

Somewhere in the back of my mind, I could hear wood popping and crackling, the fire eating its way through. The image encouraged the energy, pushing it, feeding it, until the warmth of it spilled down my arm, my fingers pulsing with it.

The coal in my hand hissed to life as a tiny plume of smoke rose to tickle my nostrils. Only then did I open my eyes and place the coal down carefully, safely sheltered by stone to prevent it from going out or starting a fire.

I heard Rosalin whisper, "Hell yeah."

Zaphara had returned to kneel beside me, overseeing, I guess.

"I didn't know I could do that."

She cocked her head in a manner that would've made any crow proud. "Had you ever tried?"

"Well, no."

Her expression was a wily one. "Now you know."

"What else can I do?"

"We will get to that, eventually," she said, sounding rather furtive about it. She offered a hand to help me up and I took it. "Shall we proceed?" I realized everything was in its place. The small points of her amethyst lights glowed like will-o'-the-wisps, marking each element she'd invoked. She'd called all of them except for the one I had, except for fire. Where the charcoal piece was placed, a soft emerald glow burned.

Was that my energy? Holy shit.

A bundle of feathers hung from a tree branch in the east, marking the element of air. How long had I been visualizing? It hadn't seemed it'd been terribly long, but I couldn't remember Zaphara invoking the other element.

Zaphara returned to her bag, picked it up, and knelt in the center of the circle we'd created. Inside the circle, the cold night seemed warmer. I couldn't actually see the circle, only the marker points of it where Zaphara's and my energy shone like dim lights, infusing the items and staking the point into the ground.

She used her boots to kick clear an area of dirt, drawing an athame from the tuck of one and tracing something in the dirt itself, the thin metal blade sliding through the dirt with ease.

I stood slightly to her side, watching her work.

When she sat back on her heels, she curled her fingers around the blade.

"The chalice, Kassandra."

I found what appeared to be a silver chalice in the bag and tucked my hand inside my sleeve, not touching it with my bare fingers.

The knife hissed through Zaphara's skin and blood fell freely to the ground. She snatched the chalice and held her hand over it.

The chalice itself didn't surprise me, as many witches and wiccans would've used a chalice in ritual to symbolize the mother's womb, the divine feminine. The athame didn't surprise me either, symbolizing all that was male, phallic. It wasn't sexual. It was simply polarity at play. And though it was made to pierce, a witch's ritual dagger was often never used to draw blood.

But that was the lighter side of Wicca and witchcraft; that was the human idea.

Zaphara guided her hand over the chalice, her blood splashing down into it.

The air inside the circle seemed even hotter, making it more difficult to breathe, as though I was drawing things thicker than air into my lungs.

The wound closed in her hand, nearly as quickly as it had opened, and she split her skin again, and again, until the chalice was over halfway full of her blood.

The symbol she had drawn in the dirt was similar to the sigil I'd seen at the crime scenes. The same eight-pointed star, the same symbol in the middle, but it was the outside symbols she'd adjusted. And none of them looked familiar to me. I hate not knowing what I'm looking at. Especially when whatever we were calling could potentially kill us.

She murmured something and every freaking hair on my arm stood straight up.

Zaphara drew her hand back and flung the contents of her chalice out over the symbol.

The sound following the lash of power she flung outward thundered through the woods like an angry sky that had just opened up above us.

Chapter Twenty-six

The atmosphere inside the circle crackled with energy. I wasn't sure if I was actually hearing it or if I felt it and by feeling it, imagined I'd heard it. While the air was abuzz, Zaphara took out a length of white braided rope. The earth seemed to swallow her bloody symbol, burning deeper trenches where her drawing had been. She set about folding the rope in a neat circle around the symbol, a circle inside a circle. I thought I understood what she was doing. When she was done, she held the double-sided dagger in her hand, took my wrist between her fingers, and slashed the blade across my open palm. The cut stung, making me hiss through my teeth.

"I need you to combine your power with mine," she said, as if explaining, but she didn't really explain anything. She slashed her palm again.

"Quickly," she said, "before our wounds close. Take my blood into your body."

"You want me to drink your blood?" I asked.

"There is no time for qualms, Kassandra. I've summoned the Hag."

She raised my hand to her mouth and I felt her tongue tracing the wound, licking my skin clean as my body healed it.

Zaphara didn't offer her hand as much as shove it in my face. I frowned, but raised my hand to cup hers, bringing it to my lips. I licked the blood that had trailed down her fingers to the center of her palm where the original cut had been. The taste of Zaphara's blood was smooth and velvety, only lightly metallic. Without the taint of cinnamon from Lenorre's mouth, the taste was fresher, richer. I found it odd.

Somewhere in the back of my mind, I felt the wolf agreeing with me. Good, but odd.

Before I could ask, "What next?" Zaphara grabbed the back of my head and kissed me, her tongue delving between my lips. I staggered and was about to push her away when I felt it. She pushed her power into my mouth and it felt like honey sliding down my throat. She held me against her tightly, her arms like shackles, her lips locked on mine, sending warmth into my belly. At the touch of her lips and power, the magic awakened.

I pushed into the kiss, taking control of it, and forcing the energy that rose from me into Zaphara's lean body.

She stepped back, breaking the kiss. I could suddenly feel every movement ripple through her, her spine when it straightened, her foot being placed slightly behind her. The movement vibrated through me, as if we had been caught in a web and every time she moved, I could feel the strands pulling at my skin. But it wasn't my skin her movement tugged at, every chakra on my body felt like it had been fixed into hers.

Zaphara stood before the circle she'd created, fingering a milky stone in her hands. She mumbled more words, harshly accented. I had a second to wonder if she was speaking Gaelic when she threw the stone into the middle of the circle. The stone sparked, as if holding a cloud of lightning inside it before I could taste smoke and ashes on my tongue.

Inky blackness formed above the stone. It was the same blackness I'd seen at the police department. I was sure of it. I'd thought she would've invited the others into the circle, but she did not. I stayed close to Zaphara as the black mist shaped itself. The slitted eyes I'd seen at the police station stared at us from within the veil of mist. Limbs began to form and take shape, until I could make out the silhouette of a body nearly as tall as Zaphara's, with mimicking human arms and legs. The figure's hands and feet were tipped with curling talons like some ghoulish bird of prey.

By the silver light of the moon, the creature became whole. Hair the color of dark wood fell to her knees. Her eyes were slitted and narrowed in contempt as she gazed at Zaphara. The dark mist settled over her long body like a continuously moving cloak, sliding over and around her, allowing glimpses of what was clearly a female body underneath.

"You called, Daoine Maithe?" There was a dangerous purr to her tone.

Zaphara's voice when it came was as sharp as steel, less honeyed, more cold. "I, Zaphara, Daughter of Danann, call you and command you. Tell me your true name."

"My name," the being mused, "my name spins on the tip of a needle, is etched within ancient stone. It can be heard in the sighs between lovers."

I felt Zaphara's fingers curl into fists.

"You'll not hear my name from my lips, Daoine Maithe."

"Then I will cast you back to the black lands." Zaphara drew the dagger from the belt at her waist.

Before she'd raised the dagger high enough to place it against her palm, the being said, "Wait."

We waited.

"Why do you call?"

"Kassandra, tell her."

The being looked at me then, and it was as if she'd just seen me. She'd been so focused on Zaphara, maybe she did.

"I remember you, little one," she said, lips curling as if she were pleased.

"I don't care about your name," I said, even though I knew Zaphara sought it to gain power over the fey. "I want the name of the witch that's been helping you."

She was moving to the edge of the circle closest to us. When she reached the white rope, she looked down, stopping in her tracks.

The expression on her face when she looked at me was dark and calculating. She moved close enough to us that I stepped back.

Her nostrils flared as she inhaled a sharp breath, her face contorting into an expression more animal than the human form should have allowed.

"Make me whole," she said. "I'll not only give you the witch, I'll take you to her myself."

I shook my head. "I don't know how to make you whole, and considering the possible repercussions, I'd rather not."

She shrugged her shoulders. "Then you'll not gain anything from me." She glared at Zaphara. "You, Daoine Maithe, you know how to make me whole. Give me what I ask, and I'll give you what you ask in kind."

"You were exiled for a reason, harpy."

The fey laughed bitterly, her voice ringing throughout the woods. "You think?" she asked. "And what reason was that other than for the satisfaction of an envious queen?" She spat on the ground.

Zaphara was utterly quiet, her only response the steely blankness of her features.

"What does she mean?" I asked.

"She hasn't told you?" The fey crossed her arms over her chest, looking none-too-happy as she stared down Zaphara. "Her kind would have wiped out our entire existence, if they could have. As it was, they could not. Lesser though they view us, we are not so easily killed, and so her *queen* banished us to the black lands, the land of eternal night, out of her own jealous spite."

"She banished you for a very good reason, hag."

"I am one of the Leanan Sidhe, Daoine Maithe. Use my title," she snarled. "Your precious queen had a horde of Leanan lovers and when one, her favorite, betrayed her by sleeping with one of her elite, she cast us all into the hell she'd created."

"She banished you because you were killing our people."

"You're a fool," she said. "We didn't begin killing until we were thrust into the dark world and only then for means of survival."

"I saw the corpses," Zaphara said. "You'll not fill my head with lies and illusions. I was there when the queen exiled you."

"Queen's corpses!" she retorted. "She killed her own brethren and used us as scapegoats. Easy to believe, for those who do not know that the Queen is part Leanan herself."

"Zaphara, what the hell is she talking about?"

"She's implying the Queen of the Daoine Maithe is part Leanan and murdered her own people."

"Implying?" Her chestnut brows rose high on her elegant brow. "I do not imply. I know it to be fact. I saw it before I was *banished*."

"So what you're saying is that you've been framed?" I asked, not bothering to conceal that I wasn't quite buying her story.

"Yes, witch."

"Why should I believe that?" I asked, holding up a finger. "One, you've murdered on this plane." I held up another finger. "Two, you attacked me." I held up another finger. "Three, you attacked another woman. And four," I said, "you attacked me *again*. If you were so wrongfully accused and you are not a creature of ill intent, why the track record?"

"I have no other choice," she said. "I want out. We were a peaceful people once. Don't you remember, Zaphara?"

Zaphara seemed to be thinking very hard.

"Who had you known or heard of that had been murdered by our kind before the mass death among the Daoine? Who had you known before your queen went on her killing spree?" she asked. "No one, I assure you. We are lovers, not fighters or murderers." She looked at me. "Release me and I will prove it to you."

I was unsure what to do. My own internal idea of justice seemed to be battling it out with my caution and distrust. What if it were all a trick?

Zaphara remained silent and so I asked, "Do you believe her?"

"I do not know," Zaphara said and I was pretty sure it was the first time I'd ever truly heard her sound uncertain about something. "I'll not fall for any tricks. If you want me to believe you, if what you say is true, then give me your true name."

"So you can command me for all eternity? I think not."

"Then your mind will rot in the black lands. We're done here. If you'll not give your name or the name of the witch that's leashed you, we have nothing to gain from each other."

"Wait! Wait!"

Zaphara lowered the blade again. "Yes?"

"I want your oath you'll not make of me a puppet thing."

"I do not seek your name to make of you a puppet," Zaphara said. "You know why I seek it."

The Leanan Sidhe waved a hand in the air. "Yes, yes, to ensure that I do not go on a murderous rampage, as your queen did centuries ago."

"Tell me your name."

The Leanan raised those eerie inhuman eyes and said, "My name is Avaliah."

Zaphara said, "Shit."

Avaliah grinned widely in response.

Zaphara moved, but she was too late. Avaliah stepped out of the circle and grabbed me. The world went black.

I hit the ground with a heavy thud, feeling hard rock beneath my hands and knees. If I had fallen, I didn't know where exactly I'd fallen from.

Avaliah's voice crept from the darkness.

"Welcome to Oíche," she said. "Land of eternal night. Beautiful, isn't it?"

A white flame flared to life in her cupped palm, illuminating the impenetrable darkness.

As far as I could see, there was nothing, nothing but mountains and black sky.

"Can you imagine spending all of an eternity here?" she continued. "No food, no water, no sustenance, no life, no death. A vast nothingness, a meaningless existence."

The shadows that had been cloaked around her figure became a black cloak in truth. Owl feathers decorated the long brown waves of her hair. She turned to me, and her eyes had changed, reminding me more of Rosalin's honeyed gaze.

"Why have you brought me here?" I sat back on my heels, feeling uncomfortable and cursing myself for not wearing a weapon.

"I will tell you a story before the Daoine Maithe calls me back and retrieves you from my clutches," she said, coming to kneel in front of me. She touched my jaw and I recoiled from her. "You do not know who I am?"

"Should I?" I asked.

She seemed to consider me before lightly shaking her head. "No, you are too young and not one of the Daoine. I can smell the fey in you, but you are not like them." She rose, giving me the view of her back.

"Make yourself comfortable," she said. "So long as you do not raise hand against me, I will not harm you."

"Why the sudden change of heart?" I asked. "You seemed more than ready and willing to kill me when you attacked me. Twice."

She looked down her perfect nose at me. "What I told you is truth. If I wanted to kill you, I would not have brought you here."

I got to my feet. "Then what do you want?"

"Justice."

The word hung heavy in the air, like an apple swinging from a branch.

"Medb is not the perfect queen she'd have everyone believe."

"Wait," I said. "The Medb? The Queen of Connacht, Cattle-Raid of Cooley, Medb?"

Avaliah's answer was smooth, "The Queen of the Daoine Maithe, *Medb*. The Medb in your mythology texts only bears resemblance in name and the amount of lovers. The mythos has become tangled and there have been several rulers bearing the same name. I would not rely on it for what I am about to tell you. Humans have always recorded history according to the whims of power and perception, not truth and fact."

"Why did Zaphara startle when you told her your name?"

"Allow me to introduce myself." She turned to face me more fully and for the first time, I realized the Leanan Sidhe in front of me bore a certain resemblance to the Daoine Maithe I'd grown to know. Her cheekbones were high, her jawline smooth and slightly pointed. "I am Avaliah, Queen of the Leanan Sidhe, Daughter of Óengus the young."

I let Avaliah know with a look that whatever she'd just fucking said went completely over my head.

She sighed. "Medb was my lover, once."

"That means what, exactly?"

"Well," she said, almost thoughtfully, "it means that Medb is a bleedin' hypocrite. I did mention she had multiple lovers, did I not?"

Slowly, I nodded.

"We were to unite our courts," she said, "the Leanan Sidhe and the Daoine. The one truth I will give her is that I did seduce a noblewoman of her court, but the Leanan have never been the murderers she's painted us as."

I still found that hard to believe. I mean, she had attacked me twice, and I'd seen the ruins of the mortal woman she'd left behind.

As if she had heard my thoughts, she said, "I have only killed because I have no other choice, Kassandra. I cannot live this damned existence, and if I must kill to break its hold on me, I will."

Where was Zaphara? What had happened to the woods? Lenorre? Rosalin? Eris?

"I'll follow the Daoine Maithe's orders. If she binds me I won't be able to kill anyone, but I will set things right and fight with every breath in me for our place in the world."

"I've seen that look before and it's usually followed by blood and vengeance."

"It's true, it stirs in my breast," she said. "But I've no desire to be chained to your human witch. When you wake, you will know everything about her that I do and may call upon your human police to find her." She touched my hair, and again, I recoiled. An expression of perplexity and deep thought passed over her features. "We'll meet again, raven witch."

"Wait," I said and she waited.

"Yes?"

"Why bring me here? Why couldn't you have told me these things in front of Zaphara and the others?"

"Because there are two sides to every story," she said, appearing amused. "And I wanted *you* to hear mine."

She touched me and the dark world of Oíche fell away.

Chapter Twenty-seven

True to her word, I woke. I came back to myself in the woods behind Lenorre's house. Rosalin was with me.

"Where's my phone?" I asked. "Where are the others?"

Rosalin startled. "They went with Zaphara to look for you. I volunteered to wait here just in case."

I nodded, shoving my hands into the pockets of my jeans. They were empty.

Rosalin handed me her cell phone. "Here, use mine," she said.

I could've sworn I'd grabbed my phone before coming out to the woods, but took the one she offered and dialed Arthur's number. Avaliah's knowledge filled my head like weeks' worth of experience, as if I'd been the one summoned and not her.

Arthur answered on the second ring.

"Did it work?"

"Yeah," I said. Sure, why not? It might not have gone quite like we'd wanted it to, but everyone was still standing. I hoped. "Miranda Blevins," I said, "she's staying in a motel room a few blocks away from the police station." I closed my eyes, seeing the sign, room number. I spouted the information off to him.

"She's the one that's been summoning and controlling the fey. She's your murderer. She killed her husband. You'll find his body somewhere along the northern edge of Kielder Lake, along with the car stashed in a bunch of trees."

It seemed as though Avaliah had seen everything. I knew there were traces of blood left in Miranda's silver Impala. Knew she'd used the car to transport her Great Dane and Landon's body to the lake. I knew that his frame was smaller than hers. For some reason, I'd imagined Miranda to be petite, but in Avaliah's memories, she wasn't.

I knew what she knew, and her knowledge haunted me.

Leana Davey.

I shook my head, not wanting that specific memory.

Avaliah had pleasured her while she killed her, using her magic to make Leana completely compliant and utterly willing as she strangled her, taking her half-fey life force and using it for her own personal gain as she sought to escape the astral realm.

"Got it," he said. "I'm heading out there with Ackerman to find Miranda Blevins and sending another team out to search for the body and the vehicle."

"There's blood in the vehicle," I said. "Any word on pulling that guy in from out of town? You're going to need an expert."

"Leave that to me," Arthur said. "I'll call you after we make the arrest."

He hung up. I closed Ros's phone and handed it back to her.

I heard a twig snap and raised my head.

Lenorre stood several feet away, watching me. "Are you well?"

"I'm fine," I said. Why did it feel like I was saying that a lot lately? Then again, considering the possibilities, *fine* wasn't such a bad answer.

"Arthur's going to call me after they make the arrest."

"So I heard."

"Where's Zaphara?"

"Searching with Eris for Avaliah."

"Is Zaphara going to try and kill her?" I asked. "She didn't harm me."

"No, I believe she is more concerned with placing restrictions upon her."

I didn't blame her for that, not one little bit. I felt it in my bones, how easily Avaliah would kill for herself, but not just herself, for her cause, her people. If it was a matter of taking energy to get the hell out of Dodge, she'd do it. And the only reason she'd been able to set foot in our world, to reach beyond Oíche in the first place, was thanks to Miranda Blevins and the victims she'd offered up.

"Her true name allows Zaphara to control her?"

"With the fey, it is so. To know the name of a being is to have power over it. If the being willingly offers their *true* name."

I sighed. "Fuck," I said, "this is going to be a long night."

"So?" Rosalin asked. "What's going on?"

I stood, brushing off my jeans. "I'll explain on the way to the house."

We walked toward the house while I explained, relying on the portion of memories Avaliah had somehow left in my head.

Could she have tricked me? Probably, but I didn't sense she had or why she would have.

She could have killed me.

It was unnerving knowing every little detail of what had transpired between Avaliah and Miranda, hearing Miranda's words of invocation, calling Avaliah with blood sacrifice, the elven blood of her husband, an offering.

Knowing that she'd slaughtered two dogs to summon Avaliah made me grit my teeth in anger.

It was dark and dire magic, a selfish pact, Avaliah's search for freedom, for herself and her people, and Miranda's relentless desire to have a child at any cost. Even if she had to kill her husband and countless others to achieve it.

"You'll make me fertile? You'll give me the child I desire, if I do this for you? If I find the power source you need?"

"Yes," Avaliah had said, though in memory, it seemed as though my lips had spoken the words.

❖

A couple of hours later I found myself standing in Arthur's office at the police station with Zaphara in tow. If we were going to sit and have a little talk with Miranda Blevins, I actually wanted

Zaphara with me. Arthur was sitting behind his desk, leaning back in his chair, and staring at her.

"She's a faerie?"

"She's one of the Daoine Maithe," I said.

Zaphara hadn't been entirely thrilled when I asked her to join me in paying Arthur a visit. She wasn't too keen on being surrounded by human law enforcement. Lenorre had insisted and at that, Zaphara had obliged without further disagreement or protest.

The team Arthur had put together had done their job. They found Miranda in her motel room and made the arrest. The other team had found the car and Landon's body at Kielder Lake. I knew Forensics was there, collecting evidence that would hold up in court. I wondered how much of the story they'd omit for the newspapers. I'd learned from Arthur that Johnas Bardsley, a DNA expert from Kansas University, was flying down to lend a hand.

Arthur didn't nod or really acknowledge that I'd said anything. Instead, he changed the subject. "She knows what we're holding her for," he said, talking about Miranda, "but she continues to deny all of it."

"You've got the evidence," I said. "She can only deny it for so long."

"I'm going to ask you to do something I've never asked you to do," he said.

"What?" My brows went up with the question.

"Get a confession out of her."

I turned to Zaphara, searching her expression, trying to figure out if she'd help or hinder me.

The corners of Zaphara's mouth curled darkly.

"I have an idea, if the detective isn't too squeamish about it."

"What's your idea?"

"I want to bring in a witness," Zaphara said rather evasively.

"Who?" Arthur asked, folding his arms over his desk and leaning forward.

"The fey that Miranda Blevins summoned," I said, looking at Zaphara.

"The thing that fucking attacked us in the interrogation room?" Arthur's mouth practically hung open in disbelief and shock. "Hell no," he said stubbornly. "I'm not inviting that thing to come play on our playground."

"Arthur," I said, "it may be the only way to get a confession out of Miranda. If she knows the fey she was working with betrayed her, she might confess."

"No," he said again, stubbornly shaking his head. "Holbrook will have my ass for that. No."

"She was being manipulated, Detective. The witch had bound the fey with magic," Zaphara said. "I had to return her free will to her by breaking the magic the witch had wielded. She bound her with blood and sacrifice. The fey had no other choice but to act on her master's whims. I assure you, she will not harm anyone in this department."

I had Avaliah's memories and knew Zaphara's words were only partial truth. If Zaphara hadn't bound Avaliah to her, Goddess only knows what she'd do.

Arthur appeared reluctant, but said, "Our medical examiner has evidence that the hands that strangled Leana Davey were larger than human. We have evidence against her."

"You can't arrest her, Arthur, even if she was fully on this plane. She has the power and ability to evade arrest."

"If you do this, it's off the books," he said.

"You want a confession," Zaphara said. "I can give it to you."

"Then do it," Arthur said. Zaphara left the room before I could even ask her how she was going to do it.

Would she offer her blood to call Avaliah? Had she bound Avaliah to her? I didn't understand the mechanics of it and was curious to know, but some things you're really better off not knowing. I had a feeling this was one of those.

Arthur picked a file up off his desk and led the way to the interrogation room.

❖

As I remembered in Avaliah's memories, Miranda Blevins was a tall woman. Her blond hair fell in layers to her shoulders, highlights of gold and copper streaked through it. She sat behind the interrogation table, zip cuffs at her wrists and ankles.

I guess some part of me expected to see remorse in her, maybe guilt, shame, some human emotion, but the only emotion I found written on her features was anger. Anger flashed in her eyes. I knew without asking that she was angry because she was cuffed and bound and about to be subjected to another line of questioning. Such was a part of the job description: question until they break.

Getting a suspect to snap in their fury of being caught worked just as well as guilt. Sometimes, it worked even better. You just had to hope they didn't manage to kill you in the process.

Miranda Blevins hid behind the mask of her anger. The look she gave us when we entered was boiling.

Apparently, someone had a bit of *sociopathic bitch* mixed into her coffee.

I followed Arthur's lead, sitting in a chair on the opposite side of the table. Arthur didn't bother introducing me. He opened the manila folder he'd carried in and slid pictures out across the table.

Miranda Blevins didn't bother looking at them. She fixed her seething gaze on him.

I made a mental note to myself. Miranda didn't look down at the photographs on the table because she didn't want to face what she'd done. It wasn't that she didn't know what she'd done was wrong; it was that she was unwilling to face it overall. She was in a deep state of denial, refusing to acknowledge her trespasses.

"I'm sure you remember Leana Davey," Arthur said. "She belonged to a group you and your husband had once attended. We have a witness to confirm that they've seen you before and that you had ties to her."

He slid the photograph of Leana Davey's lifeless face toward Miranda, who continued to refuse to look at it.

"I believe this is your Great Dane," Arthur continued, and I looked down at the next photograph he placed on the table. I hadn't known they'd found the dog. As soon as my mind made sense of the picture, I turned away. The dog was lying in straw-like grass, its stomach slit wide open, everything falling out and pooling beside it.

Arthur dropped the folder, ignoring the contents that spilled out, acting as if he'd given up. "We know everything," he said. "The dogs you sacrificed, the murder of your husband, the ritual, the symbol…We know everything, Mrs. Blevins. We know what it means."

"I don't know what you're talking about," she said, and the sound of her voice was oddly small and childlike.

"I'm a practicing witch and a preternatural investigator, Mrs. Blevins, and yes, you do know what we're talking about. The eight-pointed star," I said, gesturing for Arthur to find the photograph and hand it to me. I took it up and continued, "The alchemical symbol for sulfur, used when summoning darker entities. Ceres, the mother, a representation of yourself, the full moon, your desire for fertility. I know everything, Miranda. You might as well give it up."

"No," she said, rather defiant. "You don't know everything, obviously."

"I know how you branded Leana Davey," I said, remembering the coal igniting between my hands. "How you marked her for the Sidhe, how you offered up a human life in exchange for the life you'd hoped to gain in your womb. A small gift of magic," I said. "You're a halfling, as was your husband, Landon. Fey and elven. I know that the elven blood in his body made him a richer, more substantial sacrifice for the fey. What I don't know is, did he offer his life willingly, Miranda, or did you rape him of it? The police have found the ritual dagger you tossed into the lake. They might not find traces of your DNA on it, but I am confident the blood you missed in the backseat of the car, near the passenger's side door, will be very beneficial in tying you to this murder."

Miranda didn't say anything. She didn't need to. I gauged her reaction, the twitch of muscle in her left arm, the flicker of an eyelid. I was hitting too close to home.

Good.

Every interrogator has a style and mine tends to be a bit subtle before I switch gears and play the game of *In Your Face*.

I was steadily shifting gears, as I'd once done with Carver, trying to reach into his darkness to get a confession from him, just like I did with Miranda Blevins.

"How did it feel, Miranda, watching your husband bleed to death from the wound you'd created? It was slow, wasn't it? Slower than you ever dreamed it would be. Did you catch him by surprise? Did he plead with you to stop? Did you consider it? Or did the rush of power thrill you?"

"Stop," she said, that one word croaked.

I pushed my chair back and placed my palms flat on the table. "Why should I?"

"Because it's not true!"

Everyone in the room startled when the door to the interrogation room opened. Zaphara entered with a woman trailing behind her. The woman's oaken-colored hair spilled past her shoulders. Her eyes were a light amber-flecked brown. Arthur didn't recognize her, but I did.

Avaliah entered the room behind Zaphara and even bound, something in the pit of my stomach turned uncomfortably. She wore a flowing brocaded cloak that looked centuries outdated, like she'd just stepped out of some medieval renaissance. Her hands moved, pinning the cloak close to her body. Her long human nails were painted a soft shade of pink.

"There's someone that begs to differ," Zaphara said, stepping away from Avaliah to give Miranda a clear view.

It seemed as though everyone in the room held their breath in anticipation, as if we could all sense what was about to happen.

Everyone except for Avaliah, who stood, tall and proud, looking down the straight line of her nose at the woman zip-tied behind the interrogation table.

The knowledge that she had been betrayed hit Miranda like a brick. I saw her flinch, flinch as if she'd been dealt a blow, and then, she went psychotic.

"You!" She tried to lunge across the table, and smartly, the cops had cuffed her ankles to the chair legs so she couldn't stand, not fully. She fought against her bonds, screaming at Avaliah, raging and threatening.

While she raged, we watched, we listened. Several times she managed to knock the chair stuck to her back into the wall, but she didn't rise; she simply ranted and fought like a rabid dog.

"You said it would work! You told me if I killed him, you would take his seed and give me a child! You lied to me! I killed my husband and you betrayed me!"

I stood and whispered, "There's your confession, Arthur." I had to walk past Zaphara and Avaliah to get to the door. Avaliah's cold expression never altered, but when I made to move past her, she looked down at me.

I had tasted her thoughts. I knew the hardened arrogance within her more intimately than I ever wanted to know.

I pushed past her and headed to the car. As far I was concerned, my part in the case was over and the rest was in Arthur's hands.

Zaphara rode with me on the way back to Lenorre's. Fortunately, Avaliah was not with her.

"You said the necklace would come in handy," I said to her, watching the road ahead lit by the car's headlights. "It didn't stop Avaliah from wolf-napping me or giving me her memories."

"I had not known that we were placed in opposition with the Queen of the Leanan," she said.

"Did you bind her?" I asked.

"Yes, how long it will hold and how far it will stretch, we will see."

I chewed on my bottom lip, a bad habit when I'm thinking. "What does it mean for you, Zaphara? She told me about your courts."

"I've not yet decided." I stopped at an intersection and turned to her. Zaphara stared expressionlessly out the window.

"I imagine it can't be good," I prompted her, as if prying would really get me anywhere with Zaphara.

Of course, it didn't, not really.

"It's not," she said. "If she is lying or telling the truth, it is not good."

"But we don't have to worry about her killing anyone else, do we?"

"For now, no," she said.

"For now," I repeated. "That's comforting."

"I would suggest you continue to wear the necklace the witch gave you. There may come a time when you need it."

"Sorry to say, but I've little faith in a necklace where Avaliah's concerned."

"As is wise," Zaphara said. "Even wiser, I recommend sleeping with it on."

"Why? You think she'll strike again?" Stupid question, really. I didn't realize how ridiculous it was until I asked. I knew that if it aided Avaliah's cause, she'd do it without second thought.

"Being bound to me," she said, "she now has a measure of freedom on top of the power she's been hoarding to move more easily between the land of night and this world. Do not underestimate her, Kassandra."

"I'll keep that in mind."

CHAPTER TWENTY-EIGHT

I was sitting behind my desk at Lyall Investigations, waiting for Hunter to arrive for our scheduled appointment. It was almost five o'clock. Rosalin was with me, perched in a silly inverted mushroom-shaped chair that she'd insisted on bringing into my office. She flipped through a magazine, the pages hissing as she exhaled a deep breath and flicked the corners.

"If you tear that magazine, Rosalin, Rit will have a fit," I said.

When I'd been staking out Kamryn's work, Rosalin had gone with me, keeping me company. A stake out is an atrociously boring and dull thing to do with one's time, which is why I didn't mind the company.

Earlier this afternoon she'd cornered me in Lenorre's kitchen and asked to come to work with me. I agreed, although I blame a lot of that on the fact that she'd asked me before I'd had any caffeine whatsoever. The other thing I blame it on is that Rosalin, for some reason, has a way of making me feel like an ass for saying no, without even saying, "Kassandra, you're being an ass." She just looks at me and I feel it.

June buzzed my desk to let me know that Hunter had arrived fifteen minutes early.

"Go ahead and send her up," I said, releasing the button when I was done speaking.

I'd left the door to my office wide-open and Hunter appeared a few seconds later, wearing a plum-colored long-sleeved shirt with a pair of faded denim jeans.

"Hi, Kassandra."

"Good afternoon, Hunter."

She stopped in front of my desk, burying her hands in the pockets of her jeans. "So?" she asked.

I'd spent the last week working on her case, trying to figure out if her girlfriend was cheating or not. As I said, Rosalin had accompanied me when I'd gone to Al's Diner to watch Kamryn Sherman. I'd parked away from the diner, obviously, finding a spot in the shadows that the Tiburon wouldn't be noticeable in. Having a black car comes in handy.

"She's not cheating," I said, pulling Hunter's file out of my drawer with copies of the photographs I'd taken.

Yes, at times in my line of work I feel like nothing more than a glorified stalker, but I'm good at it and there's a certain thrill to watching people unaware, when they're at ease with themselves, with no walls or guards. To be completely honest, if you've ever watched someone who doesn't know they're being watched (and no, it's not creepy, unless you're hiding outside their window at night), it can be disgusting. Hell, just on my way into work I'd stopped at a red light at an intersection and the guy in the car next to us was going to town chewing on his ink pen, after sticking it in his ear. Yep, we've come so far as a species.

I handed the photographs to Hunter, who took her time going through them.

I knew for sure that Kamryn Sherman wasn't cheating on her. Each night that she'd worked late, Rosalin and I sat in the car, listening to music, chatting, and watching Kamryn sweep, mop, and wipe down tables.

The other reason I knew for certain, was that the last time we'd staked the place out, Kamryn had left early for "lunch," and we'd followed her to a jewelry store several blocks away from the diner.

It was Rosalin's idea to go inside, creative that she is. I may not have gone inside if she hadn't egged me on. We stepped out of the car and Rosalin put her arm around my waist, briefly giving me the rundown of the role she was going to play and the story she'd be telling. She distracted the sales clerk, talking about how we were looking for an engagement ring for our upcoming commitment ceremony and making it sound sweet and convincing. I daresay she should have gone into theater. While Rosalin played her role and gave a marvelous performance, I was busy listening to Kamryn Sherman talking to another employee on the other side of the room. When the woman asked what kind of ring she was looking for, Kamryn explained that she'd been putting in as many hours as she could at work and wasn't too concerned with price. She mentioned Hunter's name when she told the older woman that she planned to propose on Christmas Eve.

Rosalin was shaking her head at the rings the clerk was trying to show her, seemingly unhappy and disappointed with them. The clerk gave me a weird look, probably wondering why I wasn't paying any attention.

I pulled my phone out of my pocket—which, thank the Gods, I hadn't lost—and made some excuse about having to go pick up my mother.

It surprised me to find that not only had Rosalin been slinging a believable lie, but she'd also been listening to Kamryn. On the way out to the car, she slipped her arm around me again, nothing but friendly, and remarked about how what Kamryn was doing was so sweet.

"You going to be okay?" I'd asked her.

"You keep asking me that."

"I care about you; that's all."

"I know." She'd stopped before we'd gotten into the car and gazed at the slate blue sky overhead. "And yeah," she said. "Yeah, I think I'll be okay."

I showed Hunter what she needed to see—proof she wasn't being cheated on and that her girlfriend was being truthful about having to work late. I surmised Hunter had come to me in the first place because she didn't want to feel like one of those insecure, stalker girlfriends and that she wanted someone outside her relationship with Kamryn to give her honesty and facts, not an opinion. Most people probably would've accused or done the "investigation," themselves, but not the were-feline in front of me.

I did not tell her about Kamryn's plans to propose. That, I felt, Hunter should learn on her own.

"Thank you," Hunter said, placing the photographs on my desk. "I appreciate it."

"You're welcome, Hunter."

Rosalin chose that moment to speak up. "You're a lucky woman," she said with a smile that was a bit too knowing.

"What do you mean?" Hunter asked.

"Oh," Rosalin said, "you'll see."

"Ignore her," I told Hunter, before she could start questioning Rosalin. "It'll be fine."

Hunter blinked her uncertainty, but didn't seek to question either of us further. I stood and walked her to the door. Hunter invited me to her house for dinner, and fortunately, I didn't have to come up with a lame excuse to decline.

"I have a date with my girlfriend," I told her the truth. "Maybe some other time."

It occurred to me how awkward it would be sitting down with her and her girlfriend, after I'd been hired to spy on her. How exactly would she have introduced me to Kamryn?

"Sure," Hunter said, smiling softly. "Maybe another time."

When she left, I picked my jacket up off the back of my chair. "Ready?" I asked Rosalin.

She jumped to her feet, closing the magazine and tossing it on my desk. I didn't bother picking it up to put back in Rit's office.

"Think you'll hear from her again?" Rosalin asked on our way out. "She really seems like she needs a friend and she's trying to be yours."

"Really?" I asked. "I hadn't noticed."

Rosalin laughed. "Yeah, really. Why are you so reluctant to make friends with her?"

"Because she's a client."

"Was a client," Rosalin said, giving pause. "And at one point, so was I."

To that, I didn't know what to say, aside from the fact that I obviously don't make friends easily. Besides, deep down I knew that our shared lycanthropy had brought us together as friends. Well, technically Lenorre had brought us together. It had been Lenorre all along. Lenorre who had introduced me to the preternatural community and had advised Rosalin to hire me to find her brother in the first place.

I drove to Lenorre's with a million thoughts in my head.

I didn't know what was going to happen with Sheila and the pack, or how far Sheila would press me, but I had a feeling she would and that we'd see each other again. A knot of unease cinched in my chest. I wasn't exactly relishing the prospect.

Lenorre and I had asked Zaphara to keep watch on Rosalin this evening. We were going to my parents' house for an early Yule dinner. It would be Lenorre's first time meeting my parents, so I didn't invite Rosalin to tag along.

At the end of the day, I often try to force myself not to entertain thoughts of what could happen. Goddess knows, if I went home and fretted about everything I could fret about, I'd never fucking stop.

Sheila, Avaliah, Eris…

I pushed the thoughts aside as best I could.

Tonight was about Lenorre meeting my family.

❖

As it turned out, Lenorre was the one fretting, pacing from her closet to the bathroom, armed with more clothes and hangers than any woman needed.

"Lenorre," I said as she breezed past me and toward the bathroom, stalking across the room like an impatient panther. "It's just my parents. You don't have to get all dressed up."

"It is not *just* your parents," she said, appearing as though I'd insulted her. "It is *your* parents."

I shook my head, falling back against the pillows with a sigh.

"Wear the Grateful Dead T-shirt," I said. "My mother would get a kick out of that."

Lenorre looked at me as if I'd asked her to smell something foul.

"A T-shirt?" she asked, brows arching. "To dinner?"

"You could go sky clad," I said, "but I don't think you want my family making eyes at you."

At that, she seemed even more appalled, turning and disappearing into the bathroom.

"You know," I called to her, "you're too old school for your own good sometimes."

She peeked out at me. "I only desire to leave a good impression and to be worthy of courting their daughter," she said smoothly. "Where is the harm in that?"

I went to her, toying with a curl of her hair. "A gentlewoman," I murmured, thought about my words, and said with a smirk, "Well, sometimes."

She laughed softly and I kissed her. "You'll do fine. Just be yourself. They're not judgmental. Do you think they could be with a daughter like me?"

Lenorre offered a deliberate blink, showing off her long eyelashes. "I am a vampire," she said, as if that explained everything.

It explained some. "And trust me, love, I've brought home much worse."

"That's a comfort," she murmured, before pressing her lips against mine again.

She stepped back, and for the first time, I let myself take in the mess of the bathroom. Clothes and hangers were strewn across the marble countertop like a vampiric whirlwind had hit it. She relented, slipping on a black cardigan V-neck sweater and pulling it down over her hips.

We headed out to the car. When I got behind the wheel, I took her hand in mine, giving it a reassuring squeeze before she had a full-blown panic attack. Lenorre laughed again, stroking the back of my hand with the tips of her fingers. "I'll be all right."

"Good," I said, putting the car into gear. "I was afraid for a moment there I'd lost you."

❖

I'd always been close to my parents. My eldest sibling, Keegan, and I were both closer to them than Makayla had ever been. Makayla was older than me but had estranged herself from the family. As soon as she was of age to bolt out the door, she'd done so, choosing to move in with her boyfriend and his mother. There was enough of an age difference between my siblings and me that I'd grown up almost as an only child. If it weren't for Keegan's brotherly warmth, I would have. Keegan was independent but unlike Makayla, he made an effort to be a part of the family, to be my sibling.

I spotted his dark SUV and parked the Tiburon behind it. Unsurprisingly, I didn't see Makayla's car. My parents' house wasn't anything in size compared to Lenorre's, but it was quaint, and it was home. The porch light was on as Lenorre and I ascended the steps to the porch. A wooden bench swing was set to one side of the door.

"You ready?" I asked.

Lenorre offered the barest of nods, appearing unmoved and pleasantly guarded.

I touched her arm, shaking my head lightly. "Don't," I said. "No guard, Lenorre. No mask. Just be yourself."

Lenorre gazed at me for a long time. After a few moments, she let out a breath, visibly relaxing, shedding the vampiric stoicism that shrouded her in mystery and made her appear every inch the Countess vampire.

"Better?" she asked.

"Better," I said, ringing the doorbell.

Out of all the things we'd faced since we got together, it was strange that this one thing set her slightly off balance. Strange and, well, charming.

It was almost human.

Bailey, my mother's Irish setter, started barking, announcing our arrival.

Keegan swung open the door with a wide and mischievous grin. Before I could say anything, he picked me up and hugged me as if he were trying to crush my ribcage.

"Hey, sis!"

I laughed when he set me back on my feet. Keegan had inherited my father's height, though he was several inches shorter than Lenorre. His eyes, like our parents', were bright and blue. His blond hair was shaggy and almost surfer-like.

"Hey, bro," I said, as Bailey, her tail wagging so hard it shimmied the rest of her coppery form, greeted me.

I'd been to my folks' since I was infected with lycanthropy, though I still hadn't told them or my brother. Bailey, who used to ignore my existence, had decided I was her new best friend and that when I visited, she would follow me everywhere.

My mother didn't understand it.

Whether I told them about the lycanthropy or not, Bailey seemed to know, and she didn't seem to mind.

We stepped into the foyer and I used my legs to try to body-block Bailey so that we could get in. She whimpered at me.

When we made it into the living room, I knelt to scratch her head as Keegan introduced himself to Lenorre.

Fortunately, he didn't try to pick her up and hug her as he'd done to me.

"So," Keegan said, "you're Kassandra's new girlfriend?"

Lenorre said simply, "Yes."

Keegan stared at her as an awkward silence passed between them.

He looked at me, shaking his head. "You sure do know how to pick them, Kass."

Lenorre's brows went up.

"What's that supposed to mean, Keegan?"

"Did you tell mom who your girlfriend is?" he asked.

Lenorre looked at me too, and I fought the urge to squirm under both their gazes. "Mom knows what she needs to know."

"Kassandra," Lenorre said.

"She knows what you are, Lenorre."

"Does she know who I am?"

Keegan laughed. "Judging by that look, I'd say she doesn't."

My mother chose that moment to hobble into the living room on her bad knee. "Hey, kid."

Keegan moved and my mother stopped, taking in Lenorre. Lenorre didn't hesitate; she strode forward to offer her hand. "Mrs. Lyall, 'tis a pleasure to meet you."

My mother stood there, glancing at the hand Lenorre held out. After a few moments, she laughed, shaking her head. "You just don't do anything by halves, do you?" she asked me.

I put my hands in my pockets and shrugged. "Not really. She's a good catch."

"Well," my mother said, taking Lenorre's hand and folding her other hand over their clasped palms with a sincere smile, "if that's the case, I'll take your word for it. Welcome to the family."

Lenorre, my mother, and my brother talked freely. Somewhere during their casual conversation and questions of how we met and how long we'd been together, Bailey sneaked up behind me and started begging for attention, which I gave, ruffling the top of her furry head.

"Start setting the table," my mother said to me when the timer in the kitchen beeped. To Lenorre, she said, "You're welcome to help yourself to Bailey. She's been driving me bonkers all day."

Lenorre tilted her head. I couldn't tell what she was thinking, but I reached out and touched her arm gently. "She's joking and they're harmless. Please, don't run screaming."

The corner of her mouth twitched. "I do not run screaming."

My brother put a hand on Lenorre's shoulder and said, "Then you'll fit right in."

Lenorre might not have been the type to run screaming, but if Bailey didn't get off my heels, I was considering it.

"Bailey!" I exclaimed as we made it into the dining room. "Get off my ass!" Bailey fell back, hesitating for a second with the command. I set the table, sparing glances at Lenorre.

She smiled, reassuring me that she wasn't going to slip out the back.

Halfway through my meal, I excused myself from the table to use my mother's bathroom. I turned the faucet on over the shell-shaped sink, washed my hands, and dried them on the designated blue hand towel.

"Kassandra."

I froze until a strand of hair tickled my cheek and I whipped around to face the mirror.

It was only for a moment, a split second, long enough to blink. I saw Avaliah, her eyes burning with an inner fire.

An owl hooted outside the bathroom window and I jumped, backing up too hard and too fast and hitting the towel rack behind me.

When I looked back to the mirror, the image was gone. I clutched a handful of my shirt, trying to remember how to breathe. A light tap sounded on the door, sending my heart jumping back up into my throat.

"Kassandra?" It was Lenorre's voice. "Are you well?"

I opened the door with shaking hands. "I'm fine."

"You don't look fine." She stepped into the bathroom, investigating.

She brought my attention to the towel rack. I'd knocked a screw loose, leaving it hanging in a way that my mildly OCD mother would notice.

"Shit," I said.

"What happened?"

"I ran into the towel bar, obviously," I grumbled.

"That's not all, Kassandra."

I shook my head. "Not here, Lenorre." I set about trying to push the loose screw back into the wall with my fingers, which worked out well enough to disguise the fact that I'd knocked it loose in the first place. Of course, it'd only disguise it until someone came along to use the towel to dry their hands.

Lenorre took me by the shoulders, turning me to face her, her beautiful features etched with concern. "Kassandra, what happened?"

"I'll tell you later, Lenorre. Not here. It's not a conversation for here and I'm not letting that bitch ruin my night."

Lenorre's mind worked behind her eyes.

"Avaliah?" she asked.

I nodded.

"When we go back out there, stay close to me."

"You don't think she'd try to do anything here, do you?" I asked.

"It wouldn't be in her wisest interest," Lenorre said. She took my trembling hands in hers, pulling me into the circle of her arms. I let her, breathing out a sigh and trying to force myself to relax.

"Calm your beast, Kassandra."

"I'm trying." I could feel her within me, her senses rocked to high alert, pacing uncertainly, uncomfortably, feeling my anxiety as her own.

It made my chest tight. It made me focus harder on breathing.

When I could feel my heartbeat slow against Lenorre's chest, she released me, her energy clinging to my skin like soft snow.

"Thank you." I hadn't realized until she stepped away that she'd been helping, which said something of Lenorre's subtlety.

She pressed her silken mouth against mine, murmuring, "You're welcome."

I licked my lips, tasting her coolness.

Lenorre buried her face in the bend of my neck, our scents mingling like a cool summer night.

"Lenorre?" I interrupted the moment.

"Hmm?"

"You didn't poof on my family, did you?"

Lenorre stood up straight. "Bloody hell," she said.

I laughed.

"What?" she asked.

"I'm taking that 'bloody hell,' as a yes, and well, with your track record, they were going to find out about your poofing abilities, eventually." I laughed again. The corners of her mouth twitched before she let out a quiet chuckle.

"Hey, lovebirds!" Keegan called from the dining room. "You going to join us again anytime soon?"

I peeked out the bathroom door and yelled down the hallway, "Coming!"

"Hope not!" Keegan responded. "Don't think mom would appreciate you using her bathroom for that!"

I heard my mother exclaim, "Keegan!"

When we made it back to the dining room, Keegan was grinning like a twelve-year-old boy.

I sat down, ignoring Bailey as she stirred from the floor at my mother's feet to come sit on the floor by me.

My father engaged Keegan in a conversation about sports as we finished our meal. I was only half-listening, focusing on the only slightly warm food in front of me when a chill made the back of my neck prickle.

I dropped my fork, clinging tightly to the knife in my right hand.

Not now, I thought. *Fucking hell, not again.*

A voice whispered like the dance of leaves across concrete. *Soon.*

Lenorre put her hand over mine, her energy washing over me like cool silk, drowning out that rustling sound and putting an end to the creepy sensation that crawled up my spine.

"Not tonight," Lenorre whispered low enough not to be heard, her eyes slightly misty with power.

"Dessert?" my mother asked.

Lenorre blinked, her gaze returning to normal. She smiled beautifully. "No, thank you. Kassandra?"

Slowly, I lowered the knife, keeping Lenorre's hand in mine. "Sure," I said. "I hope to hell it's chocolate."

About the Author

Winter Pennington is an author, poet, artist, and closeted musician. She is an avid practitioner of nature-based spirituality and enjoys spending her spare time studying mythology from around the world. The Celtic path is very close to her heart. She has an uncanny fascination with swords and daggers, and a fondness for feeding loud and obnoxious corvids. In the shadow of her writing, she has experience working with a plethora of animals as a pet care specialist and veterinary assistant.

Winter currently resides in Oklahoma with her partner and their family of furry kids.

Books Available from Bold Strokes Books

Worth the Risk by Karis Walsh. Investment analyst Jamie Callahan and Grand Prix show jumper Kaitlyn Brown are willing to risk it all in their careers—can they face a greater challenge and take a chance on love? (978-1-60282-587-1)

Bloody Claws by Winter Pennington. In the midst of aiding the police, Preternatural Private Investigator Kassandra Lyall finally finds herself at serious odds with Sheila Morris, the local werewolf pack's Alpha female, when Sheila abuses someone Kassandra has sworn to protect. (978-1-60282-588-8)

Awake Unto Me by Kathleen Knowles. In turn of the century San Francisco, two young women fight for love in a world where women are often invisible and passion is the privilege of the powerful. (978-1-60282-589-5)

Initiation by Desire by MJ Williamz. Jaded Sue and innocent Tulley find forbidden love and passion within the inhibiting confines of a sorority house filled with nosy sisters. (978-1-60282-590-1)

Toughskins by William Masswa. John and Bret are two twenty-something athletes who find that love can begin in the most unlikely of places, including a "mom and pop shop" wrestling league. (978-1-60282-591-8)

me@you.com by K.E. Payne. Is it possible to fall in love with someone you've never met? Imogen Summers thinks so because it's happened to her. (978-1-60282-592-5)

High Impact by Kim Baldwin. Thrill seeker Emery Lawson and Adventure Outfitter Pasha Dunn learn you can never truly appreciate what's important and what you're capable of until faced with a sudden and stark reminder of your own mortality. (978-1-60282-580-2)

Snowbound by Cari Hunter. "The policewoman got shot and she's bleeding everywhere. Get someone here in one hour or I'm going to put her out of her misery." It's an ultimatum that will forever change the lives of police officer Sam Lucas and Dr. Kate Myles. (978-1-60282-581-9)

Rescue Me by Julie Cannon. Tyler Logan reluctantly agrees to pose as the girlfriend of her in-the-closet gay BFF at his company's annual retreat, but she didn't count on falling for Kristin, the boss's wife. (978-1-60282-582-6)

Murder in the Irish Channel by Greg Herren. Chanse MacLeod investigates the disappearance of a female activist fighting the Archdiocese of New Orleans and a powerful real estate syndicate. (978-1-60282-584-0)

Franky Gets Real by Mel Bossa. A four day getaway. Five childhood friends. Five shattering confessions...and a forgotten love unearthed. (978-1-60282-585-7)

Riding the Rails: Locomotive Lust and Carnal Cabooses edited by Jerry Wheeler. Some of the hottest writers of gay erotica spin tales of Riding the Rails. (978-1-60282-586-4)

Sheltering Dunes by Radclyffe. The seventh in the award-winning Provincetown Tales. The pasts, presents, and futures of three women collide in a single moment that will alter all their lives forever. (978-1-60282-573-4)

Holy Rollers by Rob Byrnes. Partners in life and crime Grant Lambert and Chase LaMarca assemble a team of gay and lesbian criminals to steal millions from a right-wing mega-church, but the gang's plans are complicated by an "ex-gay" conference, the FBI, and a corrupt reverend with his own plans for the cash. (978-1-60282-578-9)

History's Passion: Stories of Sex Before Stonewall edited by Richard Labonté. Four acclaimed erotic authors re-imagine the past...Welcome to the hidden queer history of men loving men not so very long—and centuries—ago. (978-1-60282-576-5)

Lucky Loser by Yolanda Wallace. Top tennis pros Sinjin Smythe and Laure Fortescue reach Wimbledon desperate to claim tennis's crown jewel, but will their feelings for each other get in the way? (978-1-60282-575-8)

Mystery of The Tempest: A Fisher Key Adventure by Sam Cameron. Twin brothers Denny and Steven Anderson love helping people and fighting crime alongside their sheriff dad on sundrenched Fisher Key, Florida, but Denny doesn't dare tell anyone he's gay, and Steven has secrets of his own to keep. (978-1-60282-579-6)

Better Off Red: Vampire Sorority Sisters Book 1 by Rebekah Weatherspoon. Every sorority has its secrets, and college freshman Ginger Carmichael soon discovers that her pledge is more than a bond of sisterhood—it's a lifelong pact to serve six bloodthirsty demons with a lot more than nutritional needs. (978-1-60282-574-1)

Detours by Jeffrey Ricker. Joel Patterson is heading to Maine for his mother's funeral, and his high school friend Lincoln has invited himself along on the ride—and into Joel's bed—but when the ghost of Joel's mother joins the trip, the route is likely to be anything but straight. (978-1-60282-577-2)

Three Days by L.T. Marie. In a town like Vegas where anything can happen, Shawn and Dakota find that the stakes are love at all costs, and it's a gamble neither can afford to lose. (978-1-60282-569-7)

Swimming to Chicago by David-Matthew Barnes. As the lives of the adults around them unravel, high school students Alex and

Robby form an unbreakable bond, vowing to do anything to stay together—even if it means leaving everything behind. (978-1-60282-572-7)

Hostage Moon by AJ Quinn. Hunter Roswell thought she had left her past behind, until a serial killer begins stalking her. Can FBI profiler Sara Wilder help her find her connection to the killer before he strikes on blood moon? (978-1-60282-568-0)

Erotica Exotica: Tales of Sex, Magic, and the Supernatural edited by Richard Labonté. Today's top gay erotica authors offer sexual thrills and perverse arousal, spooky chills, and magical orgasms in these stories exploring arcane mystery, supernatural seduction, and sex that haunts in a manner both weird and wondrous. (978-1-60282-570-3)

Blue by Russ Gregory. Matt and Thatcher find themselves in the crosshairs of a psychotic killer stalking gay men in the streets of Austin, and only a 103-year-old nursing home resident holds the key to solving the murders—but can she give up her secrets in time to save them? (978-1-60282-571-0)

Balance of Forces: Toujours Ici by Ali Vali. Immortal Kendal Richoux's life began during the reign of Egypt's only female pharaoh, and history has taught her the dangers of getting too close to anyone who hasn't harnessed the power of time, but as she prepares for the most important battle of her long life, can she resist her attraction to Piper Marmande? (978-1-60282-567-3)

Wings: Subversive Gay Angel Erotica edited by Todd Gregory. A collection of powerfully written tales of passion and desire centered on the aching beauty of angels. (978-1-60282-565-9)

Contemporary Gay Romances by Felice Picano. These works of short fiction from legendary novelist and memoirist Felice Picano are as different from any standard "romances" as you can get, but they will linger in the mind and memory. (978-1-60282-639-7)

Pirate's Fortune: Supreme Constellations Book Four by Gun Brooke. Set against the backdrop of war, captured mercenary Weiss Kyakh is persuaded to work undercover with bio-android Madisyn Pimm, which foils her plans to escape, but kindles unexpected love. (978-1-60282-563-5)

Sex and Skateboards by Ashley Bartlett. Sex and skateboards and surfing on the California coast. What more could anyone want? Alden McKenna thinks that's all she needs, until she meets Weston Duvall. (978-1-60282-562-8)